Terrible Times

Over two metres tall, with a bushy beard, Philip Ardagh is not only very large and very hairy – and revered as a god in some of the less well explored areas of Camberwell – but has also written over fifty children's books for all ages. *Terrible Times* is the third book in the bestselling Eddie Dickens trilogy, which began with *Awful End* and *Dreadful Acts*, both of which were shortlisted for book awards.

Currently living as a full-time writer, with a wife and two cats in a seaside town somewhere in England, he has been – amongst other things – an advertising copywriter, a hospital cleaner, a (highly unqualified) librarian, and a reader for the blind.

Philip Ardagh

TERRIBLE TIMES

Book Three of the Eddie Dickens Trilogy

illustrated by David Roberts

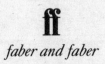

faber and faber

First published in 2002
by Faber and Faber Limited
3 Queen Square, London WC1N 3AU
This paperback edition first published in 2003

Typeset by Faber and Faber Limited
Printed in England by Mackays of Chatham plc, Chatham, Kent

Philip Ardagh is hereby identified as author of this work in accordance
with Section 77 of the Copyright, Designs and Patents Act 1988

A CIP record for this book
is available from the British Library

ISBN 978–0–571–21622–2

2 4 6 8 10 9 7 5 3

For Suzy Jenvey and Vivian French

A Message from the Author

Whose beard is now out of control

If this is the first Eddie Dickens book you've come across, DON'T PANIC!!! Each book is a self-contained adventure. For those of you who have come with me and Eddie all the way from *Awful End* to here, though, I hope you've enjoyed the ride. A number of readers – okay, a *lot* of readers – have asked why this is the last Eddie Dickens book and why I'm not going to write any more. The last Eddie Dickens book? Says who? This may be the last of the trilogy, but what's to stop me writing some 'further adventures' some day? You know, I get the feeling I might just do that. In the meantime, I hope you enjoy *Terrible Times*.

PHILIP ARDAGH
England
2002

Contents

Episode 1

Explosive News!

*In which America is mentioned, but the author gets
somewhat side-tracked*

'America?' said Eddie Dickens in amazement.
'You want me to go to America?' His mother
nodded. This was difficult because she was
wearing an enormous neck brace, which looked
rather like one of those huge plastic collars vets
sometimes put around dogs' heads, to prevent
them from licking wounds; only hers was made of
whalebone and starched linen.

Before you start crying 'Poor whale!' and
writing off letters of complaint, I wish to point out
two things: firstly, these events took place in the

19th century when things were very different to the 21st; secondly, the whale whose bones were used to make the frame for Mrs Dickens's neck brace had died of natural causes after a long and fulfilling life at sea, with plenty of singing which is, apparently, what whales like doing most.

Okay, it hadn't said, 'When I die, I hope my bones are used to make surgical appliances,' but it's better than being harpooned and killed in its prime in order to make surgical appliances. (I say 'it' simply because I don't know whether this particular whale was a he or a she. Sorry.)

Not that Eddie or his mother were thinking of such matters, as they walked up the drive of Awful End, that cold winter's afternoon. She'd just dropped the bombshell about wanting Eddie to go to America. I don't mean she'd *actually* dropped a bombshell, of course. Not a real one. That's simply an expression for a surprising piece of news. She did drop a real bombshell once, funnily enough – actually it was a mortar shell, but it was packed with explosives like a bomb and did go off which explains why she was now wearing the neck brace and, oh yes, walked with the aid of crutches.

She was lucky not to have been more seriously injured. Fortunately for her, when she'd tripped and stumbled with the shell – it was like a big brass tube, or a giant bullet, not something a hermit crab lives in on the beach – she'd tossed it over a small wall, dividing the rose garden from the sunken garden. It was the sunken garden which took much of the blast, but it wasn't badly damaged either. A lot of earth flew all over the place and an ornamental pear tree was destroyed, but little else. Less fortunately, one of Mad Uncle Jack's ex-soldier colleagues (who'd been sleeping under the rhubarb, which afforded great shade under its huge leaves) was blown to smithereens (which isn't a small seaside town near Bridlington, but means 'to bits'). Eddie's mum was horrified. She felt guilty for days, and never ate rhubarb again for the rest of her life, except in crumbles or with custard . . . or a light sprinkling of brown sugar. Or white, if there was no brown.

Mad Uncle Jack tried to reassure her by saying that, if the chap had been a half-decent soldier, he would have been heroically blown up in some battle long ago. And, anyway, he strongly suspected that the fool had been chewing the rhubarb leaves, which are highly poisonous, so he'd probably have been dead by now whether she'd tripped and tossed the shell over the wall or not.

Before we get back to Eddie and Mrs Dickens crunching up the drive to Awful End, and her telling her son about the plans for America, there may be those amongst you who are interested to

know why Mrs Dickens was carrying the shell in
the first place. Quite simply, it was because she'd
found it in her sewing box. It was summertime
(you might have guessed that from the size of the
rhubarb leaves) and she was fed up with the early
morning light coming through the crack between
the curtains, so she'd decided to sew them
together. Instead of finding her usual rows of
cotton reels, little pot of pins, her packet of
needles, and dried broad beans (graded by size)
she found the brass mortar shell and nothing else.

Puzzled, she'd gone in search of her husband, Mr Dickens, whom she knew was painting the garden.

Mr Dickens wasn't painting the garden in the sense that John Constable might paint a landscape or Turner a seascape, with oil paints on to a canvas. No, Mr Dickens was going around the garden painting some of the leaves a greener green. As he was getting older – and he wasn't *that* old – his eyesight wasn't quite what it had been, and some colours (especially browns and greens) seemed duller, which was why he was going around with a pot of bright green paint and a badger-bristle paintbrush. Unfortunately, unlike the whale, I've no idea whether this particular badger died of natural causes. I'm very, very, sorry.

Having found the shell in her otherwise empty sewing box and knowing her husband was painting the trees, the garden was a logical place for Eddie's mother to go, and how she came to drop the shell where she did.

Okay? Okay. I think that just about covers everything. So let's get back (which is really moving on, because it happened later) to Eddie and his mother, on crutches, walking up the drive to Awful End, that cold winter's afternoon.

'You want me to go to America?' said Eddie, in amazement.

No, hang on. Wait a minute. I thought I'd just about covered everything in the how-she-came-to-drop-the-mortar-shell incident, but there are two glaring omissions (things left out). Firstly; who put the shell in the sewing box; and, secondly, what it was that Mrs Dickens tripped over, causing her to throw the shell in the first place. Both can be easily explained.

The shell had been a present to Mad Uncle Jack from a local shopkeeper who didn't like him. He secretly rather hoped that MUJ would keep it over the fireplace and the heat would cause it to explode, giving Mad Uncle Jack a headache and an expensive repair bill, at the very least. That would teach him not to squish fruit and vegetables when he had no intention of buying them! Mad Uncle Jack had, indeed, put this fine, gleaming, brass mortar shell on display on one of the many mantelpieces in Awful End, but it had caught the eye of his loving wife, Even Madder Aunt Maud.

Even Madder Aunt Maud was a woman who acted on impulse. The day she first set eyes on a stuffed stoat, whom she later called Malcolm, she fell in love with him and he became her (almost) constant companion. The day she saw the snout of a hollow cow sticking over a hedgerow, her heart went all a flutter once again, and she knew there

6

and then that she would call the cow Marjorie and live inside her.

When she saw the gleaming shell case, she wanted it. I've no idea what for. She never said and, though I give a very good impression of one once in a while, when I write 'he thought' or 'she wondered', I'm not a state-registered mind reader. All I know is she wanted it, picked it up and was horrified to see that her hands left fingermarks and palm prints on the nice brass, which might tarnish the lovely gleam which had attracted her to it in the first place. She needed something to carry it in. She went into the nearest room and there, on a stool by the window, sat Mrs Dickens's sewing box. Not only was it just the right size, it also had a *handy carrying handle*.

Even Madder Aunt Maud tipped the contents out of the box, and swept them out of the way with her feet, under an old upright piano, putting the shell in the box. She was just about to carry it out to Marjorie, when she remembered that she'd left Malcolm the stuffed stoat on the mantelpiece. It was as she dashed out to retrieve him that Eddie's mum walked in and found the shell in the sewing box. It was just a case of bad luck and bad timing. If she hadn't wanted to sew up that gap in the curtain, or had come in a moment sooner and been able to ask Aunt Maud what she was up to, or come in *later*, allowing time for Even Madder Aunt Maud to have retrieved Malcolm and taken the sewing box, Mrs Dickens wouldn't be in the poor state she was in now.

Which only leaves the matter of what she tripped over, mortar shell in hand: a now-empty pot which had once contained green paint. And I don't think *that* requires further explanation!

Immediately after the explosion, Mad Uncle Jack dashed down the ladder from his tree house, three rungs at a time. Eddie, who was helping Dawkins polish the family silver, dashed out of the kitchen door and around the side of the house. Mr Dickens fell out of a laburnum tree he'd been painting, and Gibbering Jane (their retired/failed chambermaid) stayed under the stairs. Even Madder Aunt Maud was the last to appear, clutching Malcolm under her arm, and still frowning a puzzled frown at the sudden disappearance of the sewing box and shell.

Mad Uncle Jack, Eddie and Dawkins all ran to assist Mrs Dickens, whilst Even Madder Aunt Maud ambled over to Mr Dickens, who was lying on his back, moaning. She held Malcolm by the tail and prodded Eddie's father with the stuffed stoat's nose. 'What's all the fuss about, ay?' she demanded.

Meanwhile, Eddie's mum just groaned a lot and looked a bit crumpled. Back then, it wasn't simply a matter of picking up a phone and calling an ambulance. Dawkins was sent into town, on horseback, to find the doctor and it was a good hour before both men came galloping back. By then, Even Madder Aunt Maud had made the gruesome discovery of the ex-ex-soldier. Death is never nice, even in books. She told Mad Uncle Jack, who was able to identify which of his men it was – he still thought of them that way, and they did often do odd-jobs around the house – by a medal, still hot and slightly melted – in a flowerbed. On it were the words:

BEST OF BREED

'It was Gorey,' he said quietly. 'Poor chap.'

Doctor Humple took one look at Eddie's mother and assured her that she'd be fine in next to no time. He gave her the neck brace straight from his bag and arranged for crutches to be delivered, and had her up and walking about in a matter of days. Eddie's father was less lucky. The fall from the tree had hurt his back and, even as our story starts that following winter, he spent most of the time lying on his back, unable to sit up, let alone walk.

'I don't think the author likes me,' he once muttered. 'I always seem to get injured in these books.' Of course, none of the other characters had any idea what he was talking about.

It was soon after the accident that Eddie's father had a brilliant idea. He'd remembered reading somewhere about a famous artist called Michel Angelo, whom he assumed would have been called 'Mike Angel' if he'd been an Englishman – in fact 'Michelangelo' was just the artist's first name, his surname was Buonarroti – who'd painted the ceiling of a place called the Sistine Chapel. Mr Buonarroti had covered it with pictures of clouds and angels, and Adam and Eve and suchlike . . . but he'd done it all from wooden scaffolding, built to the height of just below the ceiling, and had painted the whole thing whilst lying on his back!

So, rather than lying around feeling sorry for himself, Mr Dickens had the remaining ex-soldiers build him a wooden scaffolding rig on wheels, and he started to paint the ceiling of the great hall in Awful End. His food was brought up and his chamber pot taken down. Occasionally, Gibbering Jane would clamber up and give him a sponge bath or one of the family would join him for a while to keep him company, or mix him new coloured paints. When he'd finished painting one patch of roof, they'd simply wheel the whole wooden scaffolding rig forward about a foot, and on he'd go.

There's a phrase about making triumph out of adversity, which has nothing to do with the saying about making a silk purse out of a pig's ear (natural causes or no natural causes). It means making something good out of something bad . . . and that's exactly what Mr Dickens would have done – produced a work of art when his bad back prevented him from doing just about anything else – were it not for the fact that he couldn't paint to save his life. Painting leaves on trees a brighter colour was where Eddie's dad's talent ended. If he actually tried to paint something to look like a leaf, it looked as much like an angel as his angels did, which was *not much*.

The ceiling in the great hall looked dreadful.

No, worse than that. If an unsuspecting visitor entered Awful End through the main entrance and saw the ceiling without warning, he might think that either some strange and horrifying multicoloured fungus had spread across it, or he'd eaten some mushrooms that hadn't agreed with him and was having weird and crazy hallucinations. Mr Dickens's ceiling was horrible. Today, it's painted over with several layers of very thick white paint. How very sensible.

. . . Which reminds me of the thick white snow on the ground as Eddie and his mother walked up the drive to Awful End and she raised the subject of America.

'America?' said Eddie in amazement. 'You want me to go to America?'

His mother managed a little nod, despite her huge whalebone-and-linen surgical collar. 'Well, I can't go like this, and your father can't even tie his own shoelaces the state he's still in, so, yes, I'm asking you to go to America for us. Your great-uncle will explain everything.'

Wow! This sounded the sort of adventure Eddie really could enjoy.

Episode 2

A Painful Surprise

*In which Mad Uncle Jack gets it in the end and
Even Madder Aunt Maud has an attack of guilt*

Eddie found Mad Uncle Jack in his study,
crouching under his large oak desk in the
space meant for his knees.

'It's very roomy in here!' he announced on
seeing his grand-nephew. 'Very roomy indeed . . .
so roomy, in fact, I think I shall make a room of
it.'

Before Eddie knew what was happening, Mad
Uncle Jack had leapt to his feet and was
brandishing a small ceremonial sword. Eddie
remembered Mad Uncle Jack telling him that he'd

been given it by some surrendering foreign general, long before Eddie had been born.

'I shall cut a hole for a window in the back, fit a door to the front and – hey presto – a new room just like that!'

Eddie knew better than to ask Mad Uncle Jack where he proposed to fit his knees the next time he tried to sit down at the desk.

'How nice,' said Eddie, instead.

'This is just what I need to cheer me up!' his great-uncle pronounced.

'Why do you need cheering up?' asked Eddie. MUJ seemed perfectly cheerful to him.

'With poor Gorey dead, your mother on crutches and your father up that wooden contraption of his, need you ask, dear boy?' he said, which was a surprisingly sensible thing for him to say.

Eddie seized the moment of sanity and said what he'd come in for. 'Mother says you want me to go to America,' but Mad Uncle Jack was no longer listening.

He was crawling back under the desk – head first this time – and starting to stab the wooden board at the back with the ceremonial sword. He made a high-pitched whine with every thrust: '*Aieeeeeeeeeeeeeeeeeeeeeeeeeeeeee!!!*'

At that very moment – I added the word 'very'

15

because I suspect I often use the phrase 'at that moment' in Eddie Dickens books, so I wanted to disguise it a little – Even Madder Aunt Maud entered the room by opening a window and stepping in, shaking the snow from the elephant's-foot-umbrella-stand she was wearing as a boot on each foot.

She took one look at her husband's posterior protruding – that's 'bottom sticking out' to you and me – from beneath the desk and dashed (as fast as her elephant's-foot umbrella-stands would allow her) across the study to the fireplace. Grabbing a brass toasting fork from a selection of fireside utensils, she thrust it into MUJ's buttock. It was his left, I believe, though  there were to be conflicting accounts later.

'BURGLAR!' she cried, so loudly that it almost drowned out the roar of pain and surprise coming from beneath the desk, which is really saying something!

Technically, of course, she was inaccurate. 'Burglars' do their burgling at night. In the daytime, such a person should have been called a 'housebreaker'. Then again, she was being even more inaccurate than that, wasn't she? (That was what we call a rhetorical question. I don't expect you to answer me. You're probably too far away for me to hear, anyway.) Mad Uncle Jack was neither burglar nor housebreaker. He was her husband! It was at times like these that Eddie wondered if he wouldn't be better off living in a nice quiet orphanage somewhere.

Mad Uncle Jack emerged from under the desk red-faced and enraged, his hat crumpled like a concertina (which may not be a very original simile, but is a jolly good one, along with 'as black as a bruised banana').

'WHAT IS GOING ON?' he demanded, pulling the prongs – or 'tines' if you want to be ever so accurate – of the toasting fork from his bottom.

To Eddie's utter amazement, Even Madder Aunt Maud actually looked apologetic. He'd expected her to be unrepentant, blaming her husband for being under the desk in the first place, or 'masquerading as a burglar' or something. But no. She looked positively sheepish at having pronged – or tined – poor Mad Uncle Jack.

'My sweet!' she cried, in anguish, tossing

17

Malcolm aside and throwing her arms around her injured man.

Fortunately for Eddie, he managed to catch the stuffed stoat as he came flying through the air like some thick French breadstick used as a throwing club. Eddie knew from experience that being hit by a flying Malcolm was enough to knock a fleeing convict to the ground.

Jack and Maud's hug had somehow taken on the appearance of a grapple. Losing her footing in her elephant's-foot umbrella-stand boots, Even Madder Aunt Maud was trying to use her husband to steady herself at the same time he was using her to steady *himself* as he tried to turn to inspect the damage done to his behind. The result? A terrible crash and an entanglement of Great-uncle and Great-aunt on the bearskin rug in front of the spluttering study fire. I'd love to say that the fire was 'roaring' but Mad Uncle Jack spent most of the time living in a treehouse in the garden so the fire was rarely lit. When it was, families of hibernating mice or hedgehogs had to be carefully moved some place else first, and the wood was often damp and spitting.

(If you know about real fires, you'll know about spitting logs. If you don't, you'll just have to take my word for it: a damp or sappy log can spit like an angry camel but, unlike camels, they

18

don't – according to folklore – know the 100th name of Allah, so don't have that all-knowing smug expression that camels do, which you'd have too if you knew such an important and sacred name. In fact, most logs' expressions – big or small – are quite wooden.)

And don't think I have forgotten about the poor old bear who ended up as a bearskin rug on the floor. Back in Eddie's day, animal-skin rugs were everywhere: lions, tigers, bears of all shapes and sizes. It was unusual to stand on a rug that hadn't once been running around quite happily in the sunshine. I don't know this particular bear's history but I'm sorry to say that he probably ended more with a bang than with all his family around his bed (in the bear cave) as he ended his days saying, 'I've had a good life . . .'

Which brings us back to Mad Uncle Jack lying on top of his ruggy (as opposed to rugged) remains.

'Are you all right?' asked Eddie, helping his great-aunt to her feet.

'What have I done? What have I done?' she groaned.

They both looked down at Mad Uncle Jack who lay there like a helpless upturned beetle.

'I'm sure he'll be fine,' said Eddie, trying to sound reassuring. He took MUJ by the arm and tried to help him to his feet.

19

'Leave me,' he whispered hoarsely into the boy's ear. 'You must get word to Fort Guana.'

'Fort Guana?' asked a puzzled Eddie.

'Tell them that we will hold the ridge until re-enforcements arrive . . .' He paused and took a gulp of air. 'The Bumbaloonies shall not break through our ranks!' He turned his face away and came eye-to-glass-eye with the head of the bearskin rug.

'I see that Corporal Muggins didn't make it,' he sighed, stroking the head. 'A fine soldier. Made an excellent omelette.' He turned back to Eddie, tears in his eyes. 'It's all down to you now, my boy . . . Take my horse . . .' and, with that, he fainted.

Snatching Malcolm from the occasional table where Eddie had placed him, Even Madder Aunt Maud let out a truly dreadful cry of despair and fled the study – this time through the doorway rather than the window.

Eddie looked at the unconscious form of Mad Uncle Jack. He didn't think that he'd be finding out much more about his trip to America that day!

Episode 3

A Cure for Ills?

In which Doctor Humple pays yet another visit to
Awful End and Eddie goes in search of shiny things

As it turned out, Doctor Humple was more concerned about Mad Aunt Maud's state of health than Mad Uncle Jack's. After a good night's rest and a few of Dr Humple's large blue pills, Eddie's great-uncle seemed to be back to his same old self, apart from a sore bottom, backache and a slight limp. The doctor had tucked him up in his tree house (which was made entirely from creosoted dried fish) and, by the next morning, he'd been down the ladder and building snow sculptures like he did most winter mornings, weather permitting.

Even Madder Aunt Maud, in her hollow cow in the rose garden, meanwhile, was far from her normal self. She clutched Malcolm to her, rocking backwards and forwards, muttering, 'What have I done? What have I done?' and no amount of coaxing could get her to relax and unwind.

Once Eddie's mother had taken to regularly eating raw onions and, after the habit had passed, Even Madder Aunt Maud had threaded the remaining vegetables singly – like conkers – and hung them at different heights from Marjorie's 'ceiling'. There was nothing she liked more than passing the dark evenings by hitting the suspended onions with Malcolm's nose, singing as she went; as though each onion somehow represented a particular musical note.

Eddie tried hitting them and singing now – there was no way that he could prise Malcolm from her grasp, so he'd used a wooden spoon. No reaction. Even Madder Aunt Maud simply continued to snivel. Even Dr Humple's mixture of big blue, small pink and medium-sized yellow pills had no effect. Even Madder Aunt Maud was awash with guilt at stabbing and then knocking out her beloved Jack.

They brought Mad Uncle Jack to see her, to

show her that he was, in his own words, 'as right as rain'(apart from the sore bottom, backache and slight limp, in the *other* leg now) but this made no difference. She was still terribly upset. MUJ soon grew tired of trying to 'make her snap out of it' – his words again – so he stomped off back through the snow to his treehouse, in a huff.

Dr Humple put his arm on Eddie's shoulder. 'I really am at a loss as to how to help your poor great-aunt, at present,' he said. 'Fortunately for us, Time is the great healer.'

Although Eddie was hearing the words come from the doctor's mouth, rather than seeing them on the printed page as you are, he knew that Dr Humple had just said 'Time' with a capital 'T', in the same way that people sometimes say 'Nature' with a capital 'N', when they mean Nature in an all-important way . . .

. . . From past experience, Eddie knew that Mad Aunt Maud's mood could certainly change in the time it took to blink an eye or scratch an eyebrow, but a mood change didn't necessarily make things better. Suddenly, an idea popped into his head.

'Shiny things!' he said.

The doctor stopped what he was doing – which was coiling up his stethoscope and putting it in his top hat (that's where doctors used to keep their stethoscopes. Honestly, dear reader, I promise) – and stared at Eddie. 'What do you mean by shiny things, my boy?' he asked.

'Well, you remember when you came in the summer and gave Mother the neck brace and crutches and Father the back-strengthening corset?'

'How could I forget?' said Dr Humple. 'They're both still using them . . . and that was the day poor Gorey died, beneath the spreading rhubarb leaves.'

'Exactly!' Eddie continued. 'The whole thing came about because Even Madder Aunt Maud –' He paused and looked down at his great-aunt, whom they'd managed to tuck up in bed, but seemed oblivious to (unaware of) what was going on around her. 'The whole dreadful accident happened because Mad Aunt Maud liked the look of a shiny artillery shell.'

'The idea is to make the poor lady feel less guilty about herself, young Edmund, not MORE!' the doctor reminded him.

'No, you don't understand,' said Eddie hurriedly. 'I was simply about to suggest that we try to distract her with some new shiny object she might like.'

'Aha!' said Dr Humple, his hat back on his head, the stethoscope safely tucked inside (his hat, not his head). 'That is, indeed, clever thinking!'

'Shall I go up to the house and see if I can find something really shiny?' Eddie suggested.

'An excellent idea!' said the doctor. 'In the meantime I shall check her pulse.'

Eddie slipped out of Marjorie's bottom – she was the carnival float cow they were in, remember – and crunched his way through the snow towards the back of Awful End.

He was surprised to see Gibbering Jane taking down some washing from the line near the kitchen door. As a failed chambermaid, Jane usually spent her time under the stairs, sitting in the dark, knitting her life away. When Eddie's previous home had burnt down, all she'd managed to save of her years of knitting was the charred corner of an egg cosy which she, thereafter, wore on a piece of string around her neck. She'd moved to Awful End with Eddie's parents and gentleman's gentleman Dawkins . . . directly under the stairs there, so it was unusual to see her doing anything as ordinary as bring in the washing. Not that it was straightforward. The temperature had dropped considerably overnight, and the clothes were as stiff as boards. Put a shirt above a pair of trousers, and it would look as though a very flat person was inside them.

Gibbering Jane gibbered as she tried to bend the clothes to fit inside the wicker washing basket.

She was fighting a losing battle. When she saw
Eddie, she dropped the basket – a rigid sock
sticking in the snow like a knitted boomerang –
and ran (you guessed it) still gibbering into the
house. By the time Eddie had entered the warm
glow of the kitchen, he could hear the door under
the stairs slamming shut.

Eddie's mum, Mrs Dickens, was sitting at the
kitchen table, cutting the crusts off a pile of
triangular sandwiches with a pair of carpet scissors.

'Hello, Jonathan.' She beamed when she saw
her son. (Don't ask.)

'Hello, Mother,' said Eddie.

'I'm making these for your father's breakfast,'
she said.

27

If you're trying to work out what time of day it was, don't let the whole breakfast business put you off. We're in the DICKENS household, remember. Breakfast could be served at any time during a twenty-four-hour period (if at all) depending upon who was doing the serving.

'How is Father?' asked Eddie, who hadn't climbed up the scaffolding in the hall for the past few days.

'Having great difficulty drawing the serpent in the Garden of Eden,' said Mrs Dickens. 'Apparently, it keeps coming out looking like a liver sausage.'

'Oh,' said Eddie, who secretly thought that his father's paintings of both Adam and Eve looked rather like liver sausages, too.

'Would you like something to eat?' asked his mother. 'There are plenty of crusts.' She trimmed another sandwich, adding the crusts to an already impressive pile.

'No, thank you,' said Eddie. 'I'm actually looking for something shiny . . . something which might distract poor Even Madder Aunt Maud from feeling so guilty about stabbing and knocking out Mad Uncle Jack.'

'Poor Jack,' said Mrs Dickens, placing the carpet scissors on the table and dabbing her eyes with the corner of a lacy hanky she kept up her sleeve. 'We shall all miss him so.'

'Miss him? But he's alive and well, Mother!' Eddie protested. 'He was with us inside Marjorie just now, trying to comfort Even Madder Aunt Maud.'

'Then whose funeral did I attend the other day?' asked Mrs Dickens, a confused look passing across her handsome features.

Funeral? There hadn't been any funerals lately. The last time Eddie could remember seeing a coffin was when he'd ended up in one, in the book called *Dreadful Acts* (not that he'd realised that he was in a book called *Dreadful Acts*, or called anything else, for that matter). Then he remembered the hen.

Dawkins kept hens for their eggs, one of which (hen not egg) Mad Aunt Maud was particularly fond of. Sadly she had died of old age a few days previously. Maud had insisted that Ethel, the chicken, be buried, and all members of the (human) family had been required to attend the brief service.

'You're not thinking of the chicken's funeral are you, Mother?' Eddie asked.

'Why, of course! How silly of me,' said Mrs Dickens, trimming the final sandwich and arranging the pile neatly on the plate. 'An easy mistake. They're both so plump and feathery.'

Eddie could see how Mad Uncle Jack's whiskeriness might be compared to feathers, but plump? He was about as thin as a person could be and still be classified as a person. Any thinner and he might be a stick man . . . but Eddie knew better than to say anything. He decided to resume his quest for something shiny.

★

Eddie finally found just what he was looking for in one of the upstairs rooms that nobody used any more. It had once contained furniture covered in white sheets, to stop it getting dusty. That had been done back in the days when Mad Uncle Jack and Even Madder Aunt Maud had an army of servants. Now they were all gone and – before Eddie and his parents had moved in with Dawkins and Gibbering Jane – all they'd been left with was the very small army of retired army misfits (of whom 'Best of Breed' Private Gorey had been one). Over the years, MUJ and EMAM – oooh, that's the first time I've used EMAM, and I like it! – had used the furniture under the white sheets as firewood, and used the white sheets as sheets, or to play 'ghosts'.

(By the way, I should explain that there was a fashion for calling people by their initials . . . and not necessarily their own. Don't ask me why, but the Victorian prime minister William Gladstone, for example, was often referred to as GOM, meaning 'Grand Old Man'; so my MUJs and EMAMs fit quite neatly into the period, thank you.)

When Eddie entered the room, it was bare; bare floor, bare walls, bare ceiling . . . well, not quite a bare ceiling for, although there were no carpets or rugs on the floor and no paintings or fixtures on the walls, from the middle of the ceiling hung a huge chandelier, glinting in the weak winter sunlight that had managed to make it through the slats of the closed shutters across the windows.

Most of the chandelier was covered in years of dust, and was loosely wrapped in what looked like a giant hairnet, but it still managed to wink in places at Eddie, as if to share the secret that brilliant cut-glass crystal lay beneath. From the bottom of the chandelier, nestling in the net, hung a glass bauble the size of an orange. Eddie felt sure that if he could reach this bauble, unhook it and polish it, it would be just the kind of shiny object to fascinate his great-aunt. The problem was the first part: reaching it. He looked around for something to stand on. Zilch. Zero. Then he remembered the library steps his mother kept in the bathroom for diving practice and he hurried off to find them.

By the time that Eddie was striding back down towards Marjorie, through the snow, the crystal-cut bauble in his gloved hand was sparkling and glinting like the world's biggest diamond. Eddie wasn't wearing the gloves to keep out the cold, but to keep from smudging the bauble. He didn't want a few fingerprints to spoil what he hoped would be the effect this shiny thing would have on Even Madder Aunt Maud.

Episode 4

A Brief Family History

*In which Eddie learns more about
his family and the reasons for going to America*

Eddie's mind wasn't entirely on curing Mad Aunt Maud as he stamped the snow off his shoes and clambered inside Marjorie. He was still thinking about the trip to America, whatever that was about. If only his mother or Mad Uncle Jack had had a chance to explain things to him before Mad Uncle Jack and Even Madder Aunt Maud had joined the list of casualties.

Dr Humple was giving the boy's great-aunt another large blue pill, with a sip of water from a glass when Eddie entered.

'What are in those pills, Doctor?' Eddie asked.

'The large blue ones?'

Eddie nodded.

'Mainly blue dye. It's very expensive, which is why my bills are so high . . . What's that amazing jewel you have there?' Dr Humple was eyeing the crystal-cut bauble the size of an orange, nestling in Eddie's gloved hands.

'A shiny thing!' said Eddie, passing it to the doctor.

Dr Humple held it up in front of Even Madder Aunt Maud, just out of her reach. She sat bolt upright in bed and tried to snatch it. The doctor jerked his hand away. 'I think it's working, Eddie!' said the doctor, obviously impressed.

'Ah, my precious!' said Even Madder Aunt Maud, which would have been a quote from a character called Golom in a book called *The Hobbit*, except that *The Hobbit* hadn't been written yet, which made Even Madder Aunt Maud way, way, way ahead of her time.

Even Madder Aunt Maud made another swipe for the bauble and Dr Humple almost dropped it. He fumblingly saved it from falling to the floor and tossed it over to Eddie who caught it with ease. His great-aunt was out of the bed now, clutching Malcolm by the tail, but she only had eyes for one item: the shiny thing.

She launched herself at Eddie who stood by the opening in Marjorie's bottom, and threw the crystal-cut bauble out into the garden, aiming for the deepest snowdrift so as not to damage it.

Even Madder Aunt Maud bounded after it like a dog after a ball thrown by its master. And it should remind anyone who's read *Dreadful Acts* of a certain escaped convict who seemed to think he was a hound.

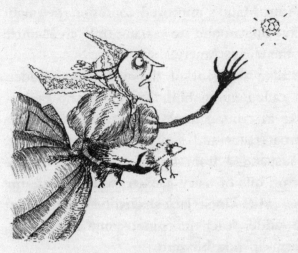

'Well, Master Edmund,' said the doctor, 'she's up and about again, but now what?'

'You're the doctor,' said Eddie. 'Shouldn't you decide?'

Dr Humple and Eddie watched Even Madder Aunt Maud dig the bauble out of the snowdrift and hold it triumphantly to the sky.

'Well,' said the doctor hesitantly, 'she seems fine to me. Fully cured.'

'Certainly back to her old self,' Eddie agreed.

Dr Humple stepped out of the hollow cow. 'Why don't you go and tell your great-uncle the excellent news?' he suggested. 'And please inform him that I shall be sending him my bill in due course.'

Eddie hurried off through the snow to Mad Uncle Jack's treehouse. Once he'd told him about Mad Aunt Maud's improved condition, he might actually get around to asking his great-uncle about the trip to America.

Reaching the foot of the tree house ladder, Eddie called up to him. There was no bell or knocker at ground level, just Mad Uncle Jack's cut-throat razor and a piece of broken mirror, each suspended from hooks in the side of the ladder on bits of hairy garden twine of differing lengths. (Mad Uncle Jack shaved here, at the foot of the ladder, each morning, come rain, shine, hailstorm or snow blizzard.)

'Uncle Jack!' Eddie called. 'Uncle Jack?'

The beakiest of beaky noses appeared through an unglazed window up above. An unglazed window is a window without any glass in it, which means that it's really just another phrase for a hole. The word 'window' actually comes from the Old Norse word *vindauga* which means 'wind eye' – useful for keeping an eye on the wind – and Old Norse windows certainly didn't have glass in them either.

'Who is it?' Mad Uncle Jack called down.

'Eddie!'

'What's the password?' Mad Uncle Jack shouted.

Eddie sighed. He'd never needed a password to be allowed up into the tree house before, so why now? 'I didn't know there was one!' he groaned.

'Correct!' cried Mad Uncle Jack triumphantly. 'Come on up, my boy! Come on up!'

A somewhat relieved Eddie shinned up the ladder. (People often shin up ladders in books. Have you noticed that? They sometimes shin up drainpipes, too . . . but you very rarely get people shinning up stairs.)

Mad Uncle Jack was delighted to see Eddie. 'Come in and sit yourself down,' he said. 'You're probably here to ask me about the American trip, aren't you?'

Mad Uncle Jack was sitting on one of the elephant's-foot umbrella-stands that Even Madder Aunt Maud had been using as a boot. 'Yes,' said Eddie. He sat himself down on a small upturned wooden crate marked 'MANGOES'. Behind his great-uncle was a bed and between them a rather wobbly table, and that was about all there was room for in the tree house. 'And also to tell you that Even Madder Aunt Maud is back to her old self again.'

'Oh dear,' said Mad Uncle Jack. 'I'm very sorry to hear that.' Eddie didn't know what to say, so he wisely said nothing. 'Well, before I explain what I – what *we* – need you to do in America, I think I should give you a little Dickens family history,' said his great-uncle, at last.

'Fine.' Eddie nodded, hoping beyond hope that Mad Uncle Jack wouldn't get too side-tracked.

'Your Great-uncle George is probably the most famous of the recent Dickenses,' MUJ began, tilting back on the elephant's foot. 'He burnt down the Houses of Parliament in 1834, which is why we have the nice new gothicy one with Big Ben and all . . .'

'You mean your brother George was a kind of Guy Fawkes?' gasped Eddie.

'What, the gunpowder, treason and plot chap? I think the difference is that Guy Fawkes *planned* to burn down the Houses of Parliament and *didn't*, and Brother George *didn't* plan to burn down the Houses of Parliament . . .'

'But *did*!' said Eddie, in amazement. 'So it was an accident! Did he get into trouble?'

'Of course not,' said Mad Uncle Jack.

'Why not?' asked Eddie. He imagined that burning down the Houses of Parliament, by mistake or not, would be a getting-into-serious-trouble offence.

'Because he never told anybody in authority,' said MUJ. 'That's why.'

'So he's only famous in the family for having done it? Not the history books?'

'Exactly,' said his great-uncle. 'But that's no less an achievement. If it hadn't been for my brother, we wouldn't have that fabulous new building with all the twiddly bits.'

'How did he – er – accidentally set fire to the old Parliament building?' Eddie asked. 'A smouldering cigar butt, a casually discarded match?'

'Over-zealous stoking,' said Mad Uncle Jack. 'It could have happened to anybody. It was the sixteenth of October – George's birthday – and, as a treat, a friend of his sneaked him into the Parliament's boiler room to let him help stoke the furnaces.

'Even as a boy, George was mad keen on fire, you know. Nothing he loved more than a smouldering carpet or a blazing curtain. Set fire to local tradespeople on numerous occasions, when we were lads, but always in the spirit of fun! They stopped calling at the house. They've always lacked humour, the lower classes.'

'And this friend of his let him stoke the furnaces underneath Parliament?!' said Eddie, in disbelief.

'As I said, it was his birthday . . . Anyhow, Brother George over-fed the furnaces. He filled them up with much too much stuff . . . far too many tally sticks.'

'Tally whats?'

'No, tally sticks. Right up until the twenties, the government used wooden sticks, rather than paper or dried fish, to work out tax. By 1834, the practice was as dead as Private Gorey and they were using them as firewood –'

'And Great Uncle George stuffed too many into the furnaces?' asked Eddie, trying to get a clear picture of events.

Mad Uncle Jack tried to suppress a giggle. 'I'm afraid so. George says it was a beautiful sight, the orange flames and smoke blowing out across the River Thames.'

'Didn't he feel guilty?' said Eddie.

Mad Uncle Jack nodded. 'Not for long though.

He was killed soon after.'

'Set fire to himself?'

'No, as a result of an accident arising from his conviction that he was a fish,' Eddie's great-uncle explained. 'He took to living in a large tank in a rented space near the Manufacturers Museum and – refusing to come up for air one Thursday – he died.' (Today the museum is called the V & A.)

Eddie looked around the inside of the tree house made of dried fish, and thought of the rockpool dug into the floor of the study. What was it about the Dickens family and fish? Great Uncle George had died thinking he was one, and Mad [Great] Uncle Jack even tried to *pay* for everything with dried fish! He wondered whether Grandpa Percy had ever had any fishy habits, too.

For those of you who might doubt Mad Uncle Jack's claims – and why not, he's not been the most reliable of people throughout the trilogy, has he? – I should say that the Houses of Parliament in London were indeed destroyed by fire in 1834 *and* as a result of overloading the furnaces with tally sticks, though whether his brother really had a part in it I can't say. From his childhood behaviour, it seems just the sort of thing he would have done, though.

Fortunately, London had formed its first single fire service the year before the fire. Prior to that, if your house caught alight it would only have been put out by the firemen (they were all men) working for the particular insurance company your house was insured with. Otherwise, they'd just stand there on the other side of the road and watch.

A couple of important bits of the old buildings were saved: the Great Hall (which was great) and the Jewel Tower (which was good news, too). This was partly thanks to the London Fire Engine Establishment (the fire brigade) and partly thanks to a chap called Lord Melbourne who happened to be Prime Minister at the time, so was good at being bossy, and told the firemen what to do. These old bits were incorporated into the new building which is still there today (or, at the very least, at the time I'm writing this).

'I met Chance, once, you know,' said Mad Uncle Jack, picking up the dried swordfish he used as a letter opener from the rickety table, and sticking the tip of its nose into his ear, giving it a quick joggle. 'An itch,' he explained on seeing Eddie's startled expression.

'Who was Chance?' asked Eddie.

'A dog belonging to the Watling Street Fire Station,' said Mad Uncle Jack. 'Born for search and rescue work, he was. No one had to train him. He would dash up the escape ladder into a burning building and start hunting for survivors.

If he found someone, he'd sniff out his master and bark to tell him that someone was in trouble. Saved lots of lives, he did. Quite the hero.'

Eddie looked doubtful but, amazingly, his great-uncle was telling the truth. Chance was a bit of a celebrity in his day and wore a special collar with a message on it which read: '*Stop me not but onward let me jog, for I am the London firemen's dog.*'

Chance's life is just the sort of thing which will get made into one of those children's feel-good costume-drama programmes they put on television around Christmas time, mark my words. And when it does, you can say, 'I know where they pinched the idea from; that nice Mr Ardagh and his brilliant book *Terrible Times*,' and you can write to the TV company and demand that I get a special payment for coming up with it.

What Mad Uncle Jack didn't mention (and probably didn't know) and the television programme might, possibly, leave out is that – after his death – Chance was stuffed and shown off at fairgrounds . . . which wasn't the most dignified end for such a heroic hound.

'Er . . . what does your dead brother George have to do with my going to America, Mad Uncle Jack?' Eddie asked, trying to steer the topic of conversation back on course.

The empty mango crate wasn't the most comfortable seat in the world and, anyhow, it was getting cold in the tree house.

'My father had three sons,' Mad Uncle Jack explained. 'There was my elder brother George. There was me – if there hadn't been, he wouldn't have been my father, now, would he? – and there was my younger brother Percy, who was your grandfather.'

'Father has a picture of him in his room,' Eddie recalled. His parents' room at Awful End wasn't the one they'd first occupied when they moved into the house. That had been damaged in a gas explosion. Though the damage had been repaired, it had been repaired by Mad Uncle Jack's faithful ragbag of ex-soldiers . . . which brings the word 'repair' into question, if not disrepute. So Mr and Mrs Dickens had moved into another, smaller room and it was there, by their wash-stand, that the small portrait of Grandpa Percy hung.

44

He was from the very heavily bearded era of Queen Victoria's reign. Percy Dickens was more beard than just about anything else. You could just make out the eyes and there was a hint of a nose in there somewhere, but it would be a complete waste of time searching for a mouth, though it must have been *somewhere* under all that facial hair. Despite being all beard – he needn't have worn a collar and tie, for example, because the bushiness of the beard hid all of his neck and most of his torso down to his tummy button – he still managed to look stern in the portrait, which is quite an achievement when you consider there was little room for any features. Whenever Eddie looked at the picture, he imagined his grandfather was being disapproving or saying 'no!' to something; anything; *everything*.

45

'What was he like, Uncle Jack?' asked Eddie.

MUJ shook his head, sadly. 'Percy was a very strange boy,' he said. 'He showed no interest in fish, the army, or any of the games George and I played as children. He always had his nose stuck in a book. I don't mean that he did a great deal of reading. I simply mean that he had his nose stuck in a book . . . the same book, and stuck between the same two pages for about thirty-two years. He even slept that way, which made him prone to snoring and, if he ever got a cold, you can imagine how soggy that book became after all that sneezing and constant nose-dripping.'

'But why did he do that?' asked Eddie, wondering if anyone in the world had normal relatives or whether all families were secretly barmy.

'I've absolutely no idea, m'boy,' said Mad Uncle Jack. 'I never thought to ask him.'

Eddie sighed. Why did grown-ups never ask the sort of questions any sensible ordinary kid would? 'Can you remember what the book was?' he asked.

Eddie's great-uncle tilted precariously on the elephant's foot, the back of his head brushing against the creosoted fish wall. 'Of course I can!' he said indignantly, then fell silent. (Why people *fall* silent rather than *go* silent is one of those

46

mysteries, like why wire coat-hangers multiply if left alone long enough in a wardrobe: you start off with six and, by the following month, you end up with a tangle of about four hundred and twenty-eight.)

Eddie waited for Mad Uncle Jack to tell him the book's title. Nothing. 'Er, what was it?' he asked, when he could bear it no longer.

'Oh, *Old Roxbee's Compendium of All Knowledge: Volume Three,*' said Mad Uncle Jack. 'Of course, I've no idea what it was about because I could never get it off Percy. He was too busy sticking his nose in it.'

Eddie reflected on that generation of Dickenses. Three brothers: George, the arsonist, Jack, the general all-round nutter, and Percy the man with the book on his face . . .

47

What had the neighbours thought? How had they coped in polite society? The truth be told, a lot of the upper classes in those days were a bit bonkers but, *because* they were upper class, they were called 'eccentric' and everyone thought, 'Oh, that's all right, then.'

After another period of silence, Eddie asked: 'What does your telling me about your brothers George and Percy have to do with your wanting me to travel to America?'

'Good question!' said Uncle Jack, picking up the stuffed swordfish for a second time, this time employing it as a back-scratcher. (I don't mean 'employing' it as in putting it on the payroll and giving it a regular wage – what would be the point of paying a dead fish? – but employing as in using . . . which means that if I'd simply employed the word used, or should that be used the word used, I wouldn't be in this mess now.) 'In fact, an excellent question!' he continued. 'You see our father, Dr Malcontent Dickens, had a number of interests in America, the most important of which was the ownership of a newspaper which was not afraid of telling the news as it really was. It was – and still is – called the *Terrible Times* and has an extremely high readership, I am informed, on the Eastern Seaboard.'

Eddie had no idea what the Eastern Seaboard

was, so he asked his great-uncle, who had no idea either.

'Sounds rather like a sideboard to me, only larger,' he said. 'Everything in America is larger. I'm told the mice are the size of rats and the rats are the size of dogs.'

'What about the dogs?' Eddie asked, wondering how big they might be (so as not to be confused with the rats).

'What about them?' asked Mad Uncle Jack.

'Oh, nothing,' said Eddie. 'You were telling me about the *Terrible Times*.'

'Was I? I mean, I was. It was originally my father's newspaper, then, when he was killed by the human cannon ball, it was passed on to us three boys. George never married so, when he died, his share was divided in two and passed on to me and young Percy, so we both owned half the paper. Then, when your Grandpa Percy died, his share went to your father.'

'So you and Father own a daily newspaper in America called the *Terrible Times*?' he said, making a mental note to ask him about the human cannon ball another time, because he didn't want to risk getting off the main subject now.

'Exactly,' nodded Mad Uncle Jack, his beak-like nose casting an interestingly shaped shadow on the tree house wall.

'And you don't just mean a copy of an old newspaper, you mean a company which produces a newspaper every day –'

'Except Sundays,' his great-uncle interjected (which, in this case, is the same as interrupting).

'– except Sundays – which is read by a large number of people on the Eastern Seaboard –'

'Whatever that might be,' said Mad Uncle Jack.

'Whatever that might be,' Eddie conceded, 'in America?'

'Spot-on, my boy! Spot-on!' cried Mad Uncle Jack. 'For years everything's run smoothly, and the editor has been in touch every six months with a report as to how the paper's been doing and a cheque for the profits to be shared between me and your father . . . except that we haven't heard from him of late, and we need someone to go from the family. Your father's bad back means that he can't go. Your mother's on crutches and, like your great-aunt, is also a woman, which leaves you or me, Edmund. I can't go, because I'm completely mad, so that leaves you. We want you to go to America as the representative of the Dickens family, to find out what's gone wrong in the offices of the *Terrible Times*.'

Eddie actually gasped out loud. What an adventure that would be!

Episode 5

Looking Backward, Looking Forward

In which we learn more of Eddie's past and more of his excitement at the upcoming voyage

When Eddie was very little, there was a fashion for sending boys to sea to toughen them up, particularly if they'd 'gone bad'. Eddie's parents had sent him to sea – in other words to work on a ship – not because he was a handful, but by mistake. They had meant to send a trunk, containing printing inks, to America by ship and Eddie to a school for extremely-young young gentlemen (him not being old enough to go to an ordinary school then). As it was, Eddie ended up on the vessel, and the trunk had a second-rate education for a boy, but a first-class education for a trunk. It sat at the back of the class and never said or did anything, which meant that it never did anything *wrong* and it didn't need feeding either, which made it very popular with the teachers. That trunk got better marks and end-of-term reports than the majority of the boys, so Eddie's parents were blissfully unaware that Eddie wasn't at the school (because it was a boarding school and he wasn't supposed to come home for the holidays either).

Eddie, meanwhile, grew up amongst sailors on a cargo ship. It was obvious to the sailors that Eddie wasn't a trunk – except for someone called the purser who said that if Eddie was down on the ship's inventory as a trunk then that's exactly what he was – but they were out at sea and they weren't going back just to put Eddie ashore. So Eddie spent his early years amongst the creaking rigging and was used to sleeping in a hammock, having the salty spray of the sea in his face and living off the toughest beef imaginable, which was packed in salt and stored in barrels. For some reason, it was full of maggots or weevils or maggots *and* weevils, but they added a bit of variety to the flavour as well as giving extra protein.

Eddie never reached America – the intended

destination for the now well-educated trunk – but he did learn to love a life on the ocean waves. He spent about eight years aboard ship in total and, by the end of it, could do some pretty impressive knots; could read a compass; had scrubbed the decks more hours than you've watched television in your entire life so far; and knew the workings of a ship from the tip of the main mast to the bilges below the waterline.

By one of those strange quirks of fate that God or Mother Nature throws up to show that He or She has a great sense of humour, Eddie finally landed back on English soil just as the trunk finished its schooling for extremely-young young gentlemen, and they both arrived back at home about the same time. Eddie was very excited and told his parents (who were pretty much strangers to him) about his exciting life on board ship. Being grown-ups, they only half-listened and, knowing full well that he'd actually been at school all this time, simply assumed that their only child had an overactive imagination.

They were puzzled by the trunk's return because they'd assumed it was lost at sea. Mr Brockenfeld, the editor of the *Terrible Times*, had sent a message saying that the inks had never arrived and now, all this time later, they'd somehow found their way back to their house (which later burnt down in the events outlined in *Awful End*).

One other side-effect of this strange mix-up was that, later in life, Eddie was to meet a few pupils of Glumberry School For Young Boys who assumed that they'd been at school with him – the trunk was always referred to as Edmund Dickens, remember – and were surprised how different he'd become.

'I remember you being much squarer shouldered when you were younger,' one Old Glumberry told him, for example.

A trip to America now, to try to find out what was going on at the *Terrible Times* offices, meant that Eddie would have a chance to re-acquaint himself with life at sea. (In those days, with the wind in your favour and no unexpected hitches or cock-ups, it took a clipper – a fast-sailing cargo ship – about two weeks to sail from England to the shores of North America. Steam ships were often slower, more expensive and, once in a while, blew up.) Eddie was really, really, *really* looking forward to it! He found an old atlas in Awful End's library and pored over it to try to work out the route the ship would be taking.

Eddie felt something jab him in the back. He turned to find that it was Malcolm the stuffed stoat's nose. Even Madder Aunt Maud had him tucked under her arm. She was dressed in her nightclothes and her slippers were covered in snow which was melting on the library floor.

'What are you doing?' she demanded.

'Trying to see what route the ship will take that's carrying me to America,' he explained, holding up the huge atlas with enthusiasm.

'You're being carried to America?' asked Even Madder Aunt Maud.

'Not by a person,' Eddie explained. 'By ship.'

'We're on board ship?' asked Even Madder Aunt Maud, looking a little confused.

'No,' said Eddie. 'But I will be soon.'

'Then why lie to me?' his great-aunt demanded. 'I suppose you think it's clever to try to muddle an old lady?'

'I'm sorry if I didn't make myself clear,' said Eddie. 'I didn't mean to –'

Even Madder Aunt Maud raised Malcolm in the air by his tail. The meaning was obvious. It meant: *Silence, young man, or I might hit you over the head with this here stuffed stoat.*

'I don't like tricks,' she said. 'I haven't forgotten the time you dressed as a tree and jumped out at me!'

Eddie had certainly forgotten it. Or, to be more accurate, had no recollection of this event and rather suspected that (if it really had happened) it

55

had been nothing to do with him.

'I don't think I've ever dressed as a tree, Even Madder Aunt Maud,' he protested.

'Exactly!' cried his great-aunt, her voice like someone drilling through a wall. 'You don't think! You don't think. Well, perhaps if you *did* think before you went and covered yourself in bark and leaves and jumped out on a poor old lady, then you wouldn't have done it.' She turned on her heels. 'Come, Malcolm,' she said, and left the library.

Eddie knew better than to try and protest his innocence any further, and went back to studying the atlas. After a while, he had the feeling that he was being watched, and looked around to see who, if anyone, was there. Framed in the doorway stood a complete stranger: a woman dressed in the finest of clothes.

'Master Dickens?' she enquired. (If you were that posh you didn't ask, you made enquiries.)

'Yes?' he said, politely.

'My name is Bustle, Lady Constance Bustle,' she said. 'Your father has asked me to act as your companion upon the upcoming voyage.'

Companion? It hadn't occurred to Eddie that his parents might worry about him travelling to America alone. It wasn't as if he wasn't used to a life at sea but, then again, there was still that confusion in his parents' minds.

'I'm delighted to meet you, Lady Constance,' said Eddie. She put out her gloved hand, and he strode across the library floor and kissed it. 'You've spoken to my father, you say?'

'Yes,' said Lady Constance. 'I've just come down from the scaffolding. He's currently painting an angel playing the harp, though I have to confess that, to me, it looks as if the angel is clutching an enormous vegetable and appears to be sitting on a large liver sausage.'

'That sounds like one of his clouds,' said Eddie.

'I suspected as much,' said Lady Constance. She had striking features (which doesn't mean that one wanted to hit her but that her face would stand out in a crowd, even though it would be a whopper to call her conventionally beautiful).

'My father isn't the world's greatest painter,' Eddie confessed. 'But he is most enthusiastic. What kind of vegetable, by the way?'

'A sprout,' said Lady Constance, 'though if it were that large in real life it would probably feed a family of four!' She laughed at her own joke in a snorty, horsy kind of way.

Eddie grinned. If he was going to have to have a companion on a long sea voyage, he could do worse than Lady Constance Bustle. Or so he thought.

'How did my father come to ask you to be my companion?' he asked. He'd never heard anyone mention her.

'I answered an advertisement,' she said. 'I was recently a companion to an elderly lady but she died.'

'I am sorry,' said Eddie, because that was the kind of thing you were expected to say when someone mentioned a death.

'I'm not,' replied Lady Constance. 'She was as sour as a bag of lemons . . . It was quite a relief when the railings on the edge of the ferry gave way and her bath chair tipped into the rapids.'

A bath chair's a kind of wheelchair. The one the old lady had been in was made of wicker. Her name had been Winifred Snafflebaum and her death caused quite a splash, both in the river and the local newspaper. The report said that Lady Constance had had to be restrained from jumping in after her employer to try to save her, though another eye-witness said that someone looking very like Lady Constance had brushed past him with a spanner in her hand not ten minutes before the ferry's railing had mysteriously 'given way'!

'So you're a companion by profession?' Eddie asked.

'Oh yes,' she nodded. 'Before the old lady, I was companion to a French woman. Sadly, she choked to death on a door handle.'

'How dreadful!' said Eddie.

'Most inconvenient,' Lady Constance agreed. 'I did so like living in Paris.'

'You must get to meet lots of different people,' said Eddie.

She nodded again. 'Though titled –' by which she meant being a 'lady', '– my family is a large one and the family fortune is small. In truth, it's not so much a fortune now as a large sock full of pennies under my father's bed. It has, therefore, been up to my eleven sisters and I to make our own way in the world. I could, of course, try to find some rich duke or baronet to marry, but I'd far rather travel the world as a companion. There's so much more freedom. It was simply bad luck that I was lumbered with such an objectionable old duck. She did leave me all her money though, which was nice.'

'I'm sure we'll have plenty of fun on the way to America and back,' said Eddie. He was a very well-mannered lad.

'There is one thing I should tell you whilst I remember,' said Lady Constance. 'I suffer from Dalton's Disease. Have you heard of it?'

Eddie had.

Dalton is probably famous for three things. Firstly, his Atomic Theory of 1808. In it, he claimed that if you kept cutting up something smaller and smaller and smaller you'd eventually come to something so small that it couldn't be cut up any more, and he called these smallest-of-small things atoms. Actually, he was wrong, because atoms can be cut up into sub-atomic particles and these can probably be broken up into sub-sub-atomic particles. Still awake? Excellent. But Dalton's Atomic Theory was *almost* right and way ahead of its time. It changed the way that every-one who thought about such things thought about such things, except for a small man in Alfriston, East Sussex, who stuck a finger in each ear and hummed loudly, stopping only occasionally only to shout: 'I'M NOT LISTENING!'

The second thing Dalton is famous for is keeping records of the local weather for just about every day of his adult life. Don't ask me why he did it. He just did. If he wanted to find out if it'd been raining in his back garden on a Wednesday twenty-five years previously, he could just look it up.

Thirdly, Dalton studied the problem he had with his vision. He was what we now call 'colour blind', and he did much to spread awareness of the condition. He even donated his eyeballs to science . . . for study *after* he died, of course. And that's why, in Eddie's day, colour-blindness was called Dalton's Disease. See? You pick up a book because of the funny picture on the cover and end up learning about some strange bloke who died in 1844. Isn't life just full of surprises?

Episode 6

Going . . . Going . . . ?

In which Eddie and the reader are almost halfway through the book and neither is sure whether he is ever going to get to America

The following Thursday, Mad Uncle Jack held a family meeting inside Marjorie the hollow cow. It was to have been in the library up at the main house, rather than inside a converted carnival float amongst the rose bushes, with onions hanging from the ceiling on strings, but Even Madder Aunt Maud had caught a cold from all that romping about in the snowdrifts after her shiny bauble, and was now in bed, and her husband had felt it important that she attend.

Also present were: Mad Uncle Jack himself, Mr and Mrs Dickens, their son Eddie, Lady Constance Bustle – who'd never been inside a hollow cow before – and Dawkins the gentleman's gentleman who was there to provide drinks . . . oh, and Malcolm, of course, if you count stuffed stoats. Jane, the failed chambermaid, was up in the house on her own, gibbering under the stairs, no doubt.

'This meeting is now in order!' Mad Uncle Jack announced, beating Even Madder Aunt Maud's bed with his dried swordfish for silence.

It hit her knees under the woolly blankets and she let out a cry: 'There's a dog on the bed! There's a dog on the bed!' Her cold had turned to a fever and she was slightly delirious. Make someone already as mad as Even Madder Aunt Maud *slightly* delirious and you get what by normal standards is *very* delirious.

'Where?' said MUJ, lifting the blankets to try to find the dog.

Eddie's father raised his hand, stiffly. 'Please ignore poor Aunt Maud, Uncle,' he said. 'And let's get on with the meeting, shall we?'

'What? Er, oh yes . . .' said MUJ. 'I wanted us to discuss plans for Eddie's voyage to America and visit to the offices of the *Terrible Times*. I'd like you to meet Eddie's travelling companion Lady Constance Bustle.'

Lady Constance stepped forward, parting the onions-on-strings above her head, as though pushing aside the leaves of an overhanging branch. 'I'm delighted to meet you all,' she said.

Even Madder Aunt Maud sat bolt upright in bed. 'You're pug ugly!' she gasped, which is another way of describing someone with striking or memorable features; a pug being a not-so-handsome breed of dog.

'Forgive my wife,' laughed Mad Uncle Jack. 'She's inclined to say what she thinks.'

Lady Constance wasn't sure what to say to *that*.

'A walking pair of nostrils!' cackled Even Madder Aunt Maud.

Mr Dickens was positioned between his aunt in bed and Eddie's travelling companion. 'Enchanted to meet you, Lady Constance,' he said, trying to lean forward to kiss her gloved hand but missing the target.

'Stay back, lady!' cried Even Madder Aunt Maud, with a barely suppressed guffaw. 'You'll frighten the stoat!' She waved Malcolm high above her head.

'I'm so pleased to know that my boy will be in your capable hands,' said Eddie's mother, Mrs Dickens. When Maud had started saying those embarrassing things to the titled newcomer, Mrs Dickens had become agitated and comforted

64

herself by filling her mouth with the nearest thing to hand – the tassel of Even Madder Aunt Maud's dressing-gown – so what she actually said was: 'Um thow pweed cha now vat my bow wiw be inyaw caypabuw ands.'

Eddie's father was well used to understanding his wife when she had a mouth full of ice-cubes shaped like famous generals or anti-panic pills or acorns, for example, but no one else had the slightest idea what she'd just said, the corner of EMAM's dressing-gown cord trailing from the edge of her mouth, like a half-eaten snake.

If Lady Constance Bustle wished that she was anywhere except inside a cow-shaped carnival float with a bunch of misfits, she hid it very well. Perhaps it was her good breeding. Perhaps it was something else.

'Lady Constance comes to me with impeccable references,' said Eddie's father. 'I'm sure if they hadn't all died, each and every one of her previous employers would have been reluctant to let her go.'

Her list of previous employers was, indeed, impressive. They included: Sir Adrian Carter, the author, who died during a visit to the Royal Zoological Gardens when Lady Constance slipped on a discarded banana skin and pushed him into the gorilla cage; the philosopher and forward-thinker John Knoxford John, who drowned in game soup during a visit to the famous Barnum Soup Factory when an apparently involuntary spasm in the leg, possibly brought on by the cooking fumes, caused Lady Constance to kick him off a viewing platform and into a giant vat; the Duchess of Underbridge, who fell to her death in her own home, unaware that Lady Constance had had the stairs removed that night 'for cleaning'. The list was a long one.

As well as being well-known or wealthy people, they all had something else in common. According to the letters and wills presented by the distraught Lady Constance after their untimely deaths, they all left their money – often small fortunes, sometimes not so small – to their devoted companion, Lady Constance. Oh yes, and there was one *other* thing they all had in common, judging from these letters and wills: surprisingly similar handwriting.

'I feel sure that Eddie is in safe hands,' said Mad Uncle Jack.

'Pug ugly hands!' cried Even Madder Aunt Maud from her bed.

'Should somebody fetch the doctor?' suggested Lady Constance.

'Should somebody fetch a bag for your head?' suggested Even Madder Aunt Maud, which would be considered rude even by today's standards but in Eddie's day such a comment would have been considered OUTRAGEOUS.

'I really must apologise for my husband's aunt's behaviour,' said Mrs Dickens. 'She's not a well woman.' If only life were that simple because, of course, what she actually said was: 'Oy weierwy muscht apowoguys faw mow hushbangs awunts beavyvaw. Sheech nowtta weow woomang.'

On the word 'woman', or 'woomang', the tassel of Even Madder Aunt Maud's dressing-gown shot out of Eddie's mum's mouth and hit Lady Constance slap bang/slam bam/full-square in her striking (and/or pug ugly) face.

Her ladyship snarled – yes *snarled* – like a cornered cat and hit Mrs Dickens across her face with her muffler.

67

Those of you wondering why Lady Constance was holding a car component designed to keep exhaust pipes from being too noisy have got the wrong end of the stick . . . It wasn't *that* kind of muffler, which some folk call 'silencers'. Let me turn the stick around the other way so that you can hold the right end. The kind of muffler Eddie's mother was hit with was a piece of fur sewn into an open-ended cylinder in which well-to-do ladies stuck a hand into either end to keep them warm.

This meant that Mrs Dickens wasn't actually hurt by Lady Constance's attack, but was deeply shocked by it. She'd been apologising to her for her husband's aunt's rudeness and the spitting out of the dressing-gown tassel had obviously been an accident. And what did she get by way of thanks? A literal as well as a metaphorical slap in the face with a muffler!

Matters were made worse by the fact that, in the dim light of Marjorie's insides, Even Madder Aunt Maud mistook Lady Constance Bustle's furry muffler for her own beloved stuffed stoat, Malcolm.

'How dare you treat my Malcolm in that way!' she protested, grabbing the nearest thing – which happened to be the *real* Malcolm, resting by her pillow – and used him to lash out at the next nearest thing . . . which, or I should say who, happened to be poor old Mad Uncle Jack. The victim of yet another attack from his wife, MUJ fell to the floor of the cow with a terrible yell.

Lady Constance, meanwhile, was apologising to Mrs Dickens. 'Do forgive my hitting you in the face,' she said. 'It was a reflex action by my right arm as a direct result of having been hit on the nose by the regurgitated dressing-gown cord. Hitting my nose is like pressing a button. My arm swipes out like a lever. I'm only glad that it was my muffler which hit you and not my *fist*.' She said the last word as though she had experience of just what damage her fist could do.

'We quite understand,' said Mr Dickens hurriedly. 'I'm only sorry that my wife spat at you first.'

Eddie, who was helping his poor winded great-uncle to his feet, studied Lady Constance with interest. He was beginning to suspect that there was much more to her than met the eye.

I can't actually tell you what part of Mad Uncle Jack got hit by Malcolm – it's far too rude – but suffice it to say that it hurt a great deal for a while, but he soon recovered and there was no real harm done. It did, however, put an end to the meeting so it was agreed that Lady Constance should stay the night at Awful End and that they discuss the trip the following morning.

Now it's time to sort out the smart readers (anyone sensible enough to be reading such an excellent book as this) from the *very* smart readers. If you were wondering how on Earth Mr Dickens was suddenly able to attend a meeting inside Marjorie when, just a few pages ago, he was spending all his time on his back at the top of a wooden scaffolding rig, you fall into the very smart category. If you didn't spot that, don't worry. I write such beautiful prose that you were probably so engrossed in marvelling at my storytelling skills that you didn't let something as insignificant as how someone got to be somewhere bother you. Well, it's no big mystery, so let me explain:

Mad Uncle Jack had thought it important that everyone attend the Eddie-going-to-America meeting, so Dawkins (the gentleman's gentleman) and Gibbering Jane (the failed chambermaid) had been sent up the scaffolding to lash Mr Dickens to a plank of wood and lower him down to the ground on a pulley usually reserved for the chamber pot. Once on the floor of the hall of Awful End he was tipped upright (still lashed to the plank) and tied to a porter's trolley – one of those two-wheeled trolleys with a high back that railway porters sometimes still use to carry luggage – and wheeled down the garden to the hollow cow. Even this was harder than it sounded. Dawkins did the wheeling whilst Gibbering Jane ran ahead, gibbering, with a coal shovel, clearing a path through the snow.

It had been lashed to a plank and a porter's trolley, parked in the upright but rigid position inside the cow, that Mr Dickens had conducted himself at the meeting as I just outlined. If you think this is ridiculous, I should remind you that, near the end of the 20th century there was a film/movie/flick/motion picture called *The Silence of the Lambs* based on a book of the same name written by Thomas  Harris. In the film (which I have seen) and possibly the book (which I haven't read) the baddy (played by a very well-respected Welsh-born actor) is, at one stage, wheeled around on a porter's trolley AND he's wearing a silly mask, and everyone took that very seriously; so you can understand why, in the oh-so-polite 19th century, Lady Constance Bustle was far too polite to giggle or to ask what was going on . . . and the others probably just accepted it as perfectly normal. We are talking about the *Dickens* family, don't forget.

With the meeting now over, Mr Dickens was untied from the porter's trolley, winched back up the wooden scaffolding rig, untied from the plank, which was then slid out from under him, and left in his usual position, staring up at the ceiling. He was in the process of painting 'Joseph and his coat of many colours' which, the truth be told – I am informed by someone who saw it before it was painted over years later – looked more like 'a mutant melting rainbow with a head, and fingers like liver sausages'. See? Just about everything he painted on that ceiling sounds as if it had at least something sausagy about it!

Mad Uncle Jack retired to his tree house, still winded. Even Madder Aunt Maud drifted off to sleep in Marjorie, dreaming about a pair of giant nostrils, and Eddie and his mother had supper at the kitchen table.

'I made the soup myself,' said his mother.

'What is it?' asked Eddie, studying the contents of his bowl. It looked very clear, except for the odd tiny leaf and what might possibly have been a dead fly.

'I used ingredients I found in the garden,' she said proudly.

'I thought the ground was far too hard to dig up vegetables,' said Eddie. 'Frozen solid.' He tasted the soup. It was like drinking hot water.

'I used melted snow,' she said. 'Oh look.' She took something out of her mouth. 'Here's one of Private Gorey's brass buttons.' She put it on the edge of her plate like a prune stone.

Eddie let out one of his silent sighs. He wished he was in America already!

Episode 7

. . . Gone!

In which, to everyone's amazement, including the author's, Eddie actually sets sail for America

I n Eddie's mind, he had imagined saying goodbye to his mother on a quayside and then striding up a gangplank to a ship. When the time came – and amazingly, it did come – only Mad Uncle Jack accompanied him and Lady Constance on his farewell trip, and the ship was anchored at the mouth of an estuary in deeper water. The only way to reach the ship was by rowing boat and climbing up a rope ladder.

When Eddie first met Mad Uncle Jack, he – Uncle Jack – used to go just about everywhere by horse (inside and out). But then, following Eddie's escape from an orphanage his horse bolted at the first sight of a giant hollow cow, whom we now know as Marjorie. When the poor frightened creature finally let itself be caught, it was a changed animal. Whereas before it was happy to do just about anything Mad Uncle Jack asked of it, now it dug its hooves in (which is, I suppose, the horsy equivalent of 'put its foot down') and regularly refused to gallop upstairs or jump over chimney sweeps . . . so MUJ spent much more time on foot.

He had acquired a new horse at the same time; Marjorie having been pulled along by one belonging to Mr and Mrs Cruel-Streak who'd run the St Horrid's Home for Grateful Orphans, from which Eddie (and the orphans) had escaped. Now it was obvious that the Cruel-Streaks cared more for their horse than the orphans in their so-called 'care', but the Dickenses were in no mood to return the animal to such nasty owners, so they kept him. Technically, this was theft but, as someone jolly famous was to announce a number of years later: all property is theft. (Wow! Think about that . . . You don't have to agree with it. Just think about it!)

This particular horse (whom they named

Edgar) was so used to being pampered that he spent much of his time sipping a small glass of sherry, reading *Bradfield's Horse & Hounds*. (The horse read *Bradfield's Horse & Hounds*, not the sherry. Sherry can't read. Come to think of it . . .)

Rather than travelling by pony and trap or horse and carriage, therefore, Mad Uncle Jack, Eddie and Lady Constance had travelled to the port by train.

Trains were at their most exciting back then. Locomotives made brilliant noises and belched out great billows of smoke from their gleaming funnels, and next to the driver on the open footplate stood the fireman, frantically stoking the furnace with fuel to create the steam to power the engine to turn the wheels.

Possibly the most famous engine driver of the steam-train era was the American Casey Jones. There are songs about him, a railway-station-based chain of burger outlets was named after him and there was even a long-running TV series about him and his heroic deeds . . . which is a bit strange when you realise that, in real life, he crashed his train, 'the old 638', and was killed in a terrible accident which was, according to the official investigation at the time, entirely his fault 'as a consequence of not having properly responded to flag signals'. Weird, huh? But I digress. Back to Eddie's train:

As well as first- and second-class carriages there were third-class ones too, which were usually jam-packed full of slightly grubby people carrying bulging sacks or live chickens. They may not have started out the journey grubby, but – jam-packed with all those other people – they always ended it that way. Some third-class passengers also ended up with chickens they hadn't set off with. Such people are technically known as 'thieves'.

MUJ, Eddie and Lady Constance were in the first-class carriages, which were very different. In the first-class dining car, pink flamingos stood on one leg each in an ornamental pond with plush velvet seats neatly arranged around it in semicircles. The windows in first class had shutters, blinds *and* curtains – whereas in third class they relied on the grime to keep out the light, when travelling at night – and all the fixtures and fittings were either made of gleaming metal or highly polished wood. In fact the insides of the first-class carriage and dining car were probably a lot nicer than most people's homes!

Eddie's travelling trunk was far too big to fit in the train carriage, let alone put on a rack, so it had been loaded into the guard's van. Eddie, however, was not so lucky. Mad Uncle Jack insisted that he spend much of the journey lying in one of the luggage racks above the seats.

'It's to get you used to life at sea, m'boy!' he explained. 'They don't have beds on board ship, you know, they have hummocks.'

'H*a*mmocks,' Eddie corrected him. (Hummocks are very small hills.) He'd tried to tell Mad Uncle Jack that he'd had plenty of experience of life on the ocean waves and couldn't he please sit in a seat like anyone else . . . but failed.

The luggage rack was uncomfortable enough as it was but when Lady Constance stuck her parasol – a small umbrella designed to keep off the sun rather than the rain – up there alongside him, it was really uncomfortable . . . but nothing could dampen his excitement of going to America to find out what had gone wrong at the offices of the *Terrible Times*.

When they finally reached the port and Mad Uncle Jack lifted Eddie off the luggage rack, the poor boy had mesh-marks all over his clothes and bare arms.

'It suits you,' whispered Lady Constance.

Eddie grinned. O, foolish, foolish child. (I'm allowed to say things like that because I know what's going to happen later.)

Somehow a porter managed to wheel Eddie's huge trunk, with Lady Constance's bags balanced precariously on top, out of the busy station, with one single journey of a porter's trolley. It was similar to the one that Dawkins and Gibbering Jane had used to transport Eddie's father to and from Marjorie. They passed a ragbag of street vendors trying to sell everything from newspapers and fresh(-ish) fruit to quack remedies (which are not cures for quacking but so-called cures that didn't really offer any relief except, of course, relieving you of your money to pay for them). Mad Uncle Jack hailed a cab in his own inimitable way. He rummaged in his coat and, producing a large dried puffer fish from his pocket, he threw it with all his might at a passing cab-driver; knocking the poor man's hat clean off.

'Strewth!' said the cabbie, swerving his cab in the direction the projectile had been thrown. I think I'd have said a lot worse if the dried puffer fish had hit me. The puffer fish gets its name from puffing out into a big spiky ball, and note the adjective 'spiky'. A dried one of those thrown at your head could cause quite an 'OUCH!!!'

'Who threw that?' demanded the enraged driver.

'It was me,' said Mad Uncle Jack. 'You can keep the change.' To those who knew him, this made complete sense. He 'paid' for everything with dried fish and, by his reckoning, a puffer fish was quite high currency (more of a twenty-pound note than nickel and dime change). Of course, those who knew him also knew to parcel up the fish and send them to Eddie's father, Mr Dickens, who then sent them actual money in exchange. Those who didn't know Mad Uncle Jack and his unusual ways thought that he was either someone trying to make a fool out of them, or that he was a nutter. Or both. Which was exactly what the angry cabbie was thinking as he charged horse and cab towards the kerb.

'Do you take me for some kind of a fool?' he demanded.

'I take you to be a cab driver waiting for a fare and we are a fare waiting for a cab-driver,' said MUJ, blissfully unaware that he'd caused minor injury and major offence. (A 'fare' not only meant payment but also a passenger in the cab.) He patted the cabbie's horse.

While Mad Uncle Jack and the cab driver were talking – you can't really call it an argument because it takes two to argue – Eddie opened a door of the cab and Lady Constance stepped inside and sat down. Next Eddie stepped in and sat down beside her. With more strength than his stick-like body suggested was possible, Mad Uncle Jack helped the porter heave the heavy trunk off the porter's trolley and on to the roof of the cab, then threw Lady Constance's luggage up after it, piece by piece.

The cabbie knew he was beaten and let the thin, beaky man climb inside the cab without further fuss or delay. 'Where to, guv'nor?' he asked, which is what they still teach cab-drivers to say at cab-driving school today.

'To the *Pompous Pig*,' said MUJ. 'She's due to set sail today.'

'To America,' Eddie added excitedly.

'Aha!' said the cabbie, obviously pleased to know something they didn't. 'She's too big to dock in the port in this tide, so they've dropped anchor at the river's mouth. You'll have to get a boat out to it from Muddy Straits. I'll take you there.' He swished his horse's reins and they were off.

'Muddy Straits sounds rather *muddy*,' Eddie called out.

'It did indeed get its name on account of the

mud,' said the cabbie, knowledgeably.

Muddy Straits was a large area of grey, damp mud which birdwatchers so love and which the rest of us find so boring that you're almost guaranteed that nowadays it would be turned into an area of Special Scientific Interest, with its own leaflet explaining why it was important not to turn this boggy habitat into a new four-runway airport. The snow had long since melted, so the mud was there in all its glory, for all to see.

'It's a shame this mud can't be put to some good use,' said Mad Uncle Jack when he stepped out of the cab and took in his surroundings. 'Put in a brightly coloured fancy package, with a pretty bow on top, and I'm sure it would appeal to ladies.'

'But what would they use it for?' asked Eddie, who had paid the driver with real money – he'd been given some for the voyage – before the whole payment-with-fish approach could rear its ugly head and upset the poor man again. The luggage was then heaved to the ground.

'What do ladies *do* with half the things they own: china ornaments, trinkets, mementoes? They leave them cluttering up the place, that's what they do. Little packets of mud needn't be different. They don't have to be *for* anything.'

'The skin,' said Lady Constance, dusting the top of the trunk with a handkerchief, removed from her sleeve, before sitting down upon it and rearranging her dress.

'I beg your pardon?' said Eddie.

'The skin,' said Lady Constance. 'Some types of mud are said to be particularly good for the skin. Ladies have been known to wear mud packs upon their faces. There are even some in society who believe a mud bath to be most revivifying.'

Eddie hadn't the foggiest what 'revivifying' meant, but he didn't much like the idea of having a bath in mud . . . Well, certainly not in the mud around Muddy Straits. It looked gloopy and smelly, with tufts of marshy weeds sprouting out in places, reminding him of the nostril hairs Even Madder Aunt Maud had trimmed from the nose of her stuffed stoat.

'I cannot imagine my beloved,' (which is pronounced as though spelled belove-ed, as in the name 'Ed' short for Eddie, short for Edmund) 'wearing a mud pack upon her face!' said Mad Uncle Jack in obvious amazement.

Eddie could imagine quite the opposite. If anyone was mad enough to smear mud all over her face, then Even Madder Aunt Maud was the one!

'Poor Mrs Riversedge,' (which is spelled like 'rivers edge' but pronounced 'river sedge') 'suffocated whilst wearing a homemade mud pack

I had prepared,' said Lady Constance.

'One of your employers?' asked Eddie.

Lady Constance nodded, wiping a non-existent tear from her eye. 'I'm afraid so.'

The cabbie, meanwhile, had raised his hat and left them at the water's edge. It was only when he'd clattered off with his cab that it occurred to MUJ that he'd need a ride back to the railway station once he'd seen off his great-nephew and the boy's travelling companion on the *Pompous Pig*.

'Now what?' asked Eddie. 'Are we supposed to swim out to the boat?'

'Ship,' said Lady Constance.

'I beg your pardon?' said Eddie.

'It's a ship, not a boat,' said Lady Constance.

'What's the difference?' asked Eddie.

For all I know, Lady Constance was about to reply 'about three points in Scrabble with the letters on ordinary squares' – except, of course, Scrabble hadn't been invented back then – because she never got to tell Eddie the difference. They were interrupted by a loud whistle.

'Look!' said Mad Uncle Jack, pointing excitedly at a sparrow passing them overhead. 'An albatross!' He never was very good at identifying wildlife and once mistook a badger for a lance-corporal in his regiment. 'I'd recognise that cry anywhere!'

'Er, that was a whistle,' said Eddie.

'Coming from that rowing boat,' said Lady Constance pointing at the little boat heading for them.

The oarsman reached the shallows and jumped out into the water, his feet protected by a pair of high leather boots. He dragged the boat behind him.

'Lady Constance Bustle and Master Edmund Dickens?' he asked, in that 'oo-arr' accent which sailors always seem to have in pirate stories.

'Yes,' said Eddie excitedly.

'Indeed,' nodded Lady Constance.

'I'm Jolly,' said the sailor.

'I'm somewhat cheerful myself,' said Eddie's great-uncle, 'despite most of my family being ill or injured.'

'You misunderstand, sir,' said the sailor. 'My name be Jolly.'

'Aha!' nodded Mad Uncle Jack. 'You're Mr B Jolly . . . What does the "B" stand for? Brian?'

'No sir, you see –'

'Benjamin?'

'No, I –'

'Benedict? Bernard? Balthazar?'

'I –'

'Bill?'

'No, my –'

'No, if you were Bill your initial would be "W" and not "B" because your first name would be William –'

'ROGER!' shouted the sailor in desperation.

'I beg your pardon?' said Mad Uncle Jack.

'My name, sir . . . My name be Roger but me shipmates call me Jolly.'

'I see,' said Eddie with glee. 'Because the skull-and-crossbones flag is called the Jolly Roger!'

'That be right, young gentleman!' said the sailor with a toothless grin.

'I do hope the *Pompous Pig* isn't a pirate vessel!' said Lady Constance.

'I wouldn't let Captain Skrimshank hear you speak like that, m'lady,' said Jolly. 'He prides himself on being one of Her Majesty's most loyal subjects. He carries a picture of her with him everywhere.'

'I, on the other hand,' said Mad Uncle Jack, 'carry portraits of my own family with me everywhere.' He opened his long checked coat to reveal a series of small oil paintings somehow fixed to the lining, the tail of the dried swordfish he used as an ear-cleaner-cum-back-scratcher sticking from an inner pocket. Eddie had first laid eyes on these pictures when his great-uncle had nailed them up on a visit to his house, since destroyed by fire.

86

Jolly eyed the oil paintings. He eyed the tail of the dried fish. He eyed Mad Uncle Jack. 'I think we'd better be gettin' to the *Pompous Pig*,' he said. Then he eyed the large trunk. 'That'll leave us low in the water.' Soon they, and their luggage, were in the rowing boat.

The goodbyes were brief and, in next to no time, Mad Uncle Jack was just a small dot in the distance. Soon Eddie was stepping off the boat and climbing up the rope ladder after Lady Constance, to find himself on the deck of the ship that was intended to carry them to foreign shores.

*

Unlike his many years at sea 'below decks', Eddie now had a proper cabin to himself, connected by an inner 'adjoining door' to Lady Constance's. He had a proper bed, too, not the hammock (nor, to be more accurately inaccurate, the hummock) MUJ had predicted.

According to the first mate, Mr Spartacus Briggs, who had greeted them and shown them around the ship on their arrival, there was only one other paying passenger on board, but Eddie had yet to meet him. This was not a pleasure cruise, nor a ship full of immigrants wanting to start a new life in the fairly new (but not quite so new as it used to be) New World of the Americas. It was, first and foremost, a merchant vessel taking cargo to America, with the intention of filling up with other goods in America and bringing them home to Britain. The paying passengers were an added source of income – more money, money, money – for the ship's owners.

When Eddie did finally lay eyes on their fellow passenger he couldn't believe them. A feeling of horror, which started at his heels and spread all over his body like a hot flush, soon engulfed him. It couldn't be . . . surely?

But it was.

There on the deck stood a man he'd last seen in an arrowed suit, with a ball and chain fitted to his ankle. It was the escaped convict Swags.

The man's hooded eyes met his with a piercing stare. There was no doubt in Eddie's mind that the villain recognised him in return. It was unlikely that Swags would have forgotten him. Eddie had helped in the capture of one of his fellow convicts – the leader of his little group, in fact – which probably made him not only memorable but *very unpopular*, too!

What made matters even worse, of course, was that, on board ship, there was nowhere to run . . .

Episode 8

Discoveries

In which Eddie may be at sea, but we seem to spend most of the time amongst familiar faces on dry land

How Even Madder Aunt Maud came to be in Eddie's large sea trunk no one knows to this day. It became a regular topic of conversation in the Dickens family and many theories have been put forward over the years, even from Dickenses who weren't even born at the time, but the truth went with Even Madder Aunt Maud to her grave – buried inside Marjorie in her beloved rose garden – not long after her 126th birthday (which is nearly a quarter of a century after Eddie, Lady Constance and Maud-in-the-trunk set sail for America).

What *is* known is that it took nearly a week at sea before Even Madder Aunt Maud was discovered aboard the *Pompous Pig*, because she soon vacated the trunk and moved about the ship, sleeping in a variety of places from the cook's cauldron in the galley to the crow's nest at the top of the main mast.

There had been rumours spreading around the ship of a strange being cackling to herself and taking things but Eddie knew from experience that sailors were a superstitious bunch who drank a lot, which didn't make them the best eye-witnesses when apparently 'seeing things'. It was only when Eddie heard a number of reports of this apparition – variously described as a 'water witch' and 'sea hag' and everything in between – wielding some kind of animal, possibly a rigid ferret, that Eddie began to fear the worst; that his great-aunt and Malcolm had somehow got on board!

It took almost as long for the folks back at Awful End to discover that Even Madder Aunt Maud had gone missing. With Mr Dickens up his wooden scaffolding rig, Gibbering Jane under the stairs, Mad Uncle Jack back in his tree house, Mrs Dickens pootling about doing whatever she did and poor old Dawkins, the gentleman's gentleman, doing everyone's bidding, they probably assumed that Even Madder Aunt Maud was in Marjorie or, on finding the cow empty, had just nipped out with Malcolm for a breath of fresh air. When they did finally realise that she was well and truly GONE, they had no idea where. There were no telephones, no ship-to-shore telegraphs or radios, and the word 'email' was nothing more than a misspelling of 'female', with the 'f' missing; so there was no way that those aboard the *Pompous Pig* could let them know she was safe and well. To put it bluntly, the folk at Awful End were baffled. She seemed to have vanished into thin air.

MUJ went to the local police station to report his wife missing. He knew the detective inspector from a previous encounter and demanded to see him. Knowing that Mad Uncle Jack was the gentleman living up at 'the big house' and completely mad, of course, the sergeant at the front desk led him straight through to the inspector's office. The front desk was a new idea and the sergeant was still in the looking-at-it-admiringly stage, and was keen to get back to it. He'd bought a tin of beeswax with his own money (and he didn't get paid very much so this was beyond the call of duty). He intended to wax and polish the front desk in his lunch hour which was, for some inexplicable reason, only 45 minutes long.

'There's this madman to see you, sir,' said the

sergeant, showing MUJ into the inspector's office. The inspector was sitting behind his desk on a pile of gazetteers (which are a kind of book). He was a very large man and his desk chair had recently broken under the weight of him. The detective inspector struggled to his feet. 'Ah, Mad Mr Dickens,' he said in greeting. 'How may I be of service?'

Mad Uncle Jack fumbled in his pocket and pulled out a dried halibut. A halibut is a flat fish and therefore, if you're that way inclined, an ideal fish to write on. 'My wife has disappeared,' he explained. 'I've made some notes on her last known movements.'

'Disappeared, you say?' said the detective inspector.

'Disappeared,' MUJ nodded. He handed the policeman the dried halibut.

The inspector could not read so did not know that MUJ's scribbles were writing. He simply assumed that the dried fish had strange markings and was being proffered as a snack – in much the same way that you or I might offer someone a crisp/potato chip – so he tried to take a bite out of it. He nearly broke his teeth.

'What are you doing?' demanded Mad Uncle Jack, wanting to know why the detective was eating his carefully written notes.

'What are *you* doing?' demanded the inspector, wanting to know why on Earth he had been handed an uneatable snack. (And, no, the word shouldn't be 'inedible'. If something's inedible, it means that you can physically eat it but it's so horrible that no one in their right mind would want to. If something's uneatable, you physically can't eat it; such as a chunk of rock . . . or one of Mad Uncle Jack's dried fish.)

'I want you to read my notes!' Mad Uncle Jack protested. He had been around to every member of the household asking them when they'd last actually seen Even Madder Aunt Maud and had carefully written down their responses. Now he could see that there were teeth marks on his notes and that the detective's saliva had smudged some of the replies . . . and he'd been very proud of his initial investigations!

The inspector was equally angry. 'I may not be able to read,' he said, 'but I know the difference between a piece of paper and a dried fish, and I don't take kindly to you trying to make a fool out of me!'

'Can't read?' spluttered Mad Uncle Jack. 'Who ever heard of a police inspector who can't read?'

'Me for one, sir,' said the sergeant from the front desk who'd come back into the office to ask to borrow a cloth for the polishing. 'The detective inspector, here, can't read and he's the best detective inspector for miles around.'

'Thank you, Sergeant,' said the inspector, returning to his seat of books and sitting back down behind his desk.

'I expect you're the ONLY detective inspector for miles around!' said the clearly agitated Mad Uncle Jack.

'Not true!' said the inspector and was about to pull out a map marked with the county's police stations when he thought better of it. He placed the dried halibut on his desk and then folded his arms across his stomach. 'Do, please, sit down, Mad Mr Dickens, and tell me all about your dear lady wife's disappearance.'

The detective inspector may not have been able to read but he was certainly a very good detective inspector. He listened very carefully to what MUJ had to say and, based on the facts laid out before him, made an initial hypothesis (not to be confused with an initialled hippopotamus . . . which is rather unlikely, come to think of it).

'It would seem that no one has seen your wife since you, your great-nephew Edmund and his travelling companion Lady Constance left to catch the *Pompous Pig*,' said the inspector, 'which leads me to conclude that she either disappeared during your brief absence or, somehow, went with you.'

'How do you mean went with us?' asked Mad Uncle Jack, so deep in concentration that he was unaware that he was combing his moustache with the serrated edge of his dried swordfish's nose.

'That she hung on to the back or underside of your coach, or somehow got inside your great-nephew's luggage,' said the police officer, which would have sounded crazy if they weren't talking about Even Madder Aunt Maud. He'd met her once before and had built up an extremely accurate psychological profile of her: completely bonkers.

'Well . . .' said Mad Uncle Jack, a little

hesitantly, 'I suppose that's a possibility. In our early years of marriage, she did once glue herself to the underside of a performing African elephant when the circus came to town, so went with them to the next venue, though she did reassure me afterwards that it'd been by mistake . . . She's a truly remarkable woman.'

'Remarkable,' repeated the inspector, as he was prone to do; though he said the word as though it wasn't necessarily the one he'd have chosen first and foremost to describe Mad Uncle Jack's missing spouse.

'And what about the other possibility? Her disappearing during my absence instead?' asked MUJ, slipping the dried fish back into his pocket.

'That would be more of a coincidence,' the detective pointed out, 'but not an impossibility. If she'd disappeared during the period when there were all those breakouts from Grimpen Jail and escaped convicts on the loose, I'd be concerned for her safety. But all the escapees, bar one, were recaptured a long, long time ago and the single one still at large will have fled the district long ago, too. No, in my professional opinion, your wife has probably ended up aboard the *Pompous Pig*.'

'If she was simply hanging on to the back or underside of our carriage, she might have dropped off at the station before we got on the train,' Mad Uncle Jack pointed out.

'If that was the case, she, or someone who ran into her, would have probably been in contact with you by now,' the inspector reasoned. 'She has a . . . er, very distinctive way about her.' What he actually meant was that a potty woman wielding a stuffed stoat would stick out like a pyramid in a sandpit.

'But what makes you so sure that she's actually aboard my great-nephew's ship?' asked Mad Uncle Jack.

'The very fact that there's been no report of anyone having seen her,' said the detective inspector. 'If she's on the *Pompous Pig*, neither she nor the crew can contact us unless they land and send someone ashore with a message . . . and the first stop after Ireland is America itself.' He struggled to his feet once more. 'Just to be doubly sure, I'll have my sergeant check the daily reports from other districts to see whether there have been any sightings, but I'm sure I'd have remembered them from the morning briefings. I'll also have him fill in a full missing person's report. I have all the information I need stored in here.' He tapped the side of his head and a small, round peppermint fell out of his ear on the opposite side, and rolled across the floor.

The policeman was more startled than Mad Uncle Jack, who simply assumed that the detective inspector had a head full of them. What had actually happened was that the inspector'd had a peppermint in his hand before dozing off at his desk, resting his head in said hand. The peppermint had got pushed into his ear and, when he'd been awoken by the sergeant knocking at the door to his office, he'd sat bolt upright, blissfully unaware that the peppermint had been lodged there . . . until now.

'If you find anything out, please inform me immediately,' said Mad Uncle Jack. 'You can usually find me in my tree house.'

'If *you* find anything out, please inform *me* immediately,' added the detective inspector. 'You can usually find me in *my* tree house.'

'You have a tree house?' asked Mad Uncle Jack.

'No,' confessed the detective inspector. 'I don't

know what made me say that. Sorry.'

Mad Uncle Jack left the police station, striding past the desk sergeant who was watching the hands of the police station clock approach the hour. He was itching to get out his beeswax and make a start on his desk.

Episode 9

That Sinking Feeling

*In which both Eddie and Mad Uncle Jack make plans
regarding the 'recapture' of Even Madder Aunt Maud*

The first thing Eddie did on seeing Swags, the escaped convict on board the *Pompous Pig*, was to tell Lady Constance.

'Are you sure that it's him?' she asked when he'd told her the whole story.

'I'm sure,' nodded Eddie, wishing that there was some room for doubt.

'And is Swags his real name?'

He thought hard. 'I think it was short for Swagman, but that was only a nickname, too.'

'I believe that a swagman is an Australian drifter,' said Lady Constance, with a puzzled frown.

'That's it!' said Eddie. 'I remember now. He was given the nickname because he'd been sent on a convict ship to Australia but had somehow escaped back to England . . . only to be jailed for something else and to escape again. This time to the moors.'

'And it looks like he's now trying to escape to America,' said Lady Constance, letting it sink in.

'So what should we do? Inform the captain?' asked Eddie. 'He could be dangerous.'

'Do you know what Swags was in jail for?' asked his travelling companion.

'No,' Eddie confessed.

'So he could be harmless,' said Lady Constance. 'I've heard stories of men being convicted for stealing a loaf of bread, and I don't think a loaf-thief will do much harm . . .'

'He might do if he's afraid of being caught!' protested Eddie. 'And, anyway, for all we know, Swag could be a murderer!'

They were in Eddie's cabin, him sitting on his bed and Lady Constance in a chair. She stood up and sat down next to him on the bed, taking his hand. 'Eddie,' she said. 'You don't even know his real name. You don't know what he was originally

102

locked up for and it's your word against his that he's an escaped convict. Don't you think it would be better to say nothing?'

'I . . . I . . .' Eddie was speechless. This wasn't what he'd expected her to say at all.

'Not only that, he's unlikely to try to harm you if he wants to get to America, isn't he? It's in his best interest to behave himself and to keep a low profile. If he goes around threatening people he'll simply draw attention to himself but, if he does try anything, then we should go straight to Mr Briggs or Captain Skrimshank. Agreed?' asked Lady Constance.

'Agreed,' sighed Eddie but, in his heart of hearts, he wanted to inform the captain right then.

*

When Eddie later told Lady Constance of his suspicions – his *conviction* – that Even Madder Aunt Maud had somehow got on board the ship, her reaction was completely different.

'We must warn . . . er, that is *tell* Mr Briggs at once. We must find your poor great-aunt before she harms herself or, possibly, the *Pompous Pig*. Who knows what she and that stuffed stoat of hers might get up to unchecked!'

They hurried off together to find the first mate.

He was on the smaller upper deck, where the huge steering wheel thingy was – I don't know the nautical term – standing by a scruffy young boy who was actually 'at the wheel', steering the vessel.

'We have reason to believe that there's a stowaway on board,' said Lady Constance, whom Eddie noticed was fluttering her eyebrows at the handsome Mr Spartacus Briggs in a way he'd never seen her flutter them in front of anyone else.

'Really, Lady Constance?' asked the first mate, straightening himself to his full height in his fine uniform. 'Do you have any idea who it is?'

'Young Master Edmund's great-aunt,' said Lady Constance.

The boy – for he was no more than that – at the wheel smirked at Eddie. He was in a tattered sailor suit and had gaps in his teeth. He reminded Eddie of the orphans he'd helped escape from St Horrid's a while back.

Mr Briggs looked disappointed. 'Your great-aunt?' he said, turning his attention to Eddie.

'I'm afraid so, Mr Briggs,' he said. The first mate had insisted, at their first meeting, that it would be wrong to call him 'sir'. 'She's the sea witch with the ferret your men have been reporting seeing . . . only she's not a witch, just Even Madder Aunt Maud, and it's not a ferret but her stuffed stoat Malcolm.'

'I see,' said Mr Spartacus Briggs, though he obviously didn't. It was hard for Eddie to explain his relatives to someone who'd not met them face to face. 'How do you think she got on board?'

'She must have been inside my trunk,' said Eddie. 'It was very heavy but, when I opened it after your men put it in my cabin, there was only an apple core and a single handkerchief inside.'

'And you didn't think to report it?' asked Mr Briggs. 'I mean, didn't you consider the possibility that say, for example, some of the men aboard this ship might have stolen its contents?'

'It was mainly clothes,' said Eddie, 'and, with the way things happen in my family, I assumed one of my relatives must simply have unpacked what I'd packed.'

'The Dickenses are a most unusual family,' Lady Constance added helpfully. 'Unique, I hope.'

Eddie wasn't listening. 'Now it's obvious that Even Madder Aunt Maud must have emptied the trunk and climbed inside.'

'But why would she want to be a stowaway on a ship to America?' pondered Mr Briggs.

'Oh, I doubt she planned anything like that,' said Eddie, surprised that the first mate should even consider that his great-aunt would have had anything sensible, like a plan! 'I expect she saw the trunk and thought it was a comfortable place to have a quick sleep, or some such thing.'

'I see,' said Mr Briggs. 'Er, I have just two more questions before I report this to the captain.'

'Yes?'

'Firstly, have you any idea how we might – er – get your great-aunt to come out into the open?'

'I'm sorry?' asked Eddie.

'He means do you have any thoughts on how they might capture her?' explained Lady Constance.

A big grin spread across Eddie's face. He'd just had a brilliant idea. It was obvious! Why hadn't he thought of it before? He needn't have involved the crew. 'Shiny things!' he cried. 'It's worked before and it'll work again. Shiny things!'

'Shiny fings?' asked the boy at the wheel.

'Quiet, Powder Monkey!' the first mate ordered. 'Concentrate on steering.'

'Yes, sir,' said the boy, looking down at the ship's wheel deck with a sheepish look on his face.

'Shiny things?' asked Mr Spartacus Briggs and Lady Constance Bustle as one.

Eddie nodded. 'My great-aunt's a bit like a jackdaw,' Eddie began.

'But your great-*uncle*'s the one with a nose like a beak,' said Lady Constance, which was another of her not-so-ladylike comments.

'I mean that she seems to love collecting shiny objects nowadays. Last summer there was a highly polished mortar shell . . . recently there was the crystal bauble from a chandelier . . . She can't resist them.'

'So if we were to bait a trap with a shiny object, we could lie in wait and – er – encourage her to stay in your cabin with you rather than frighten the men?' nodded Mr Briggs. 'I think we have the makings of a plan here, Master Dickens. Well done!'

'That's all very well, Mr Briggs,' said Eddie's travelling companion. 'But do you have anything particularly shiny on board?'

'There's always the sextant,' said Mr Briggs.

'The what?' asked Lady Constance.

'It's the instrument used for calculating latitude, by working out the angle of the sun from the horizon,' said Eddie, to their amazement. 'It's often made of polished brass.' (This boy had been to sea before, remember.)

'Exactly!' said Mr Briggs. He slapped Eddie on the back. 'Well done, lad.' Eddie only just managed to stop himself falling to the deck. That was some slap!

'Sorry to spoil the party,' said Lady Constance, 'but you must have been using your sextant throughout the voyage already.'

'And?' asked Mr Briggs.

'It ain't attracted the dotty old lady yet, so why should it now?' said Powder Monkey, getting a thwack around the ear for his trouble.

'Back down to the galley with you!' ordered the first mate, but he didn't look too angry. Powder Monkey scurried off between their legs and Mr Briggs took the wheel.

'He seems rather young to be steering this ship,' said Lady Constance.

Mr Briggs smiled. 'He's really a galley hand – a kitchen helper – but he's a good lad and has been pestering me to show him the ropes.'

'You're a kind man,' said Lady Constance, fluttering those eyelashes of hers again.

'You have a good point about the sextant,' said

Eddie. 'We'll have to think of something really shiny to bring Even Madder Aunt Maud out of hiding.'

With one hand on the wheel, and his eyes on the horizon – not literally, of course, or they'd have to be on very long stalks – the first mate rubbed his chin, deep in thought. 'I can think of just the thing to attract her,' he said. 'The shiniest of shiny things. It can't fail . . . but I must talk with Captain Skrimshank first.'

'Excellent!' said Lady Constance.

'What was your second question?' asked Eddie.

'I beg your pardon?'

'You originally said you had two questions for me, Mr Briggs.'

'Ah, yes,' said the first mate. 'I was wondering why you didn't have any clothes on?'

Of course Eddie wasn't *naked* naked, he was *almost* naked – he was in his undies – but that was still a very odd way for a paying passenger (back then) to be wandering around a ship.

'As I said, Mr Briggs, all my clothes were missing from my trunk. I've only got the ones I came aboard with and Lady Constance has kindly washed those because they were beginning to . . . to . . .'

'Smell a little ripe,' said his professional companion, finding the right words. 'They're currently drying in the rigging.' She nodded in the direction of one of the masts where, sure enough, Eddie's clothes were tied to a rope like flags, fluttering in the breeze.

'Remarkable,' said Mr Briggs. 'Truly remarkable. Now, if you will excuse me, I shall have Jolly take the wheel and will consult the captain about our plan.'

Despite his various aches and pains from attacks with a toasting fork and a stuffed stoat, Mad Uncle Jack somehow made it to the top of his nephew's wooden scaffolding rig, in the hallway of Awful End. Eddie's father was, of course, lying at the top, busy painting something which looked suspiciously like – you guessed it – a liver sausage.

'We have to get her back,' said Mad Uncle Jack. 'I can't live without her for that long, you know.'

'I know,' said Mr Dickens.

'She may live in a hollow cow and me in my tree

house,' MUJ continued, 'but we're always in the same vicinity. She is my love, my joy, my reason for living . . . I cannot bear to be away from her grating voice and violent attacks.'

'I quite understand,' said Mr Dickens, wiping his paintbrush on a stained rag before dabbing it in a different colour on the palette that lay on his chest. 'But what if the detective inspector is wrong, Mad Uncle Jack? What if Even Madder Aunt Maud isn't on board the *Pompous Pig* but riding the trains up and down the line, or living on wild berries up on the moors? She was very taken with the place after we all crash-landed there in that hot-air balloon, remember?'

This would be an excellent place for me to go on about one of my earlier books again, but I'm writing this part on a Sunday and it somehow doesn't feel right . . . but perhaps Suzy, my editor, will read it on a weekday and say: 'Go on! Mention the title. It'd be a waste not to!' We'll just have to wait and see.

'I cannot take the risk that my darling love-pumpkin is aboard the *Pompous Pig* with young Edmund and do nothing about it,' said Mad Uncle Jack. He was distracted for a moment by something Eddie's father had finished painting on the ceiling the day before. To any sane person, what it most resembled was a large marrow, or

111

some such vegetable, with arms and legs, clutching a large – yup – liver sausage. 'Moses holding the Ten Commandments?' he asked.

'Yes,' Mr Dickens beamed with pride.

'Such delicate brushwork!' said Mad Uncle Jack. 'Breathtaking!' He began to wheeze.

'But how can anyone hope to catch up with Simon's ship?' asked Mr Dickens. By Simon he, of course, meant his son Eddie. 'They have over a week's start on us.'

'I have a plan!' said Mad Uncle Jack dramatically throwing his arms wide which, in his crouched position, caused him to topple off the edge of the scaffolding.

Gibbering Jane emerged from under the stairs, with a sinking feeling, to find out what had caused the nasty 'CRUNCH'.

Episode 10

Dazzling Events

In which not only Even Madder Aunt Maud shows an interest in a priceless shiny thing

Later that same day, Eddie and Lady Constance were taken to the captain's cabin. In fact, Captain Skrimshank had a suite of rooms, including the dining room where Eddie and Lady Constance ate their evening meals with the captain and first mate, served by the steward.

They'd only been in this room once before, though, and that had been when they had first been introduced to Skrimshank. It was like an office, with a big table laid out with charts, a compass on some kind of gyroscope so that it was always level, even when the ship listed (which is nautical/maritime/sailor-speak for tilted or rocked about), and various other brass implements from a magnifying glass to a pair of dividers. There were books on shelves on the walls and a small safe in the corner, by the door. Behind the captain and his table were the biggest windows in a ship where some of the rooms below decks had none.

Captain Skrimshank was busy writing in a ledger marked 'LOG BOOK' as Mr Briggs knocked on the door and led Eddie and Lady Constance into the cabin. He was dressed as he was always dressed, in a beautifully clean and pressed uniform, which looked fresh on that morning.

Eddie had never actually seen Captain Skrimshank do much, except walk about the various decks, once in a while, with his hands clasped behind his back, whilst his men acknowledged him with a salute, a nod, a greeting of 'Cap'n', or all three. He certainly looked the part, though. Eddie could imagine him being a Royal Navy captain with a ship bristling with cannons, rather than the captain of a clipper – a merchant ship.

When Eddie had been confused with that other trunk all those years ago and first sent to sea, the sailing ship he'd been on had been entirely made of wood. Although, at first glance, the *Pompous Pig* also looked wooden, she – yup, ships were referred to as though they were women back then, something which only changed at Lloyds of London (the mighty ship insurers) in the year 2002, which sounds pretty recent to me – was what was called a 'composite'; planks of wood over an iron frame.

If you think it odd that Eddie and Lady Constance were travelling in a sailing ship – relying on the wind and currents – long after steamships had been invented, I should point out that a nifty sail-powered clipper could easily do 16 to 18 knots an hour (a 'knot' being a measure of distance, as well as something to do with string) whereas, back then, most big, bulky steamships could only do a mere 12 knots and needed to carry huge amounts of coal to burn.

'Mr Briggs tells me that you have a plan for enticing your errant great-aunt out of hiding,' said Captain Skrimshank rising from his seat and nodding his head in deference to Lady Constance, pausing for a brief second or two to admire his features in a small, circular looking-glass riveted to the wall. 'And that something shiny is in order.'

'The shinier the better, Captain,' said Eddie, still in his underwear because his dried clothes had mysteriously gone missing.

The captain unbuttoned the top of his tunic and pulled a gold chain from around his neck. On it was a large key. He handed it to Spartacus Briggs. 'If you would do the honours, Mr Briggs?' he said. While Mr Briggs took the key and proceeded to open the safe with it, Captain Skrimshank continued to talk. 'Are you aware what cargo it is that we're carrying to America on this particular voyage?' he asked.

'From what I was able to gather from your men, you have a cargo hold full of shoes,' said Eddie.

'Left shoes,' added Lady Constance.

'Exactly right,' said the captain. 'A recently mechanised shoe factory in Nottingham ran into serious problems with its machinery and could only produce shoes for the left foot, as opposed to matching pairs. This would have led to serious financial losses and even the loss of jobs had it not been for the brilliance of the owner's son, Young Mr Dunkle – as opposed to the owner himself, who was called "Old Mr Dunkle", that is. Mr Dunkle Junior was aware of the newly opened Ooops Hospital in Boston Massachusetts set up specifically for those who have lost limbs in accidents. He has secured the sole contract, no pun intended, for supplying shoes for one-legged patients whose remaining leg is of the left variety. The patients are delighted to be wearing the latest fashions. The hospital is delighted at the reasonable price they have agreed upon, and Dunkle Footwear of Nottingham are delighted that their future is safe.'

'How very . . .' Eddie wondered what the captain's anecdote had to do with the Even Madder Aunt Maud situation, unless some of these left shoes had very shiny buckles which were placed in the safe for safe-keeping. (Hence the word safe.) '. . . interesting,' he said.

'Interesting in that the shoes are not the only cargo,' said Captain Skrimshank with a dramatic air. Mr Briggs had opened the safe and pulled out a red leather box about the size of one that could hold a single cricket ball. He handed it to the captain with great care. 'There is also this,' said the captain, twisting a gold clasp and slowly opening the lid of the box, 'and it is worth more than this entire ship and all those shoes put together.'

Eddie actually gasped. There, nestling in the crushed red velvet lining of the box, was a dazzling jewel. It reminded Eddie of the bauble from the chandelier, but that had been cut crystal glass; this was obviously a real diamond, sparkling like fire, and, at the very centre, was a flaw – a dark blemish or naturally formed mark – in the almost perfect shape of a cartoon dog's bone.

'It's . . . It's beautiful,' said the stunned Lady Constance. 'Even more beautiful than I ever dreamed possible. Surely this must be the world famous Dog's Bone Diamond?'

The captain nodded proudly. 'So named because of the shape of the flaw at the very heart of it. It was recently purchased from its British owner by Dr Eli Bowser, the American dog-food tycoon, and we aboard the *Pompous Pig* have been given the honour and responsibility of transporting it.'

'Wow!' said Eddie, which wasn't an everyday Victorian expression but neatly summed up how he felt. 'But why no armed guards? And surely a steamship would have been more reliable?' He was a bright kid.

'As a precaution,' the captain explained. 'As a subterfuge, if you like. Two days after we set sail, it was announced in the British and American press that the dazzling Dog's Bone Diamond was being sent to America, with an armed escort, aboard the American steamship *Pine Cone*. There are, indeed, two detectives from the Pickleton Detective Agency now aboard the *Pine Cone* and they are, indeed, guarding a so-called diamond, but even they don't know that it is a fake. If there are any crooks out there, their attention will be centred on the wrong ship!'

Eddie immediately thought of the escaped

convict Swags aboard *this* ship. He knew that he must say something at once. He was about to speak, but his travelling companion got in first.

'Was your idea to use this as the shiny bait to lure out Master Edmund's great-aunt?' asked Lady Constance, her eyes still on the diamond and nothing else.

'Yes,' said the captain. 'Unless someone's flying overhead in a hot-air balloon, our secret is going to remain on board. We're still a good few days away from land.'

Once again Eddie opened his mouth to mention the possible dangers of Swags and, once again, Lady Constance managed to jump in first.

'Too dangerous, Captain,' she said. 'What if his great-aunt actually managed to get hold of it before we could stop her and threw it overboard?'

'But why should she do that, Lady Constance?' asked a puzzled Skrimshank.

'The clue is in the name Even *Madder* Aunt Maud, Captain,' Eddie reminded him. 'Now I must talk to you about the other paying passeng–'

He got no further because there was a terrible smashing of glass and the terrifying figure of an elderly woman, half-covered in seaweed, came crashing through the window of the captain's cabin, swinging on a thick rope, with a slightly battered-looking stuffed stoat under one arm.

Before anyone realised quite what was going on, she had landed on the floor, snatched the dazzling Dog's Bone Diamond from the stunned captain's hand and dashed out on to the wheel deck.

The others rushed out after Even Madder Aunt Maud just in time to see her trip and lose her grip on the Dog's Bone Diamond. It rolled across the wheel deck, like the peppermint from the detective inspector's ear, and over the edge and out of sight. For a moment, everyone watched in horror, frozen to the spot . . . then there was a sudden dash to look over the edge to the main deck below to see what had happened.

There had been no sound of diamond-hitting-wood. Just an eerie silence. Perhaps it had landed on a coil of rope or some burlap sacking? No. There was none directly below; just bare boards. And no sign of the diamond. That end of the deck appeared to be deserted.

Captain Skrimshank whimpered whilst Mr Briggs was already running down the wooden ladder joining the decks, two rungs at a time. Powder Monkey and Eddie, meanwhile, were helping Even Madder Aunt Maud to her feet. Fortunately, she seemed none the worse for wear for having lived rough, swung Tarzan-like through a window and fallen on the deck . . . but, at least it had subdued her. It was only later that it occurred to Eddie that Lady Constance was nowhere to be seen.

*

Despite a shipwide search, there was no sign of the missing diamond and the captain was beside himself – now there's a phrase that's impossible to act out in real life, without the aid of mirrors – with anguish. Considering Even Madder Aunt Maud had been a stowaway and entirely to blame for the gem's loss, Eddie thought the captain was being incredibly reasonable about the whole

121

thing; simply confining her to her (well, to *Eddie's*) quarters and insisting that Eddie not leave her alone for one second.

The frustrating part was that Skrimshank wouldn't let Eddie get a word in edgeways concerning his suspicions about Swags . . . suspicions which now included the one that the Dog's Bone Diamond was probably in the escaped convict's hands!

Eddie concluded that Swags must have somehow got wind of the fact that the priceless diamond was on board the *Pompous Pig* and had become a paying passenger with a view to stealing it from the safe . . . until Even Madder Aunt Maud had – almost literally – let it drop into his lap. Eddie was as sure as he could be, without having actually witnessed it, that Swags had been lucky enough to have been on the main deck when the jewel had come falling towards it. It must have seemed like a gift from heaven!

Fully aware that Even Madder Aunt Maud (and Malcolm, of course) wouldn't have set foot on the ship – and so wouldn't have created an opportunity to steal the diamond – if he hadn't been on board in the first place, and the fact that the shiny-thing-as-bait idea had been his, Eddie felt responsible for the theft of the diamond. He wanted to put things right for Captain Skrimshank, even if it meant disobeying orders and leaving his great-aunt on her own.

Eddie felt somewhat guilty, but he decided the safest thing to do would be to tie up Even Madder Aunt Maud, to stop her wandering. He didn't want to tie her wrists and ankles – that would be most painful and undignified and not something any great-nephew should ever have to do to a great-aunt, mad or otherwise – so he waited until she dropped off to sleep (in his bed, as a matter of fact) and then wrapped a coil of rope around her *and* the bed, like an extra-tight blanket. Tiptoeing to his cabin door, he heard his aunt happily muttering something to do with 'prunes' in her sleep, blissfully unaware she was a prisoner.

Taking one last glance back at her as he gingerly turned the door handle, Eddie thought how cosy she and Malcolm looked, tucked up together like that. He stepped out of the cabin and into the night.

The *Pompous Pig* seemed very different bathed in silvery moonlight. Familiar objects seemed to take on different forms. The barrel to Eddie's left, for example, appeared to be moving.

'Whatcha up to?' asked the barrel.

If this had been a TV cartoon, Eddie would have jumped out of his skin, leaving it on the deck like a discarded pile of crumpled clothes.

'Who – ?' he blurted. Then, quickly regaining his senses, he added an urgent 'sssh!' He had recognised that this was no barrel, it was the boy Powder Monkey.

'I'm sure I's heard the cap'n tells you to stay with that dotty old lady of yours,' whispered the galley hand, with a wicked grin.

'Do I know you?' asked Eddie. 'Have we met before . . . somewhere on dry land, I mean? You do look very familiar.'

''Course we 'ave,' said Powder Monkey. 'The last time you saw me, I was hittin' some strange bloke with a cucumber.'

It all made sense in an instant. 'You're an orphan from St Horrid's Home for Grateful Orphans!' said Eddie, a little louder than he should have, what with all the excitement.

'That's right,' whispered the boy, 'an' you're the one what helped us all escape an' that. What's you up to this time?'

124

Eddie quickly told his new ally about Swags, and his belief that he must have the gem. 'With you to help me, that should make things a whole lot easier,' Eddie concluded.

'How's that?' asked Powder Monkey.

'If you could knock on his door and get him out of his cabin – making some excuse about Mr Briggs wanting to see him and then leading him on some wild goose chase around the ship – that should give me time to search it for the missing diamond.'

'But I don't have no goose,' said Powder Monkey.

'No what I meant was –'

'An' if I did, it'd be a tame goose, not a wild one –'

'No, I simply meant –'

'And what if Mr Swags didn't wanta chase it anyways?'

Eddie grabbed Powder Monkey by the shoulders. 'Forget the goose!' he hissed. 'I wish I'd never mentioned the goose . . . Could you tell Swags some lie about Mr Briggs needing to see him below decks, then get him well and truly lost down there?'

'Sure I can,' said Powder Monkey, giving Eddie a strange look. 'I don't need no goose for that.'

'I asked you to forget the goose,' Eddie

reminded him.

'What goose?' grinned Powder Monkey.

'Good,' said Eddie, grinning back. At last, they were getting somewhere. 'Excellent.'

Keeping to the shadows, they made their way towards the door of Swags's cabin. Hearing footsteps on the wooden decking, they hid behind a huge coil of rope and stood as still as they humanly could.

Eddie listened. The steps were 'clackerty' and close together, which suggested short strides in women's shoes and, apart from Even Madder Aunt Maud, the only woman on board was Lady Constance Bustle. But what was she doing up and about at this hour? Especially when she'd said goodnight to Eddie, several hours earlier, just before she'd said that she was 'retiring to bed'.

Perhaps she'd got up for a glass of water, or something, and looked into his cabin to find EMAM trussed up like a chicken, and that he – Eddie – was nowhere to be seen. He sincerely hoped that wasn't the case.

The person responsible for the footsteps walked past them in the dark and, sure enough, it was indeed Lady Constance. She had a grim, determined expression on her face. She headed purposefully towards the prow – the pointy bit at the front – of the ship. Eddie and Powder Monkey followed. There was someone waiting for her. When Eddie saw who it was, his heart sank (in much the same way that Gibbering Jane's had when she'd come out from under the stairs, back home, to find out what had made that nasty 'CRUNCH' in the hallway).

Lady Constance's secret late-night rendezvous was with none other than Swags himself.

Episode 11

Going Overboard

In which various characters pick themselves up, dust themselves down and start all over again

Fortunately for Mad Uncle Jack, he was none the worse for falling from Eddie's father's scaffolding rig because he landed on top of Dawkins – Awful End's gentleman's gentleman – thus cushioning the impact.

Fortunately for Dawkins, who had happened to be crossing the floor of the hallway at exactly the right/wrong moment, a free-falling MUJ wasn't too heavy a person to be hit with. Being so thin, he was more arms and legs and beak-like nose than anything else. Still, it's not very pleasant having anyone land on top of one unexpectedly, and poor old Dawkins ended up in bed for six weeks, as a result. (It would have been seven but Mr Dickens was getting desperate to have someone tie his ties for him.)

Because Dr Humple didn't want to move Dawkins too far from the scene of the accident, for fear of doing him more harm than good, and because it was agreed that Gibbering Jane should be the one to look after him, Dawkins's bed was brought downstairs.

The head end was stuck through the doorway to the cupboard under the stairs so that Jane could feed him, mop his brow, etc., whilst still being able to remain in familiar surroundings. The rest of the bed stuck out into the hallway. Sometimes Eddie's father would shout down with words of encouragement, flat on his back, from high above.

Mad Uncle Jack and Eddie's mother, Mrs Dickens, meanwhile, were on a steam vessel heading in the direction of America. Yup, you read that right. That's what that picture over there, at the beginning of this episode, is all about!

Unable to bear any more time apart from his beloved Maud than absolutely necessary, MUJ had decided to set off in hot pursuit of the *Pompous Pig*. He had chartered the 'steamglider' *Belch II* because of its speed.

Without going into too much boring detail, which would require a few diagrams and pages and pages of explanation (when there are less than twenty-four left to finish the entire story), suffice it to stay that what powered the engine of a *steam* vessel was, as you might possibly have guessed without a degree in mechanical engineering, steam and what created the steam was water heated to boiling point by burning coal.

The problem arose if you had to go any great distance. You needed an ENORMOUS amount of coal. You didn't need a big ship simply to carry the passengers, you needed it big to house the fuel to make it go anywhere in the first place!

Whilst people were up on deck sipping lovely drinkies and saying, ''Ain't it a beautiful morning?' gangs of men were down in the bowels of the ship stoking the boilers; not with unwanted tally sticks but with shovel after shovel of coal.

Fortunately, this was sort of solved when a new kind of steam engine, called a double-expansion engine, was invented. It made much more use out of the same amount of steam so (as the mathematically minded amongst you will have gathered) this meant more distance, or speed, for less coal.

The *Belch II* was designed and built by Tobias Belch, who later became *Sir* Tobias and is best remembered today for having invented one of the first watches to be worn on the wrist, rather than kept on a chain or in a pocket, though, unfortunately, it too was steam-powered and could cause nasty burns. His 'steamglider' had an even newer and more remarkable engine which he called the 'quadruple-expansion engine' or 'Sweet Nancy' (when he was whispering to it, to try to encourage it to go faster). This, he claimed, needed so little coal that the *Belch II* could be smaller and faster, and the 'steamglider' had quadruple propellers too which, apparently, was also a good thing. The fact that Sir Tobias – then plain *Mr* Belch – was a person way ahead of his time was borne out by the fact that he wore shorts instead of trousers and, not only that, they had a bright flowery pattern on them.

He was sporting a pair of such shorts as he steered the *Belch II* with one hand and consulted a navigational chart with the other. 'Of course, the *Pompous Pig* is dependent on the winds and we may miss her altogether but, with luck on our side, we could catch up with her any day now,' he told Mad Uncle Jack, who was leaning against a railing, dressed in a sailor suit similar to one he'd worn as a boy. Mrs Dickens was, in the meantime, stoking the small boiler. Both had lost count of the number of days they'd been at sea. Mrs Dickens found that she was a natural-born stoker and was enjoying every minute of it. On more than one occasion, Tobias Belch had told her to stop stoking because it'd be a waste of fuel. The quadruple-expansion engine – Nancy – was doing very nicely without it, thank you very much.

Thanks to the brilliance of his engineering and the skill of his sailing (or whatever it is you call handling a sea-going vessel without sails), Tobias Belch finally caught up with the *Pompous Pig*, despite its many days' head start. This also had something to do with the fact that the ship was at anchor. In other words it was 'parked' and not going anywhere.

Using a big whistle to attract attention, and some flag waving (called semaphore) to explain their intention, *Belch II* was soon alongside the *Pompous Pig* and Mad Uncle Jack and Mrs Dickens were soon scaling up the side of the clipper on the rope ladder, Eddie's mother relieved that she no longer needed crutches.

'Where's my darling Maud?' cried MUJ.

'Where's little Edmund?' asked his mother.

Mr Spartacus Briggs and a small cluster of sailors were waiting for them on deck. He stepped forward. 'I have grave news,' he said, not sure where to begin.

Lady Constance Bustle made her way to the front of the welcoming party, fluttered her eyelashes at Mr Briggs and whispered, 'Let me do it, Spartacus.' She then turned to the Dickenses. 'These are truly terrible times,' she said. 'I am sad to report that a number of people – passengers and crew – were washed overboard in the early hours of the morning two days ago . . .'

'My love-cheese?' gasped Mad Uncle Jack.

'Your lady wife is fine, sir,' Mr Briggs reassured him, placing a reassuring hand upon his shoulder. 'She is currently resting with her stuffed stoat in Master Edmund's cabin, tied firmly to her bed.'

'Unbounded joy,' Mad Uncle Jack pronounced.

'And Edmund?' asked Mrs Dickens. 'My Edmund?'

'He was not so lucky, Mrs D,' said Lady Constance, who was used to imparting bad news to relatives because she did it so often. 'I'm afraid he was washed overboard . . .'

'Deep sorrow,' interjected Mad Uncle Jack.

Mrs Dickens simply wailed.

'Along with our very own Captain Skrimshank, a galley hand and another paying passenger . . .' added Mr Briggs, eager to emphasise that the shipping company as well as the Dickenses were suffering a loss. It somehow seemed less careless that way. 'We've been circling around looking for them for days,' he went on. 'I'm afraid there's no sign of them.'

Mrs Dickens sobbed some more. Well, mothers can be like that, can't they?

'The wave came out of nowhere,' said Lady Bustle. 'It was a calm sea on a moonlit night. I witnessed the whole thing with my own eyes. I was out on deck taking a midnight stroll when I saw the galley hand –'

'His name was Powder Monkey and he was on night watch,' Mr Briggs interrupted. 'He was a good lad . . . Would have made a fine sailor one day.'

'I saw the galley hand in conversation with young Master Dickens, the captain and the one other paying passenger called Mr Smith,' Lady Constance explained. She crouched down next to Mrs Dickens who had crumpled to the deck, and put a comforting arm around her. 'A jewel had gone missing and one of them had found it. They were excited and happy and I could see it in the captain's hand.' Her tone changed. 'A moment later, a huge wave came out of nowhere, washing them overboard . . . It was so fast and so unexpected that they didn't have a chance to let out so much as a cry. I dashed across the soaking deck to raise the alarm but slipped and knocked myself unconscious.' She touched a small bruise on her forehead. 'I could do nothing until I came to my senses many hours later.'

There was silence. Even those who'd heard tell of the events before were still horrified by them. That two boys and two men should be lost in that fleeting moment, not forgetting one of the most valuable and famous jewels in the world . . .

'LIAR!' said a loud voice behind them.

Members of the not-so-welcoming welcome committee that had clustered around Mad Uncle Jack and Mrs Dickens parted to reveal – yes, you guessed it (or, at least, you cheated and looked at the picture) – a bedraggled Eddie Dickens climbing aboard the ship.

'You're alive!' his mother squealed with delight and, with one of the few signs of affection he was ever to receive from her, she threw her arms around him and squeezed him tight. 'You smell of turtles!' she added.

Eddie's mother never ceased to amaze him. How did she know what turtles smelt like? But she was right. He'd ridden on the back of a turtle through the waves to get back to the ship. He'd had to help with the steering, of course, because he had a specific destination and couldn't talk Turtlese (or whatever turtles speak; I've never even heard one make a noise) but it was very friendly and seemed to thoroughly enjoy the whole experience.

'Lady Constance is a liar and, if her plan had worked, would be a murderer, too!' shouted Eddie. 'Don't worry, Mr Briggs. The captain and the others are alive and well and ready for rescue!'

'The boy is clearly deranged!' said Lady Constance. 'Loopy! Ga-ga! The whole dreadful experience has turned his mind!'

'I think I might be able to prove it,' said Eddie, walking towards her across the deck, leaving a trail of seawater behind him. Despite her being much taller than him, and him not carrying any type of weapon, she backed away. She knew what he was going to say next.

'How?' asked Mr Briggs uncertainly. He looked from the supposedly drowned boy to the titled lady.

'She said that the Dog's Bone Diamond was washed overboard, but I know where she's hidden it! She was bragging about it . . . taunting us with it . . .' He paused. 'Before she forced us into the leaking rowing boat.'

The crowd – made up of many more sailors who'd come to see what all the fuss was about – gasped (which is nice because it adds to the drama; even if they hadn't gasped, I might have *said* they did, just to make it sound better . . . but they did, anyway, so I don't have to).

'Potty, I tell you,' cried Lady Bustle. 'The boy's gone potty.'

Mr Briggs looked at her sadly. 'Then you won't mind if he shows us where he thinks it is,' said Mr Briggs.

The still-dripping Eddie led the way to his cabin and threw open the door. Even Madder Aunt Maud was still lashed to the bed, as Eddie had left her two nights previously.

'About time too!' said his great-aunt as everyone piled into the cabin. 'I am due to marry the Archbishop of Canterbury at midday and must have my moustache curled.'

'My dreamboat!' said Mad Uncle Jack, throwing

his arms around her tightly trussed body.

'Remove this man!' shouted Mad Aunt Maud. 'Have him shot!'

But Eddie wasn't listening. He pulled Malcolm the stuffed stoat out from beside her and pointed to some bright red stitching.

'Unpick that!' he said.

Lady Constance made a dash for the cabin door, only to find it barred by 'Jolly' Roger. 'I think you 'ad better be waitin' in 'ere, m'lady, until Mr Briggs says otherwise,' he said.

Briggs produced a knife from his pocket and cut through the stitching with one swipe of the blade.

Mad Aunt Maud's eyes widened in horror. 'Murderer!' she cried.

'Don't worry,' Eddie reassured her, feeling inside the stuffed stoat and pulling out the Dog's Bone Diamond with a triumphant flourish. 'A bit of fresh stuffing and Malcolm will be as right as rain!'

'How on Earth did he swallow that?' cried Even Madder Aunt Maud. 'Silly, silly boy!'

Mr Briggs took the fabulous jewel and held it up in front of Lady Constance's face. 'How do you explain this?' he asked.

'I – er – Anyone could have put it there,' she protested.

'But you said that you saw it being washed overboard,' Mr Briggs reminded her.

'I saw *him* go overboard, too,' said Lady Constance, 'and he's back.'

'The stitching,' said Eddie. 'Look at the stitching.'

'That doesn't tell you anything,' said Lady Constance. 'They looked like perfectly normal stitches to me, cleverly concealed if one didn't know where to look . . . which *you* somehow, and somewhat suspiciously, did, Master Edmund!'

'Cleverly concealed?' said a puzzled Mr Briggs and there were a few murmurs from the assembled company.

'Malcolm ate something that didn't agree with him and Eddie and that nice man operated to remove it,' Even Madder Aunt Maud was telling Mad Uncle Jack, who was now busy untying her. Both seemed blissfully unaware of the drama unfolding around them.

Eddie held up a piece of cut thread from the stitching. 'It's bright red and doesn't match Malcolm's fur in the slightest,' said Eddie. 'But, when we first met, Lady Constance told me that she has Dalton's Disease, which means that she has a kind of colour blindness . . .'

'And mistakenly thought that the stitching blended in with the ferret's fur,' said Mr Briggs.

He then added an 'ouch' because Even Madder
Aunt Maud had just hit him over the head with
Malcolm.

'He's a stoat,' she told him.

Episode 12

Back and Forth

*In which we go backwards and forwards
in order to try to make sense of it all*

When matters were explained to Tobias Belch, he quickly agreed to take his 'steamglider' to the tiny island – more of a large sandy bump in the ocean than anything else – where Eddie had informed them the others were awaiting rescue. Obviously, Eddie had to accompany him for it was only he who (he hoped) knew the way. Mr Briggs insisted on coming too because he felt it his duty to be on the rescue mission that saved his captain. Jolly was put in charge of the *Pompous Pig*, with

strict instructions that Even Madder Aunt Maud
wasn't allowed to touch anything, and that Lady
Constance must remain locked in her cabin, with
a guard on each door.

As *Belch II* steamed off, Eddie now had a
chance to tell Mr Briggs what had led to his
disappearance, along with the captain, the galley
hand and the third paying passenger . . .

. . . On that fateful moonlit night, two nights
previously, Eddie couldn't believe his eyes when
he saw Lady Constance deep in conversation with
Swags.

'They know each other!' he whispered to
Powder Monkey, who was crouching next to him
in the shadow of a huge barrel – which really was
a barrel this time – marked 'SHIP'S BISCUITS'.

'I don't fink vey do, ya know,' Powder Monkey
whispered back. 'She appears to be makin'
introductions.'

It was true. Creeping as near as he dare, Eddie
could hear Lady Constance saying: '. . . and,
though I don't know your real name, I know that
you're the escaped convict they call Swags.'

'Am I supposed to be impressed by that?' asked
Swags, with a voice that made his flesh creep. 'The
boy told you. That's all.'

'But no one has told the captain. *Yet*,' said Lady

142

Constance. Her meaning was very clear.

Eddie couldn't hear what Swags said next but he certainly didn't look the happiest person on the ship.

'Now, of course, if you and I were to share the profits from a little something you have . . .' Lady Constance paused.

'I don't have anything you want, lady,' said Swags and he made the word 'lady' sound far from ladylike, which was fair enough when you think about it. Eddie's official travelling companion was turning out to be on the nasty side of not-so-nice, and (as those of you reading these pages in order will already know) her worst was yet to come.

'You have *exactly* what I want, Mr Swags, but I'm prepared to share it,' she went on. 'I'm willing to bet my life that you have the Dog's Bone Diamond somewhere about your person' (which means 'somewhere on you'). 'Agree to split the profits when you have it cut down into smaller gems and sold, and your secret remains just that: a secret.'

Swags turned and faced out to sea and, once again, Eddie couldn't hear what he was saying, but there was absolutely no doubt what he saw. Lady Constance slipped her hand deep into an outer pocket of the convict's tatty coat and, with the nimble fingers of an experienced pickpocket, pulled out the diamond!

When Swags realised what had happened, he raised his arm as if to hit her and she grabbed his wrist. 'If you think I came to this meeting armed with nothing more than a hat pin, you've seriously underestimated me!' she hissed.

Eddie decided that it was time to report what he'd found to the captain. Leaving Powder Monkey to keep an eye on Swags and Bustle, Eddie found the captain in his cabin. Despite the hour, he was still seated at his chart-covered table and still fully dressed in his splendid uniform. What was slightly less impressive was that he was asleep, his head resting, face down, in a plate of cold shepherd's pie. (And, no, like the badger back on page 5, I'm afraid I can't tell you what the poor shepherd died of.)

When Eddie woke Skrimshank and told him about the two villains and the Dog's Bone Diamond, the captain was out of his chair and out of the cabin before Eddie had time to think.

'Shouldn't we get reinforcements?' he asked the captain, trying to keep up.

'I can handle this pair!' he reassured Eddie with confidence.

The confidence was, of course, completely unfounded. By the time Eddie and Captain Skrimshank reached Lady Constance and Swags, the scheming twosome – ooo, isn't that a nice phrase? – had already discovered Powder Monkey lurking near by; without Eddie there to hold him back, the ex-St Horrid's Home orphan had become overconfident and less cautious. Swags had grabbed the boy so had a ready-made hostage the moment Eddie and the captain arrived on the scene.

'Put that boy down!' the captain shouted.

Swags, who was holding Powder Monkey by the scruff of the neck, now lifted the boy over the edge of the ship. 'Any more shouting and the boy goes in the water,' he warned.

'I believe you have in your possession something which belongs to Dr Eli Bowser,' said Skrimshank (his voice much lower now). 'Put the boy down and return the jewel and I will go easy on you.'

145

Lady Constance laughed. 'I have a better idea,' she said. And they soon found out what it was. They were to be cast adrift in the tiny rowing boat.

Eddie was the first one forced down the side of the *Pompous Pig* into the boat. Next went the captain. He didn't resist (not only because Swags still had Powder Monkey in his vice-like grip but also because he felt it his duty to stay with a fare-paying passenger in distress). Swags came down next, with the struggling galley hand tucked under his arm. Now they were in the boat, Swags tied Eddie's, Skrimshank's and, finally, Powder Monkey's hands behind their backs, cutting the pieces of rope to length with an evil-looking knife – can knives look evil? – that conveniently glinted in the moonlight or glinted in the convenient moonlight. (Moonlight isn't really moonlight, by the way, it's simply sunlight reflected off the moon. Think about it. The moon isn't on fire like the sun, and doesn't have a great big battery inside it, so where did you think the light was coming from?)

Now where were we? Yup, that's it: Eddie, Skrimshank and Powder Monkey bound and, whilst I was doing the 'is-moonlight-moonlight?' bit, gagged so that they couldn't cry for help once cast adrift. That done, Swags began to climb back up the side of the *Pompous Pig*. A surprise greeted him at the top of the ladder. Lady Constance gave him a swift bash over the head with the Dog's Bone Diamond . . . and diamond is the hardest substance known to humankind.

The escaped convict fell into the sea with a SPLASH loud enough to attract any sailor on nightwatch, the only trouble being that Powder Monkey was the one on watch and there wasn't much he could do about it!

Lady Constance leant over the side of the ship and spoke to her captives. 'I'm so sorry it had to end this way, gentlemen,' she said and, although her tone did sound ever-so-slightly apologetic, none of them believed, for one moment, that she was sorry.

'You will be pleased to know, Master Edmund, that I have thought of the ideal place to hide the diamond. It's a place no one will ever think of looking and, once your dear sweet batty great-aunt is untied, no one will be able to get near. I shall stitch it up in that stuffed ferret of hers!'

'Oah!' cried Eddie, which is what it sounds like if you try to say 'Stoat!' through a gag when tied up in a rowing boat set adrift in the Atlantic Ocean . . . or at least it did in Eddie's case.

As it turned out, Lady Constance's cruellest act was what saved them all that night. Gagged, Eddie and his companions in the rowing boat couldn't

147

shout to attract attention or speak to each other. Bound, they couldn't take out the gags or untie each other, let alone swim. But Swags was neither bound nor gagged.

After what seemed like ages, the tiny rowing boat had drifted almost out of sight of the *Pompous Pig* and the three had given up trying to make each other understood through their gags. What was worse was that the boat appeared to have sprung a leak. Perhaps it had always been there, but now the bottom of the boat was beginning to fill with sea water, or should that be ocean water? I doubt it makes much difference when you're drowning.

Then Swags broke through the surface of the water right beside them and hauled himself aboard. Without so much as a word, he untied the captain and then collapsed, exhausted from his swim, in what little space there was. Skrimshank quickly untied Eddie who, in turn, untied Powder Monkey.

Eddie eyed the half-sleeping Swags, a cut from the Dog's Bone Diamond sending a trickle of blood down his forehead. 'He probably saved our lives!' said Eddie.

'What little good it'll do him,' said the captain. 'He put us in this predicament in the first instance,' which means 'he got us into this mess'.

'It's probably too late to save us now anyways,' said a sad and dejected Powder Monkey, who was still feeling guilty for getting himself caught and being the hostage that made the others do as they were told.

But, as we of the all's-well-that-ends-well persuasion already know, it wasn't too late. By luck or fate or a fluke of geography, when the four had to abandon the boat – then sinking – and make a swim for it, a tiny island (aka sandy hummock *not* hammock) haven had come into view within swimming distance . . . and they all made it there.

Within a matter of hours, Captain Skrimshank's uniform had dried and, with a little help from Powder Monkey, looked as good as new. Swags had lost his knife in the fall from the *Pompous Pig*, and his dignity, too. He had saved the others because he'd needed them as much as they'd needed him now that he'd been double-crossed by Lady C. They were all alone, apart from a very friendly family of giant sea turtles who had obviously never met these funny-looking shell-less animals called 'humans' that had crawled out of the sea before.

'And it was the largest turtle that finally brought me all the way back to the *Pompous Pig*,' Eddie told Mr Briggs, coming to the end of his tale, just as the first mate spotted the others on the island in the distance, and Tobias Belch steered *Belch II* in their direction. Once again, Eddie had saved the day!

So that, dear reader, just about wraps up the third and final book in the Eddie Dickens Trilogy. As I did at the end of *Awful End* and *Dreadful Acts*, though, I should, of course, tie up a few loose ends before I say 'goodbye'.

The question most of you will, no doubt, write and ask me about if I don't answer it here is whether Eddie finally got to America, the Eastern Seaboard and the offices of the *Terrible Times*? The answer is simple: no. Sad to say, he abandoned all attempts to set foot on American soil this time. He went back to England with his mother, Mad Uncle Jack, Even Madder Aunt Maud, a newly repaired Malcolm, and (the then plain 'Mr') Tobias Belch aboard *Belch II*.

As it turned out, there had indeed been what the editor called 'a few glitches' at the *Terrible Times* offices, the worst of which was the editor's wife falling into the printing presses. This particular glitch not only caused a loss of three editions whilst the presses were repaired and the pearls from her broken necklace recovered, but it also meant that Mrs Brockenfeld (the editor of the *Terrible Times* being *Mr* Brockenfeld) was never quite the same shape again. On meeting her for the first time, people found it hard to tell whether she was greeting them frontways or sideways on. She had a 'permanent profile' look about her, something which, in the following century, an artist called Pablo Picasso painted his women to look like and made a small fortune in so doing.

Mr Brockenfeld had been so embarrassed by the whole accident incident that he'd missed sending his regular report to the Dickenses in England because he hadn't known what to say. Had he known Eddie's relatives better, he needn't have worried. If Even Madder Aunt Maud had worked for the newspaper, she'd have probably clambered into the presses deliberately and on numerous occasions!

And what of the not-so-ladylike Lady Constance Bustle and Swags? They were taken to America on board the *Pompous Pig* but not allowed to set foot ashore. Once the cargo of left shoes was unloaded and the Dog's Bone Diamond delivered, they were brought back to England and ended up on trial. Swags, whose real name turned out to be Albert Grubb, was eventually sent back to Australia for thirty years' more hard labour and ended his days breaking rocks. Lady Constance ended up marrying the trial judge who died soon after. Apparently he and Lady Constance had been practising an amateur knife-throwing routine when she'd slipped on a bar of soap and stabbed him through the heart.

The Dog's Bone Diamond was duly handed over to Dr Eli Bowser 'the dog-food baron' who, on learning of a certain Eddie Dickens's part in saving it from harm, sent the boy an envelope stuffed with one thousand dollar bills, by way of a 'thank you'. Unfortunately for Eddie, the envelope somehow found its way to Even Madder Aunt Maud instead of him. She tore the money into tiny strips and wallpapered the inside of Marjorie with it. The truth be told, it certainly looked better than the ceiling of Awful End once Mr Dickens had finished painting it.

But, do you know what? Despite this and having some of the most embarrassing relatives in the history of humankind, on returning from his latest adventure, Eddie Dickens had to admit that there was no place like home . . . even when that home was Awful End.

Goodbye.

THE END
of the Eddie Dickens Trilogy

Awful End

Book One of the Eddie Dickens Trilogy

ISBN: 0 571 20354 X

£4.99 (Paperback)

When both of Eddie Dickens's parents catch a disease that makes them turn yellow, go a bit crinkly round the edges and smell of hot water bottles, it's agreed he should go and stay with relatives at their house Awful End. Unfortunately for Eddie, those relatives are Mad Uncle Jack and Even Madder Aunt Maud and they definitely live up to their names. This is the first book in the wildly successful Eddie Dickens Trilogy, set in a 19th-century world of blotchy skin, runaway orphans . . . and a stuffed stoat called Malcolm. One sitting and you'll be hooked.

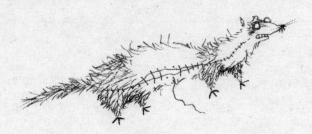

Praise for *Awful End*

'[A] scrumptious cross between Dickens and Monty Python . . . Brilliant.'
Guardian

'In this surreal world, language is never what it appears . . . It's daft but entirely engaging.'
Independent

'. . . sophisticated. . . extremely silly . . . wonderful . . . ridiculing literary conventions and turning nonsense into a fine art.'
Sunday Telegraph

'It would be a sad spirit that didn't find this book hilarious.'
Financial Times

www.philipardagh.com

Dreadful Acts

Book Two of the Eddie Dickens Trilogy

ISBN: 0 571 20947 5

£4.99 (Paperback)

In this sequel to *Awful End*, our hero Eddie Dickens narrowly avoids an explosion, being hit by a hot-air balloon and being arrested, only to find himself falling head-over heels for a girl, called Daniella, with a face like a camel's. Unfortunately for Eddie, he also falls into the hands of a murderous gang of escaped convicts who have 'one little job for him to do'. All the old favourite characters are here, along with a whole batch of crazy new ones!

Praise for *Dreadful Acts*

'One of my favourite comic characters is back . . .
Ardagh skilfully continues the comic drama of his
first Eddie Dickens story . . . and the result is
equally delicious, and ridiculous.'
The Bookseller

'Be warned, *Dreadful Acts* made me laugh so
much I had hiccups.'
Vivian French, author & reviewer

'[Readers] who enjoyed the barkingly mad world
of *Awful End* . . . will not be disappointed!'
Times Educational Supplement

www.philipardagh.com

Unlikely Exploits Book 1
The Fall of Fergal

ISBN: 0 571 21069 4
£7.99 (Hardback)

ISBN: 0 571 21521 1
£4.99 (Paperback)

This first book in a NEW series is set in an unidentified country suffering from an unexpected outbreak of holes, where the flame-haired McNally children find themselves in The Dell hotel surrounded by a strange assortment of ridiculous characters, ranging from Charlie 'Twinkle-Toes' Tweedy, the house detective, to Mr Peach, a ventriloquist with a conveniently large moustache. With young Fergal falling to his death on page one, the only way for the McNallys is up . . .

Praise for *The Fall of Fergal*

'A wacky, playful, entertaining read . . . My squeamish ten-year-old took all in her stride and pronounced it terrific!'
Irish Times

'Ardagh's writing is completely off the wall and steeped in black humour. Destined to win hearts and minds of eager readers.'
The Scotsman

'An accomplished and entertaining comedy rather than a tragedy . . . lots of fun.'
Independent

'Ardagh has a growing following among young readers who enjoy fantastical stories driven by inventive illogicality and peopled with over-the-top characters.'
Sunday Times

www.philipardagh.com

LOOK OUT FOR:

Unlikely Exploits Book 2
Heir of Mystery

ISBN: 0 571 21094 5
£7.99 (Hardback)

In this second unlikely exploit, full of surprising twists and turns, the remaining McNally children – Jackie, Le Fay and the twins Josh and Albie – are mysteriously drawn to Fishbone Forest and the forgotten crumbling mansion, which lies at its heart. Here they meet the terrifying teddy-bear clutching Mr Maggs who is planning to make sweeping changes to the world . . . which is all rather unlikely, isn't it? Packed with humour, excitement and sadness, this is another sure-fire winner.

AND COMING SOON:

Unlikely Exploits Book 3
The Rise of the House of McNally

ISBN: 0 571 21707 9
£7.99 (Hardback)

What's it all about? You'll just have to wait and see. One thing you CAN be sure of, though, is lots of laughs and lots of very silly goings-on! After all, it's an unlikely exploit and by Philip Ardagh!

www.philipardagh.com

Non-fiction by Philip Ardagh

'Philip Ardagh is one of life's fact-finders.'
The Scotsman

The Hieroglyphs Handbook
Teach Yourself Ancient Egyptian
ISBN: 0 571 19744 2
£4.99 (Paperback)

The Archaeologist's Handbook
The Insider's Guide to Digging Up The Past
ISBN: 0 571 20687 5
£4.99 (Paperback)

Did Dinosaurs Snore?
100$^{1}/_{2}$ Questions about Dinosaurs Answered
ISBN: 0 571 20653 0
£4.99 (Paperback)

Why Are Castles Castle Shaped?
100$^{1}/_{2}$ Questions About Castles Answered
ISBN: 0 571 21437 1
£4.99 (Paperback)

www.philipardagh.com

The world of Philip Ardagh is only a click away. Log on for lots of facts, fun and figures:

www.philipardagh.com

You will find many hilarious things plus the following:

☞ Strange (and normal) information about the author

☞ More details about the hilarious characters featured in the Philip Ardagh books

☞ Pictures and photographs to download

☞ Details of future Philip Ardagh books and events

☞ How to write to the author

The Philip Ardagh Club

COLLECT some fantastic **Philip Ardagh** merchandise.

WHAT YOU HAVE TO DO:
You'll find tokens to collect in all Philip Ardagh's fiction books published after 08/10/02. There are 2 tokens in each hardback and 1 token in each paperback. Cut them out and send them to us complete with the form (below) and you'll get these great gifts:

> **2 tokens** = a sheet of groovy character stickers
> **4 tokens** = an Ardagh pen
> **6 tokens** = an Ardagh rucksack

Please send with your collected tokens and the name & address form to: Philip Ardagh promotion, Faber and Faber Ltd, 3 Queen Square, London, WC1N 3AU.

1. This offer can not be used in conjunction with any other offer and is non transferable. 2. No cash alternative is offered. 3. If under 18 please get permission and help from a parent or guardian to enter. 4. Please allow for at least 28 days delivery. 5. No responsibility can be taken for items lost in the post. 6. This offer will close on 31/12/04. 7. Offer open to readers in the UK and Ireland ONLY.

Name: ....

Address: ....

....

....

Town: ....

Postcode: ....

Age & Date of Birth: ....

Girl or boy: ....

Philip Ardagh Club
token

Critical acclaim for

AWFUL END

Book One of the Eddie Dickens Trilogy

'[A] scrumptious cross between Dickens and Monty
Python . . . You can look at this book as an examination
of: 1) the absurdities of the English language; 2) the
absurdities of the 19th-century novel; 3) the absurdities of
the way the English treat their kids; 4) the absurdities of
the absurd. A child will enjoy its daftness at 10, will get
the references at 14, and will know that it is all true at 18
. . . Brilliant.'
LYN GARDNER, *Guardian*

' . . . sophisticated . . . extremely silly . . . wonderful
. . . ridiculing literary conventions and turning
nonsense into a fine art.'
DINAH HALL, *Sunday Telegraph*

'It would be a sad spirit that didn't find
this book hilarious.'
LUCY JAMES, *Financial Times*

'In this surreal world, language is never what it
appears . . . It's daft but entirely engaging.'
HILARY MACASKILL, *Independent*

'Ardagh has a brilliantly witty style of writing . . .
A future classic and no mistake.'
Crowdsurfer.com

'A delicious slice of the ridiculous. A real find.'
TARA STEPHENSON, *Bookseller*

Dreadful Acts

Over two metres tall, with a bushy beard, Philip Ardagh is not only very large and very hairy but has also written over fifty children's books for all ages. *Dreadful Acts* is the second book in the Eddie Dickens Trilogy, which began with the critically acclaimed *Awful End*.

Currently living as a full-time writer, with a wife and two cats in a seaside town somewhere in England, he has been – amongst other things – an advertising copywriter, a hospital cleaner, a (highly unqualified) librarian, and a reader for the blind.

'One of my favourite comic characters is back in the second part of his hilarious history . . . and the result is equally delicious, and ridiculous.'
TARA STEPHENSON, *Bookseller*

by the same author

FICTION

The Eddie Dickens Trilogy
Awful End
Dreadful Acts
Terrible Times

The Further Adventures of Eddie Dickens
Dubious Deeds

Unlikely Exploits
The Fall of Fergal
Heir of Mystery
The Rise of the House of McNally

NON-FICTION

The Hieroglyphs Handbook
Teach Yourself Ancient Egyptian

The Archaeologist's Handbook
The Insider's Guide to Digging Up the Past

Did Dinosaurs Snore?
100¹/₂ Questions about Dinosaurs Answered

Why Are Castles Castle-Shaped?
100¹/₂ Questions about Castles Answered

PHILIP ARDAGH

Dreadful
Acts

Book Two of the Eddie Dickens Trilogy

illustrated by David Roberts

faber and faber

First published in 2001
by Faber and Faber Limited
3 Queen Square, London WC1N 3AU

Typeset by Faber and Faber Limited
Printed in England by Mackays of Chatham plc, Chatham, Kent

© Philip Ardagh, 2001
Illustrations © David Roberts, 2001
Philip Ardagh is hereby identified as author of this work in accordance
with Section 77 of the Copyright, Designs and Patents Act 1988

A CIP record for this book
is available from the British Library

ISBN 978–0–571–20947–7

10 9

A Message from the Author

Because he likes you

*D*readful Acts is the sequel to *Awful End*, in which Eddie Dickens (and a number of other characters who lurk within these pages) were first let loose on the reading public. You don't have to have read *Awful End* for this book to make sense, it's a story in its own right . . . and I'm not sure that *Awful End* made a great deal of sense, anyway. If you enjoy this book, please be sure to tell all your friends about it. If you hate it, please be sure to keep your ill-informed opinions to yourself.

Thank you

PHILIP ARDAGH

England
2001

For everyone who has helped to
make *Awful End* the success it is.

Thank you.
You know who you are.

Contents

Episode 1

Here We Go Again

In which a hssss becomes a BOOOOM!

Eddie Dickens woke up with a shock. An electric eel had just landed on him from the top pocket of his great uncle's overcoat. And one thing that can be guaranteed to be shocking is electricity.

Eddie sat up. 'What's happening, Mad Uncle Jack?' he asked, for that was the name he called the thinnest of thin gentleman – with the beakiest of beaky noses – who was leaning over his bed.

'Come quickly, boy!' his great-uncle instructed, his top hat brushing against the gas tap of the lamp on the wall. The eel might have had electricity, but this house – Awful End – didn't.

Eddie didn't need to be asked twice. The quickest way to escape the eel was to leap from his bed, so leap from his bed he did.

Eddie and his parents lived at Awful End with his great-uncle and great-aunt (Mad Aunt Maud). If you want to find out how they all came to live together, following a series of awfully exciting adventures – though I say so myself – you'll have to read the first book in this trilogy, called (surprise, surprise) *Awful End*.

Now where were we? Oh yes: an electric eel in the bed, Eddie Dickens out of the bed, and Mad Uncle Jack's top hat brushing against the gas tap . . . What's that hissing noise? Do you think it's important? Do you think it's part of the plot?

Hsssssssssssssssssssssssssssssssssssssssssssssssssssssss.

Mad Uncle Jack snatched up the escaped eel, seemingly unconcerned as the current of electricity passed through his hand and up his arm as he popped it back in his pocket. This rather strange gentleman used dried fish (and eels) to pay his bills but, for some reason we're bound to discover later, this eel was still alive and slipping. (I can't really say 'alive and *kicking*' now, can I? Eels – electric or otherwise – don't have legs.)

Eddie glanced at the clock on the wall. It said six o'clock in the morning.

'Six o'clock in the morning,' said the clock – an old joke, but not bad for a clock.

Why was Mad Uncle Jack getting him up so

2

early, Eddie wondered? It must be important. Then again, perhaps not. After all, his great-uncle was completely mad. Stifling a yawn, Eddie pulled on his clothes.

'Hurry!' said Mad Uncle Jack through gritted teeth. He didn't have a gritted pair of his own, so he always carried a pre-gritted pair about his person for just such an occasion. He kept these in a side pocket of his coat rather than in a top pocket. This was why the electric eel, rather than the pair of pre-gritted teeth, had fallen onto his great nephew.

Out on the landing, the early light of dawn filtered through the large picture window. A picture window is a big window, usually with a large enough area of glass to permit one to see a view as pretty as a picture. (Not to be confused with a picture *of a* window, which is – er – a picture *of a* window.)

The view from this window was of Mad Uncle Jack's tree house, built entirely of dried fish, and covered in creosote. The creosote not only protected the tree house from bad weather, but also from the neighbourhood cats (who loved the smell and taste of dried fish but who hated the smell and taste of creosote). Some might think the tree house pretty in the pinky early-morning light. There was something quite *salmony* about it. That's the word: salmony.

3

Still half asleep – which, if my maths serves me correctly, means that he must also have been half awake – Eddie Dickens followed Mad Uncle Jack down the front stairs. He lost his footing a couple of times but managed to remain upright and stumble on.

The heavy velvet curtains were closed in the hallway and it was pitch-black. Pitch is a kind of gooey tar which is very, very black, so pitch-black is a way of saying 'very, very black' using fewer letters . . . so long as you don't then have to explain what 'pitch' is, as I've just done.

Mad Uncle Jack found the front door by walking into it. The advantage of having the beakiest of beaky noses was that it reached the door way in front of the rest of him, so he managed to limit his injuries.

'Oooof!' he said, which is the universal noise a person makes when walking into a door, unless he or she stubs a toe, that is. The universal noise for stubbing a toe is 'Arrrgh!!!' (but you can choose the number of exclamation marks that best suits).

'Are you all right?' asked Eddie, blinded moments later as his great-uncle threw the door open wide, letting in the morning sunshine.

'There's no time to lose, boy,' said Mad Uncle Jack, a trickle of blood running from his beak– nose, I mean *nose*.

4

The picture window on the landing looked out onto his tree house at the back of the building. The front door opened onto the *front* – the clue is in the name – and there, right in the middle of the huge sweep of gravel driveway, was a hearse.

A hearse served the same purpose then as a hearse serves today. It was for transporting dead bodies in coffins from A to B (assuming that you *wanted* the coffin taken from A to B – it might be taken from A to Z if you asked very nicely). The difference is that hearses today are sleek black motor cars, whereas motor cars hadn't been invented in Eddie Dickens's day. For that reason, hearses were often glass-sided carriages pulled – or 'drawn', as horsy folk would say – by a pair of black horses with plumes of black feathers. The driver of a hearse would be dressed in black too . . . only this hearse didn't appear to have a driver and the coffin was half in and half out of the back.

The horses appeared nervous, skittish even (whatever that may mean), and they were shuffling their hooves around uneasily. Their flesh looked sweaty and their eyes were wide.

Mad Uncle Jack was already scrunching across the gravel. Eddie ran to keep up. 'W-What's happening?' he gasped. 'Who . . . who's died?'

'Your parents are asleep upstairs and Mad Aunt Maud is safely tucked up in Marjorie,' Mad Uncle Jack reassured him. Marjorie was a cow-shaped carnival float that Eddie's great-aunt lived inside in the gardens of Awful End. If you don't know why, I wouldn't let it bother you. It won't really lessen your reading enjoyment. 'I was awoken by the sound of frightened horses and this is what I found . . . a riderless hearse.'

'And this is what you got me up to see?' asked Eddie, nervously. If these pitch-black – yes, that word 'pitch' again – horses bolted, the coffin was bound to fall to the driveway and smash open . . . and who knew what or *who* might spill out onto the ground.

'Indeed. I do not want your great-aunt troubled by such a sight. She is a sensitive creature. And your parents need their sleep with the busy day that lies ahead. I feel confident that, with your experience of training horses, we'll soon have this carriage off the premises.'

'But I've never trained horses,' Eddie Dickens explained, patiently. Living with Mad Uncle Jack and Mad Aunt Maud, you had to be patient.

'So you've lied to me all these years then, have you, Edmund?' said his great-uncle sternly. 'Next you'll be telling me that you never fought alongside Colonel Marley at the Fall of St Geobad.'

'I think you're confusing me with someone else,' Eddie protested. 'I'm only thirteen. Well, almost.'

Mad Uncle Jack frowned. 'You've never trained horses?'

Eddie shook his head.

'And you never fought alongside Colonel Marley at the Fall of St Geobad?'

'No, sir,' said Eddie. 'I don't even know what the Fall of St Geobad is.'

'Me neither,' said Mad Uncle Jack, 'and there'd be no point in asking you now.'

'Do you think it might have been a waterfall?' Eddie suggested, helpfully.

'St Geobad seems a ridiculous name for a waterfall to me, boy. Preposterous! I've often wondered whether St Geobad was a church.'

'A church that fell down?' Eddie mused. 'But

why would Colonel Marley be fighting by a falling-down church?'

'A point well made! Well made, sir!' said his great-uncle. 'Perhaps it means "fall" as in "autumn".'

One of the horses at the front of the hearse snorted, causing steam to rise from its nostrils and the reader to remember the hearse, which was in serious danger of being forgotten because Uncle Jack – *Mad* Uncle Jack, that is – and Eddie Dickens were getting sidetracked.

'Well, you're here now, boy,' said Mad Uncle Jack, 'so what I want you to do is to calm the horses whilst I go to the back of the hearse and push the coffin back inside.'

Eddie would have preferred it if his great-uncle had done the calming-of-the-horses and he'd gone round to the back of the hearse. He knew from books he'd read – such as *Life After Being Kicked* and *Horsy Horrors*, for starters – that nervous horses were inclined to kick out at people who turned up uninvited to try to calm them down . . . but, then again, Mad Uncle Jack was a lot stronger than he was. He'd be able to slide the coffin back inside much more easily.

'G-G-Good horses . . . nice horses . . .' said Eddie in the kind of voice some people use when they're cooing over a baby in a pram, saying 'Doesn't he have his mother's eyes?' (If a baby *really* had his mother's eyes, she'd be screaming her head off and calling for child psychologist, police and ambulance and trying to get the eyes back off him.)

He took a step forward. *Scrunch.*

Both horses fixed their wide eyes on his. They reminded Eddie of the glass eyes on Mad Aunt Maud's stuffed stoat, Malcolm.

He took another step forward. *Scrunch.*

The horses' eyes looked even more wild . . . even more crazy, if that was possible. Forget Malcolm. They reminded Eddie of Even Madder Aunt Maud herself, now.

Scrunch.

One of the horses whinnied.

Eddie dug his hand inside the pockets of his

trousers. In one was a carrot and in the other a fistful of sugar lumps. What a lucky break! What were the chances of having a carrot and a fistful of sugar lumps in your pocket when you wanted to try and make friends with a couple of frightened horses attached to a hearse, eh? In Eddie's case, quite high, actually.

Sugar lumps were still considered an exciting innovation by Eddie's mother, Mrs Dickens (or 'that nice Mrs Dickens' to her friends), even though they'd been around since 1790. To her, they were one of the many marvels of the age, like gas lighting. No more candles! Simply turn the gas tap, light the gas and – hey presto! – instant light. (Knock the gas tap on with your top hat, don't light the gas and hssssssssssssssssssssssssssssssssssssssssss, big explosion sooner or later.) Sugar lumps . . . sugar in a perfect cube. How's it done? Who knows? *Why*'s it done? Because we can! Eddie's mother loved gimmicks, and sugar lumps certainly fell into that category. She had recently insisted that Eddie carry a fistful with him everywhere.

The carrot was for a more practical purpose. Mr Dickens (Eddie's father) thought that a boy of Eddie's age should carry a knife with him for protection and for whittling. Mrs Dickens thought that Eddie might cut himself, so a compromise was reached. Eddie would carry a carrot for protection and for whittling instead. Eddie knew better than to argue. Anyway, he didn't feel he needed protection (having once organised a mass escape from an orphanage, single-handedly) and had no idea what 'whittling' was anyhow.

The horses smelled the sugar lumps and the carrot and suddenly looked a whole lot happier. Eddie *scrunch-scrunch-scrunched* over to them with increasing confidence, and started to feed them the treats, patting their muzzles and muttering what he hoped were encouraging words.

Much to Eddie's amazement, Mad Uncle Jack had stuck to his side of the plan and was successfully pushing the coffin back into the glass-sided hearse without a hitch.

'There,' said Mad Uncle Jack. 'All done.'

At that precise moment, there was an enormous explosion, the sound of shattering glass and a plume of smoke appeared above the proud rooftops of Awful End.

Waking early to the sound of scrunching gravel, Eddie's father, Mr Dickens, had struck a match to light his first cigar of the day – he had recently taken to smoking boxes of the things to improve his cough – but had ignited some escaped gas. The hssssssssssssssssssssssssssssssssssss had turned to BOOOOOOOOOOOOOOOOOOOOOOOM!!!

11

Episode 2

BOOOOM!

In which someone or something
flips his lid

Even the calmest of horses, with a mouthful of carrot or sugar lumps, isn't going to take kindly to a massive explosion. This black-plumed pair had been on the unnerved side of uneasy before the BOOOOM . . . now they were tearing off halfway down the drive, with the hearse in tow.

Mad Uncle Jack hadn't actually had time to twist the catch on the back of the carriage, and the coffin shot out of the hearse like a half-hearted cannonball from a cannon packed with not quite enough gunpowder.

It hit the gravel with a thud but, much to Eddie's relief, didn't split open to reveal its occupant. All of this seemed to have happened in an instant but, now that he had his wits about him, Eddie turned and ran inside the house to see if anyone had been hurt.

His mother was coming down the stairs with a stunned look on her face and the tattered remains of his father's nightcap in her hand.

'What happened, mother?' asked Eddie, running over to her and helping her to a chair. 'Are you all right? Where's father?'

Mrs Dickens pointed to her ears. Mad Uncle Jack would have taken that to mean that she was telling him that Mr Dickens was *in* her ears, but Eddie knew better. His mother was trying to tell him that she couldn't hear. The BOOOM must have affected her hearing.

'W-A-I-T H-E-R-E,' Eddie said very loudly and very slowly, then dashed up the stairs two at a time to see if he could find his father. When he reached his parents' bedroom, next to his own – or, more accurately, when he reached where his parents' bedroom should have been, next to where his own bedroom should have been – Eddie found . . . found . . . Well, it's rather difficult to describe, really.

He found a smouldering mess. Everything seemed to have been blown apart. Nothing was whole. There were bits of chairs, bits of wardrobes, bits of chamber pots, bits of bits and bits of bits of bits. And a slipper. His father's slipper, with a wisp of smoke coiling out of it, as if on cue. Where the outside wall had been was now just outside . . . a huge gaping hole opening onto the back garden and morning sky.

There was a thud. Not a heavy thud, like the one when the coffin had hit the gravel on the driveway. This was more of a mini-thud. The thud of an unsmoked cigar falling from the rafters.

Eddie looked up. There, where the ceiling had once been, were exposed roof beams and, straddled across one, like an outsized kid on a rocking horse, was Mr Dickens, in nothing but a nightshirt.

Eddie's heart leapt for joy. Suddenly nothing else mattered. His father was alive.

'It's a miracle!' shouted Eddie at the top of his voice. 'It's a miracle.'

Though even more deafened by the explosion than his good lady wife had been, Mr Dickens could hear his son's cries of joy. 'A miracle? Not really,' said Mr Dickens philosophically. 'It'd be a bit sad to kill one of us off in Episode Two . . . maybe in a tragic climax, but not in Episode Two.'

Not realising that he was *in* any Episode Two, Eddie had no idea what his father was on about, but he didn't care. Running into one of the rooms that hadn't been destroyed when the hsssssssssssssssssssssssssssssssssssssssssss became a BOOOOOOOOOOOM, Eddie returned with a pair of library steps. They were designed for wheeling in front of bookshelves, but his mother often took them into the bathroom to use for diving practice – she'd climb up them and jump off into the tub.

Eddie dashed up them and helped his father down off the beam. He was covered in a fine powdering of dust which made him and his nightgown look grey. 'Powdered ceiling plaster,' he explained. 'Someone must have left the gas on.' Apart from his (hopefully) temporary loss of hearing, Mr Dickens seemed little the worse for wear.

15

Mad Aunt Maud appeared in what would have been the doorway from the landing if the inner wall had still been standing. 'See!' she said, with a steely look of rage in her eyes. 'I told you no good would come of these rowdy parties.' Neither of the Dickenses knew what she was on about – Mr Dickens because he hadn't heard a word she'd said, and Eddie because Mad Aunt Maud never made much sense anyway. She marched off the way she'd come.

It was only later that Eddie realised that was one of the few occasions since he'd met his great-aunt when she hadn't been carrying Malcolm, her stuffed stoat.

Back in the hallway, Eddie's parents were reunited. Unable to see her husband up in the rafters and unable to hear his cries, Mrs Dickens had assumed that he'd been blown to bits . . . To find him alive was the best thing that could happen

16

before breakfast. There was plenty of hugging and kissing. This is always embarrassing to watch if it's your own parents doing it, and even more so in those days for some reason, so Eddie hurried back outside, leaving them to it.

He found Mad Uncle Jack in the driveway issuing instructions to the servants – ex-footsoldiers once under his command in some faraway place in some long-forgotten war – whose job it would be to clear up the mess. Eddie suggested that they also be given strict instructions *not* to light any fires or make any sparks until the gas pipes damaged in the explosion were repaired.

Mad Uncle Jack looked at him admiringly. 'I can see why Colonel Marley was glad to have you at his side at the Fall of St Geobad, my boy,' he beamed proudly.

Eddie was about to say something, but decided against it.

Mad Aunt Maud appeared, pushing between them. 'I said such rowdiness would end in tears,' she muttered, stomping off around the east side of Awful End, back to Marjorie, her hollow cow.

'Where's Malcolm, Mad Uncle Jack?' Eddie asked.

'Malcolm?'

'Her stoat.'

'I believe her stoat's name is Sally,' said Mad

17

Uncle Jack, which was a common error on his part, unless, of course, it was Mad Aunt Maud who consistently got the name wrong. 'Is that her?' He pointed at a stone birdbath on a pedestal. In it was Malcolm, floating on his back. It was a strange morning all round.

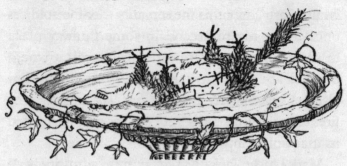

Relieved that no one was injured from the explosion, Mad Uncle Jack and Eddie returned their attention to the lonely coffin lying further down the driveway.

'What's your father's gentleman's gentleman called?' asked Uncle Jack.

'Dawkins,' said Eddie. Dawkins had moved to Awful End with Eddie and his parents, along with a failed chambermaid called Gibbering Jane.

'I thought it was something like Daphne,' said Mad Uncle Jack, a thin, puzzled frown fighting to find enough space to fit on his thinnest of thin faces.

'So does Father,' Eddie explained, 'which must be where you got the idea from.'

'Well, would you please go and find Dawkins and ask him to help us move this coffin to the stable block, where it will be free from casual discovery,' said Mad Uncle Jack. 'Who knows what distress it might cause your poor dear mother or my dear wife to stumble upon such a thing by accident . . . particularly after this morning's other events?'

Eddie was impressed by his great-uncle's clear thinking and complete lack of concern for the state of his property. He returned with Dawkins who, through years of training as a gentleman's gentleman didn't bat an eyelid at being instructed to assist in hiding a coffin in a stable block.

It was only when the coffin was nestling on a bed of straw that Eddie had time to read the inscription on a small brass plate screwed to the lid with four small brass screws. There were no dates for birth or death, just a name . . . but no ordinary name. It seemed more like a title, in fact. It read:

THE GREAT ZUCCHINI

Eddie felt sure that he'd heard the name somewhere before. Was it something to do with ice cream, perhaps?

In the days before people had learnt to harness the power of electricity, people didn't have electric fridges – I'll leave you to work out why – and ice cream was a new and exciting food brought over from Italy. It was sold in big towns and cities by Italians, out of little carts (a bit like prams) kept cool with big blocks of ice. The ice-cream sellers often painted their names on their carts. Eddie thought he'd probably seen the name 'Zucchini' on just such a cart . . . no, that wasn't it.

Eddie Dickens was so busy trying to remember where he'd seen or heard the name 'The Great Zucchini' before, that he didn't pay much attention to the creaking sound at first. Then he did. Especially when he realised where it was coming from . . .

The coffin was creaking. Correction, the *lid* of the coffin was creaking as someone was opening it *from the inside*.

Episode 3

To the Very Top!

*In which Mad Aunt Maud is hit
by a low-flying object*

The man who sat up in the coffin certainly didn't look very dead. Eddie was surprised to find that he was actually a little *disappointed* that the occupant didn't have a skinless skull for a head, or at least scary teeth. In fact, he reminded Eddie of Mr Collins who worked in the ironmonger's. He had a very round head with very little hair and sparkling eyes.

He looked very surprised when he saw Eddie.

'Where on earth am I?' he asked. 'Where are the crowds . . . Mr Skillet and Mr Merryweather?

Where is my Daniella?'

Eddie had no idea what he was talking about. 'You're in the stable block of Awful End, sir,' he explained politely.

'Awful what?' asked the man. He certainly didn't sound 'Great', or Italian.

'Awful End, sir,' said Eddie. 'The home of the Dickens family . . . I'm Eddie Dickens.' He put out his hand. The man in the coffin shook it.

'I'm the Great Zucchini,' said the Great Zucchini.

'You're not dead, are you?' asked Eddie then, realising how stupid he sounded, added hurriedly: 'I mean, you didn't think you were?'

'Whatever makes you think that?' asked the Great Zucchini, swinging his legs over the edge of the coffin and onto the straw.

'Oh, just little clues,' said Eddie, 'such as finding you in a coffin with your name on it, in the back of a hearse.'

The man nodded. 'A good point, young man. I see what you're alluding to. No, I went into this coffin very much alive and intended to come out that way, which is, as you can see, what has occurred. Unfortunately, instead of emerging to the applause and approbation of an eager crowd, I find myself in a private stable block with an audience of one.'

The word 'audience' made Eddie feel a little uneasy. He'd once had a run-in with a man by the name of Mr Pumblesnook – an actor-manager of a band of wandering theatricals – who had caused poor old Eddie nothing but Grief with a capital 'G' (which is how I just spelled it, anyway).

'You're not a wandering theatrical, are you, sir?' asked Eddie, trying to keep the revulsion out of his voice but failing spectacularly.

The man leapt to his feet and looked even less 'Great' and even more like Mr Collins, the iron-monger. Eddie noticed that what little hair the Great Zucchini did have – a patch just above each ear – was dyed black rather than naturally black. If the truth be told, from the smell of boot polish Eddie'd just detected, 'dyed' was probably too strong a word for it. Eddie suspected that the hair was *polished* black. The man was quivering.

23

'Indeed I am NOT a wandering theatrical,' he protested, and was obviously upset.

'I didn't mean to offend you,' Eddie assured him. 'I was simply trying to make sense of what you were doing in a coffin in the back of a hearse.'

'And I'm still trying to puzzle out how I came to be here,' said the Great Zucchini.

'My great-uncle woke me at six o'clock this morning to say that he'd found a hearse in our driveway,' said Eddie. 'He sleeps in a tree house at the rear but has excellent hearing and was probably aroused by the horses' hooves on the gravel. There was no driver and, by the time I came to look, your coffin was half in and half out of the vehicle.'

'Your great-uncle sleeps in a tree house?'

'Yes,' said Eddie, wishing he hadn't mentioned that part. He'd so have liked his family to be normal. He certainly had no intention of telling the Great Zucchini about Mad Aunt Maud living in Marjorie.

'And my hearse turned up riderless in your driveway?'

'Yes,' said Eddie. He led the man out of the stable block and over to the spot where he'd first seen the hearse.

'Where is the hearse now?' asked the Great Zucchini. Standing next to each other as they now were, Eddie realised that the man wasn't actually

24

that much taller than he was.

'There was an explosion in the house –'

'In the tree house?'

'In the main house –'

'An explosion?'

'Yes, and it frightened the horses and your coffin fell out of the back and we carried the coffin – you – into the stable, and here we are,' said Eddie.

'Here we are indeed, Mr Eddie Dickens, and what an extraordinary story it is too,' said the Great Zucchini. He slapped Eddie on the back.

'Would you be good enough to explain your part of it?' asked Eddie, as they scrunched their way up the drive towards the front door.

'I am an escapologist, young man. An escapologist. Do you know what that is?'

'Someone who studies pyramids and mummies . . . The kind in bandages, I mean?' Eddie suggested.

'You're thinking of an Egyptologist,' grinned the man and, when he grinned, he looked so like Mr Collins, the ironmonger, that Eddie half-expected him to try to sell him a box of screws or a new shovel for the coal scuttle because that's what iron-mongers do, you see: they monger iron. (And no, if the truth be told, I'm not 100 per cent sure what 'monger' actually means either.) 'An escapologist is a professional escaper,' he explained.

'I escaped from an orphanage once,' said Eddie proudly. 'Does that make me a professional escapologist?'

'Were you paid for it?' asked the Great Zucchini.

Eddie shook his head.

'Then I'm afraid not,' said the man from the coffin. 'Escaping is how I earn my daily bread. Anyone can escape – just think of all those convicts who keep escaping to the moors.' He looked in the direction of the nearby moors, neatly bringing them into the story and lodging them in the reader's mind for later. (M-O-O-R-S. E-S-C-A-P-E-D C-O-N-V-I-C-T-S. Okay? Good . . . as if you'd forgotten the brilliant picture of them on the cover.) 'The skill is to escape from something interesting in an exciting way, and in front of a paying audience.'

Mad Uncle Jack appeared at the side of the house and fished the stuffed stoat out of the bird-bath. 'Your great-aunt wants Sally,' he said, on seeing Eddie. 'She's inside the cow. Take it to her, would you?' Then he noticed the Great Zucchini. 'Good morning, Mr Collins,' he said. 'I wasn't aware that ironmongers made house calls.'

The escapologist looked confused. 'You have mistaken me for someone else, sir,' he said.

'I think not, Mr Collins,' said Mad Uncle Jack.

'I would recognise your hair anywhere.'

'But I have no hair,' said the Great Zucchini. 'At least, very little.'

'Exactly, Mr Collins! Exactly!' said Mad Uncle Jack, as though he'd cleverly proved his point. With that, he thrust the dripping-wet Malcolm into Eddie's arms and marched indoors.

Eddie held the stoat by its rigid tail and let the water run off its nose onto the gravel: *drip drip drip*.

'I take it that that is your great-uncle?' said the Great Zucchini.

'Yes, sir,' said Eddie.

'The one who lives in a tree house?'

'Yes, sir,' said Eddie.

'And Sally?' asked the Great Zucchini, looking at Malcolm, with eyebrows raised.

'My great-aunt's companion,' Eddie tried to explain. 'A stuffed stoat.'

'It looks more like a ferret to me,' said the escapologist. 'Stoats have rounder noses.'

'Perhaps it was stuffed by someone who'd never seen a live stoat?' Eddie suggested

and, keen to steer the subject away from the strangeness of his relatives – I'm sure you know the feeling – he said: 'You were telling me about being an escapologist.'

'Indeed I was,' said the Great Zucchini, following Eddie, who'd given Malcolm one final shake and was striding off around the side of the house in search of Mad Aunt Maud. 'I specialise in Dreadful Acts – which is, in fact, the name of my travelling escapology show. I face death at every turn, escaping from a water tank filled with flesh-eating fish, from a flaming trunk suspended high in the air . . . but the great escape which brought me to this place was entitled "Back From the Dead" – a rather good title, though I say so myself. Mr Merryweather had suggested we call it "Arisen!" but I thought it too subtle.'

'Mr Merryweather?'

'My manager,' said the Great Zucchini, 'though I can't say that he's managed *this* particular escape very successfully!'

'What was supposed to happen?' asked Eddie. They wove through the narrow paths of the rose garden and emerged in a large area given over to lawn. Unfamiliar with Mad Aunt Maud's unusual living arrangements, the escapologist – with more than a passing resemblance to Mr Collins, the ironmonger – was surprised to see what appeared to be a giant cow in amongst some flowering shrubs.

'What was supposed to happen was that my assistant Daniella was supposed to bind me hand and foot, gag me and, with the aid of Mr Skillet, place me in the coffin,' he explained. 'The coffin would be screwed shut and placed in the back of a hearse. Mr Skillet would then ride the hearse, at a respectfully slow speed, with the audience walking behind – hopefully attracting more attention and more followers as others became interested and joined our most unusual of funeral cortèges.'

They had reached the back end of the cow, from which a crazy-eyed woman peered at them both through an opening. When she saw that Eddie was carrying Malcolm, she eagerly took her pet, stroking him between the glass eyes.

'Did Malcolm have a nice bath? Did he?' she asked. She suddenly noticed the Great Zucchini and glared at him. 'I know you, don't I?' she demanded in a voice that was enough to frighten an army of well-armed badgers.

'It seems that I bear a resemblance to someone named Mr Collins,' sighed the escapologist.

'The ironmonger?'

'Apparently,' he said.

'Ridiculous!' snapped Mad Aunt Maud. 'Mr Collins has great long droopy ears and shaggy fur. You, on the other hand, have no ears worthy of mention and certainly no hair, let alone fur. Ridiculous!'

'The one with great long droopy ears and shaggy fur is Mr Collins's cocker spaniel, Aunt Maud,' said Eddie hurriedly.

'Well, I know you from somewhere, I'm sure of it,' said Eddie's great-aunt, through narrowed eyes. 'What I can't remember, offhand, is whether I like you or not.'

'See you later, Aunt Maud!' said Eddie with false cheerfulness. He took the escapologist's elbow and steered him behind a box hedge. 'Forgive my great-aunt,' he said in a loud whisper. 'I'm sure she doesn't mean to offend.'

'I'm sure not,' said the Great Zucchini.

'Please carry on with what you were telling me,' said Eddie. 'It's most intriguing.'

'What was supposed to happen was that I would be taken to a field next to the churchyard of St Botolph's –'

'That's St Botolph's there,' said Eddie, excitedly. He pointed to a distant church spire, poking above a line of trees.

'We wanted the atmosphere of a churchyard for my great escape,' the Great Zucchini explained, 'but it would have been disrespectful to actually bury me in the consecrated ground of a churchyard.'

'You were going to be buried . . . in the ground?' gasped Eddie.

'That was the plan. Daniella and Mr Skillet were to lower the coffin into the ground, shovel earth on top and then erect a screen around it. A large clock would be started to indicate the exact amount of time it took me to escape, bound hand and foot, from my premature grave, to emerge from behind the screen. In the meantime, Daniella would keep the audience occupied, and the tension high, by playing stirring tunes upon a portable church organ.'

'Incredible!' said Eddie. 'Absolutely incredible.'

The Great Zucchini looked sad. 'This was to have been my crowning glory,' he said, the quiver returning to his voice. (What do you mean, you don't remember the quiver? I first mentioned it back on page 23.) 'Mr Merryweather had arranged for the gentlemen of the press to be present at the grave side. This was going to be bigger than "The Underwater Box" trick . . . more daring than escaping from "The Lions' Den" . . . and look what happened.'

'What did happen?'

'How should I know!' he quivered – see, it's spread from his voice to his whole body now – 'I was bound and gagged in a coffin with the lid screwed down in the back of the hearse. It's obvious that we never made it to the field by the churchyard!'

The Great Zucchini saw a garden bench and sat on it. He looked tired. Eddie had seen Mr Collins look like that after a hard day selling ironmongery, on one of his very rare visits to the shops. As you'll discover later, Eddie didn't get out much.

'Something must have frightened the horses,' Eddie suggested. 'They must have bolted and made off with you in the back . . . but how come you weren't bound and gagged back in the stable? And I thought you said the coffin lid was screwed down? You opened it easily enough.'

'For the very reason that I'm a professional escapologist!' said the Great Zucchini. 'I freed myself from my bonds within the coffin and unscrewed the screws from the inside. All I had to do was lift the lid off.'

Eddie sat down next to the escapologist and looked up at the gaping hole in the side of the house where he and his parents' bedrooms had once been. He was thinking. 'I can see how you might be able to open the coffin lid back in the stable block . . . but how would you have been able to open it with tons of earth on top of it? Surely that's impossible?'

The Great Zucchini gave Eddie a sideways glance. 'You're a clever boy, aren't you?' he said. And it didn't necessarily sound like a compliment.

'And what about air?' Eddie went on.

'Why does everyone go on about it!' cried the escapologist, leaping to his feet. 'So I have very little hair and, what little hair I do have, I dye! Is it a crime? Is it? I'm going bald and I dye my hair! Let's tell the world shall we?' He climbed onto the bench and shouted: 'I'M GOING BALD AND DYE MY HAIR!' Then he sat down with a bump. 'There? Happy now, Eddie Dickens?' he demanded.

'I said *air*,' said Eddie, in a little voice. He spelled it out: 'A-I-R . . . How could you breathe in a sealed-up coffin . . . You must have been in there for hours?'

The escapologist was obviously embarrassed about the little hair/air misunderstanding and pretended to find his shoes of sudden interest. He stared at his neatly polished toecaps instead of looking at Eddie when he spoke. 'Er . . . that's a trade secret,' he said.

There was a cough. He looked up. Mad Aunt Maud was standing before them. 'Ah, Mr Collins,' she beamed. 'How nice of you to come. I'll have half a dozen three-and-a-quarter-inch galvanised nails, please,' she said. 'There's a crack in Marjorie's udder and I want to repair it whilst the weather's fine.'

The Great Zucchini put his head in his hands and wailed. It was at that exact moment that the hot-air balloon skimmed the oak tree nearest to the house and came crashing to the ground.

Episode 4

Sent From the Skies

In which Eddie does rather a lot of dribbling

'How exciting!' said Mad Aunt Maud, dragging herself from beneath the basket of the crash-landed hot-air balloon and pulling the twigs from her hair. 'I can't say I ever imagined that I'd be hit by a hot-air balloon but, now that it's happened, I must confess to having enjoyed it.' She tore off the corner of a rhubarb leaf and pressed it against a cut above her eye. 'Really most enjoyable. Yes.' She crawled off into the bushes and back towards Marjorie, dragging a sprained ankle behind her.

Eddie and Zucchini took the accident far less calmly. You don't expect to be sitting in the back garden, quietly enjoying the sunshine and occasionally glancing through a hole in the wall created by a gas explosion, and suddenly have a balloon land with a crash right next to you.

Eddie's heart was pounding like a steam train and the escapologist looked as white as Mr Dickens had with all that plaster dust on him twenty-one pages ago . . . but it was the woman from the basket of the balloon who'd come off worse.

The balloon had come down at great speed, with the basket skimming the tree tops then dragging *through* the trees before coming to rest on the ground . . . though 'rest' is rather too nice a word for it. 'Rest' makes one think of relaxing under cool sheets in a shaded room on a sunny day with ones favourite cuddly toy. 'Rest' makes one think of 'having a little lie down'. No, the balloon didn't come to rest, the balloon came to a *sudden stop*, but its occupant didn't. The occupant of the basket became the occupant OUT of the basket (which, technically speaking, means that she wasn't really an occupant any more). She went flying through the air and landed in a rose bush.

Eddie had never seen anyone like her. He'd never seen a woman tangled up in a rose bush

36

before, that's true, but that's not what I mean. Eddie had never seen a young woman with such a tight corset and quite so many layers of wonderfully frilly petticoats . . .

'Daniella!' cried the Great Zucchini, running forward to untangle her from the thorns.

'Harold!' cried the woman, in what novelists of the day would have called 'unbridled joy'. Because a bridle is something you put on a horse, it's hardly surprising that you don't find one on joy. And, anyway, this wasn't Joy but Daniella.

The name rang a bell with Eddie. What was one of the first things the Great Zucchini had said when he'd stepped from his coffin in the stable – after that bit about 'Where on earth am I?' . . .? 'Where is my Daniella?' – that was it.

Well, here she was, and what an extraordinary effect she was having on Eddie.

Okay, so crash-landing in a balloon and being catapulted into a rose bush is a pretty attention-grabbing way of making an entrance, but Eddie suspected that Daniella would have had a similar effect on him if she'd just strolled up to him and said, 'Good morning, Master Dickens.'

Most of the girls and women Eddie ever met wore dresses in such exciting colours as grey or black, or greyish-black. Not only that, these dresses began just below the chin and ended on the ground. Eddie was about nine years old before he even realised that his own mother actually had legs.

Yet here was this beautiful young creature – with a face a bit like the photographic plate of a camel Eddie had seen in a book called *Animals Other Than Horses Which Kick Too* – who had a neck, and ankles and lots of frilly bits under a tartan dress of red, blue and yellow . . .

'Are you an idiot?' asked Daniella, removing a snail from her ear and putting it back in the rose bush where it must have come from.

'S-S-Sorry?' asked Eddie.

'The way you're staring at me with your mouth open, and all that dribble?'

Eddie snapped his mouth shut like a clam and wiped the dribble from his chin with his sleeve.

There wasn't *that* much.

'This is Edmund Dickens,' said Harold Zucchini hurriedly. 'He rescued me.'

Daniella snorted. It was an enchanting snort, thought Eddie. It was the sort of snort that he imagined the beautiful camel in that book would have made. 'A kid rescued you? The world's greatest escapologist? I'd keep that quiet, if I was you.'

Daniella spoke with the sort of voice which shouted 'Bring out ya dead!' during the plague, or 'Who'll buy me luvverly roses?' in dreadful musicals about life in 'Good Olde London' in the time of Eddie Dickens.

This sounded strangely exotic to Eddie, who now spent most of his time at Awful End with his family, Dawkins, Gibbering Jane and an assortment of ex-soldiers. (More on them later, I expect.)

There was a lot of explaining to do, and Zucchini told his side of the story first. 'So tell me,' he said at last: 'how did I end up here in Awful End?'

Daniella looked at Eddie quizzically. 'Can I say in front of 'im?' she asked.

Zucchini sighed. 'I suppose so,' he said. 'The lad has as good as accused me of cheating anyway. He's guessed that, in the world of escapology, all is not what it seems.'

Daniella glared at Eddie. 'It ain't cheatin',' she

39

said, hotly leaping to Zucchini's defence. 'It's the tricks of the trade, that's what it is.'

'*Fuwuwuu*,' said Eddie, looking lovingly at the camel-nosed showgirl and trying not to dribble. Again.

'Are you sure 'e ain't no simpleton?' she asked.

'Just tell me what went wrong,' insisted the escapologist.

'Right you are, Harold,' said sweet Daniella, wiping her nose across the back of her sleeve.

*

Apparently, all had been going fine. The Great Zucchini had been ceremoniously loaded into the back of the glass-sided hearse and taken, in procession, up to the field next to St Botolph's. Of course, what the unsuspecting punters didn't know was that this was no *ordinary* hearse. No, this hearse had been especially constructed by Mr Skillet.

Once the Great Zucchini's coffin was on board and the hearse was moving, specially angled mirrors sprang into place that gave the impression that one was looking at the coffin but one was really looking at a picture of the coffin reflected back from the roof of the carriage. Meanwhile, the *real* coffin was shielded from the outside world. Under Zucchini's coffin was a secret compartment containing another, identical, coffin, and the two coffins could be swapped – one heightened and one lowered – by means of a rotating floor which Mr Skillet called the 'flip-flap'. So the coffin which ended up on *top* of the secret compartment and which was unloaded at the field contained nothing more than a couple of sandbags to give it weight.

I'm sure a diagram with lots of dotted arrows and 'Position A' and 'Position B' would be jolly useful here, but the Honoured Society of Escapologists forbids it, and I'm not about to risk waking up to find myself handcuffed in a trunk at the bottom of a river just so that everyone understands Mr Skillet's flip-flap.

(The sandbags adding weight to the other coffin had been sewn by the convicts at the nearby prison, by the way. They normally had to sew *mail*bags, and had sewn the *sand*bags specially, which was nice of them. Not that they'd had much choice. This had been before the mass break-out, leaving a number of escaped convicts up there on the moors – remember? – and the others locked up in their cells, with no more fun things, such as sewing, to pass the time.)

Well, you can guess what happened next. The coffin with the sandbags in it was buried and the screens erected around it, with the crowd thinking that the Great Zucchini himself was down there . . . and this, according to Daniella, was where things went wrong. What *should* have been happening in the meantime was that, with the hearse parked around the corner and away from prying eyes, Zucchini should have opened his coffin from the inside – just as he'd done in the stable block of Awful End – in the secret compartment, pressed a button flipping him and the open coffin back on top, and sneaked out of the hearse.

How he was then supposed to have got behind the screen so that he could appear to have come from the coffin and dug through the earth was deliciously simple, but Daniella had no need to reveal that part to Eddie. Why? Because everything had gone wrong before then. As Daniella told Zucchini (and the enthralled, drooling Eddie), the horses leading the hearse had bolted whilst the first coffin was still being buried.

'Suddenly, they rang the alarm bell at the prison because *more* of them convicts had escaped and it's really loud even miles away,' Daniella explained. 'It gave them poor beasts such a dreadful fright they ran, draggin' your 'earse behind 'em. John said he saw the back wheels go over such a bump that the mirrors flew back and your coffin shot up out of the hidin' place like a rabbit out of a hat.'

'Which is when I must have banged my head and knocked myself out,' gasped the escapologist. 'What happened next?'

'Well, there was the problem . . .' said Daniella.

The problem was that, interesting though a runaway hearse was, waiting to see if the Great Zucchini could escape from a coffin buried six feet underground was far more interesting, so Daniella and the others had to stay by the screens and pretend that he was down there whilst they decided what to do next. It was, as Daniella so neatly put it, 'a right pickle'.

'Me and Skillet 'ad a discussion in 'ushed tones while I played stirrin' music on me organ,' Daniella explained. 'John went off in search of the 'earse. He even borrowed an 'orse from the land-lord of the local 'ostlery, but he couldn't find 'ide nor 'air of you.'

When she said ''ostlery' she meant 'hostelry' and, before you get sick to the back teeth of trying to decipher her words with all those letters missing at the front, I'm going to use a narrator's trick: I'm going to cheat. When I report what the lovely Daniella said, I'm going to use the whole words and leave it up to you to imagine how she said them. I'll add a sprinkling of ''ere, what you lookin' at, mate?' now and then to remind you how she actually sounded, but it's up to you to remember most of the time. Fair enough?

'But the hot-air balloon,' said the Great Zucchini. 'Where on earth did you get the hot-air balloon?'

'I was just coming to that,' said Daniella, with a sniff. 'Merryweather –'

'My manager,' the escapologist reminded Eddie.

'Yeah, him,' said Daniella. 'If you remember, he invited Wolfe Tablet –'

'The famous photographer,' Zucchini explained to Eddie.

'Him,' nodded Daniella. 'Merryweather asked Wolfe Tablet if he wanted to come and take some photographs of your latest escape.'

'But I thought he wasn't interested? He failed to respond to the invitation,' said Zucchini. 'In fact, I seem to recall him saying that he thought I was a fraud and a charlatan.'

'Well, he does,' said Daniella, 'which is why he turned up in a balloon so that he could look *down* on the escape from above and see how it was done.'

The Great Zucchini's face reddened. 'The dirty rotten scoundrel!' he fumed. 'The lowdown good-for-nothing . . . I'd like to knock his block off! I'd like to . . .'

Eddie was worried that he was about to burst a blood vessel. The only time he'd ever seen Mr Collins look so angry was when one of the assistant ironmongers had muddled the three-quarter-inch nails with the half-inch nails . . . but he hadn't been half so furious as this.

Daniella mopped Zucchini's brow with the laciest of lacy handkerchiefs Eddie'd ever seen. He wished that it was *his* brow that she was mopping. (Sickening, isn't it?)

'Calm yourself, Harold,' she insisted. 'Nosy old Mr Tablet didn't get to see nothing because you wasn't there, remember. When his nasty hot-air balloon came sailing over the site where we'd buried you, he couldn't catch you sneaking behind the screen because you weren't around to do no sneaking. You was here, or in the hearse or wherever you was. But you certainly wasn't there.'

'Ha!' said Zucchini, with a triumphant snort. But Eddie didn't think it was nearly as pretty a snort as the sort of snort Daniella made. 'So for all he knew, I really was deep down in the earth inside that coffin!'

'Exactly!' grinned Daniella.

'Serves him right!' said Zucchini.

Eddie noticed black boot polish trickling out of what little hair Zucchini had left, and down his face. He'd worked himself into a right sweat. 'But

how did *you* get t-t-to be in the balloon, Daniella?'
Eddie asked, excitedly, doing his very best not to
dribble.

'Skillet and some of the crowd caught a hold of
his guy ropes that was trailing from the basket and
they pulled him to the ground. Most people
seemed to think it was part of the act and, when
they realised that he was none other than the
world famous photographer Mr Wolfe Tablet, they
was all interested in him and his equipment . . .
Havin' failed to expose any trickery and feelin'
right welcome, he agreed to go for a drink with
Merryweather and leave his precious balloon tied
up to a tree.'

'Overnight?'

'He had no choice. He kept on pestering
Merryweather to tell him some tricks of the trade,
so Merryweather agreed. Well, kind of. He bound
and gagged the photographer in his room at the
Rancid Rat and said, "Now get out of that!" He's
still there now, I suppose.'

'Pah! More fool him!' said Zucchini, with a
nervous laugh.

'Isn't he going to be a bit annoyed that you held
him prisoner, stole his balloon and wrecked it?'
asked Eddie.

Daniella was about to say something insulting
when Mad Aunt Maud came crashing back

through the undergrowth, in the distance, dragging her leg with the sprained ankle behind her. 'Peelers!' she cried. 'The place is overrun with peelers!' With that, she disappeared behind a compost heap.

'The police?' sighed Eddie. 'I wonder who they're after?'

Episode 5

Appealing to the Peelers

*In which almost everyone
is in deep doo-doos*

Now, I'm sure it's not true nowadays – though some of you are probably thinking 'He's just saying that' – but, in Eddie's day, most police officers seem to have been sent on a special course called Getting Hold of the Wrong End of the Stick. If it was possible to misunderstand something that someone – a suspect, in particular – was saying, then a peeler/police officer would take the *wrong* meaning.

Say, for example, you're a suspect and you say 'Good morning' to a peeler, the peeler will

48

immediately ask: 'What's so good about this particular morning, ay? Done something to make yourself feel particularly good, now, have ya?' and you know full well that the 'something' he's thinking of is something illegal, like stealing a diamond the size of a plover's egg or kicking a chicken, and that he's hoping to nail you for doing it, simply because you were being nice and polite and saying 'Good morning'. For, as well as getting hold of the wrong end of the proverbial stick – which is like a real stick but, somehow, less sticky – peelers were particularly fond of nailing people.

Now 'nailing' in this context doesn't actually mean nailing as in 'nailing a bookcase together' (or even on your own), or even nailing as in 'nailing poor unfortunate people to crosses' (as the ancient Roman authorities liked to do), but 'nailing you for a crime' or 'pinning a crime on you'. In other words, being able to say 'You dunnit' (even if you haven't done it, but it'd be a bonus if you had).

Today people say: 'You can never find a police officer when you need one', unless, of course, they have found a police officer when they needed one, in which case, they'll probably say nothing. In Eddie's day, people would probably have said: 'What's that funny man in the funny hat and the funny uniform?' and pointed, laughed or thrown stones. Or all three.

Anyway or anyhow, with Eddie's limited experience from an earlier adventure, he had little doubt that, whether he told the complete and utter truth or a dirty sackful of lies, the peelers wouldn't believe him either way. At the station, he, Daniella and the Great Zucchini were taken to different rooms.

'Be brave, Daniella!' Eddie called out, as he was dragged in the opposite direction from the others. Because he was trying to sound brave himself, and because he was prone to dribble at the mere thought of her, his voice sounded very strange indeed. Daniella snorted and looked more indignant than afraid.

Eddie found himself in a small room with one table, two chairs and a mousetrap in the corner with a large piece of cheese on it, suitably old and smelly.

'This is the interview room,' said the peeler, 'so called because it's where the interviews take place, see?'

Eddie nodded, politely.

'Now I have some questions for you,' said the peeler, 'and I expect some answers.'

Eddie sighed.

*

50

Eddie awoke with a start, and with a starfish on his face. It was a full three seconds before he remembered where he was. When he did, he let out a groan, wishing that the peelers would do the same for him – let him out, that is.

There was a graunching sound and the door to the cell opened. In walked a peeler with a chipped enamel mug. From it hung a label which read:

PROPERTY OF HER MAJESTY'S GOVERNMENT

'What you need is a nice hot cup of tea,' said the policeman.

'Thank you,' said Eddie, accepting the drink.

'What you get is a lukewarm mug of water. What do you think this is, the Fitz?' The Fitz was a newly opened restaurant in London which was so posh that even the doorman was the Earl of Uffington and the washer-upper was a much decorated soldier – he had three layers of wallpaper under his uniform.

'How much longer are you going to keep me here?' asked Eddie.

'Have you heard of *habeas corpus*?' asked the peeler.

Eddie shook his head. (His own head, that is. He knew that shaking the policeman's head might annoy him.)

'Then we can keep you here as long as we like,' said the peeler.

'Would it have made a difference if I knew what *habeas corpus* was?' asked Eddie, suspiciously.

'Maybe,' said the peeler, hesitantly. 'Look, I must go. I just wanted to tell you that the inspector will be here to speak with you shortly.'

He left Eddie to finish his drink alone. The minute the door was shut behind him, Eddie felt flushed with guilt. He hadn't even asked about poor Daniella! What a worthless humbug he was. All he'd been thinking about was himself, when poor Daniella might be languishing in a nearby cell or worse. 'Wait!' he cried.

A tiny door opened in the top of the cell door, to reveal a glassless window. 'What?' demanded the peeler, peering through it.

'What about the others? Daniella and Mr Zucchini?'

'Wait until the inspector comes,' said the peeler, shutting the tiny door and stomping off down the corridor.

A moment later, a strangely beaky shadow was cast across the cell floor. Eddie turned to the small window, set high in the stone wall, and there was Mad Uncle Jack's face staring back down at him through the bars.

'All right, m'boy?' he asked.

'Fine, thank you, Uncle Jack,' said Eddie, 'except that I'm locked up when I've done nothing wrong.'

'Is that a starfish?' asked Eddie's great-uncle, pointing between the bars.

'Why, yes it is,' said Eddie. 'I found it in the bed, just now.'

'Pass it up, would you?' he asked. 'It must have fallen from my pocket last night.'

'Last night?' asked Eddie, confused.

'I came to speak to you at this very window, but you were sleeping. The starfish must have fallen from my pocket then.'

Eddie thought back to the electric eel that had fallen on him at the beginning of Episode One – not that he knew it was the beginning of Episode One, of course – and wondered, once again, why Mad Uncle Jack had taken to carrying *live* sea creatures, rather than the more familiar dried variety.

He stood on the bed, on tiptoe, and passed the starfish through the bars. 'Many thanks,' said Mad Uncle Jack.

'What did you want to say to me last night?' Eddie asked, as he climbed back down onto the floor.

'Last night?'

'When you came to see me, but found me sleeping,' said Eddie.

'Did I?' Mad Uncle Jack frowned. 'I mean, I did?'

'You –' Eddie stopped. He heard voices in the corridor. 'The inspector's coming!' he said in a harsh whisper. 'You'd better go.'

'Very well,' said Mad Uncle Jack, 'but take this, quickly, just so you know that you're not alone.'

He slipped something out of his jacket and held it in his hand. Eddie jumped back onto the bed and took it from him, jumping to the floor just as a key clattered in the lock and the door to the cell swung inwards. Eddie looked to see what his great-uncle had given him.

It was the starfish.

54

The man who came into the cell with the peeler was as wide as he was tall and wore a very loud checked suit. Of course, checked suits can't really make a noise – except, of course, of material rubbing against material – but this was the kind of suit with checks so loud that if they could have talked they would have SHOUTED. It was the sort of suit that when, years later, television was invented, made the picture go fuzzy. Even when the man was standing stock-still, the checks on his suit seemed to be zinging all over the place saying – shouting – 'Look at me!' It wasn't a very new suit, Eddie noticed. The cuffs were a little frayed and the material a little grubby. He was relieved about that. The suit was giving him a headache just looking at it, and he was trying to imagine how much worse he'd feel if he'd had to look at a dazzling brand new one.

'This is the inspector,' said the peeler.

'I am the inspector,' said the inspector.

'The inspector would like to ask you some questions,' said the peeler.

'I would like to ask you some questions,' said the inspector.

The peeler gave the inspector a funny look out of the corner of his eye. To be fair, this was a deliberately funny look. Most of this particular peeler's looks were funny, whether intended or not, because he was a funny-looking peeler, but he really, really *meant* this one to be funny.

'Follow me,' said the peeler.

'Follow me,' said the inspector.

Eddie was led back to the room where he'd been interviewed or interrogated (or both) the previous day and sat in the same old chair. He looked over to the same old mouse hole in the skirting board and was pleased to see that the same old piece of cheese was in the trap, suggesting that the mouse hadn't fallen for it.

'Master Dickens,' said the inspector, who'd taken up position at the opposite side of the table but whose enormous stomach meant that the rest of him appeared to be sitting rather a long way away. 'Let me start by apologising for the way that you have been treated.'

Eddie was stunned. He was *Master* Dickens now, was he? And the policeman was actually apologising.

'You see, I would ask you to see things from our point of view. Firstly, a group of hardened convicts escapes from Grimpen Jail and are believed to be hiding somewhere on the moors. Secondly, the world-famous photographer Mr Wolfe Tablet is found bound and gagged in his room at the Rancid Rat. Thirdly, his hot-air balloon is stolen. You are aware of these facts?'

Eddie nodded. 'Yes, sir,' he said politely.

'Good,' said the inspector. His suit said nothing, but you could see that those loud checks were crying out to be heard. 'You also admit that you were found by the hot-air balloon in the company of one Daniella . . .?' He looked up at the peeler who'd been standing silently by his side since they'd sat at the table.

'No last name,' said the peeler.

'No last name,' repeated the inspector, 'who was not only seen in the stolen balloon by a number of eyewitnesses but has also admitted to being an accomplice of Mr Merryweather who attacked Mr Tablet?'

'Yes, the balloon crashed in my back garden. That is, the back garden of Awful End, my great-uncle's house,' Eddie agreed.

'Crashed, you say?' asked the inspector, sticking his little finger into his left ear and shaking it so violently that his whole tummy rippled.

Eddie noticed the peeler give the inspector another funny look – out of the *other* corner of his eye this time.

'Yes,' said Eddie. 'She – Daniella – landed in a rose bush. I told him all this yesterday,' said Eddie, nodding in the direction of the peeler. 'He wrote it down and everything. Didn't you read the report?'

'Mr Chevy's handwriting is poor and his

spelling atrocious,' said the inspector. 'What's more, I can't read.'

Eddie looked surprised.

'We haven't all had the advantage of a proper education, Master Dickens,' said the inspector, 'and, though no doubt useful, one doesn't have to be able to read to be an excellent detective inspector.' He gave his little finger another jolly good wiggle in his ear.

Eddie felt guilty again and cleared his throat. 'No, sir,' he said. 'Of course not.'

'Good,' said the inspector. 'Rather a coincidence, wouldn't you say?'

'I'm sorry?' asked Eddie Dickens, suddenly wondering whether he'd been trapped into something or other, but he couldn't quite see what.

'Rather a coincidence that Daniella should crash near the very spot where her employer, Mr Zucchini was seated.'

'Well . . . when I said crashed, I meant crash-landed. I mean she'd been on the lookout for the Great Zucchini and was trying to come in to land and –'

'Aha!' said the inspector, pushing his chair even further from the table, his weight causing it to grate across the floor. 'So she intended to land roughly where she did land and you were with Mr Zucchini?'

'Er, yes,' Eddie said.

'So you can see, Master Dickens, why we wrongly assumed you to be an accomplice in the taking prisoner of Mr Wolfe Tablet and the theft of his hot-air balloon?'

Wrongly? Had the inspector just said 'wrongly'?

'Y-Yes, I can see how you might have come to the wrong conclusion,' said Eddie, cautiously.

'Good,' said the inspector rising to his feet. 'So I do hope that you can find it in your heart of hearts to forgive us for holding you in the cell overnight.' He turned to the peeler, who Eddie – and you, dear readers – should already know was named Mr Chevy. 'The lollipop, please, Mr Chevy,' he said.

With a frown, the peeler dug his right hand into the pocket of his uniform and pulled out a round lollipop, covered in bits of blue fluff, exactly matching the colour of the fluff you sometimes find in your tummy button. (Don't think I don't know about these things.) He picked off the bits as best he could, and handed the lollipop to the inspector.

In turn, the inspector handed the lollipop to Eddie. 'Please accept this lollipop as a token of our regret for any inconvenience we might have caused you,' he said, patting Eddie on the head. Three times. Very awkwardly.

'Thank you,' said Eddie, quickly stuffing the lollipop in his own pocket. He had no intention of eating the thing.

The peeler disappeared from the room, returning a couple of minutes later with a piece of paper, a quill pen, an ink well and an old brown envelope containing the items he'd taken from Eddie before locking him up for the night: a few sugar lumps and the jagged stump of a well-chewed whittling carrot. (And if you can't remember what a whittling carrot is, I suggest you soak your brain in a mild vinegar solution overnight, or refer back to pages 10 and 11.) He handed them back to Eddie.

'We also need you to sign this special piece of paper,' said the peeler.

'We also need you to sign this special piece of paper,' said the inspector. 'What does it say?'

Eddie took it off the peeler. 'It says: "I, Eddie

Dickens, do not mind having been locked up overnight and will not go complaining to a judge, dot-dot-dot-dot-dot-dot",' he said. What it actually said was:

I Edy Dikuns doo nut mind haven bean locked up over nite and will nut gow cumplanin too a gudge

. . . . . .

'What are the dot-dot-dots, Mr Chevy?' asked the inspector.

'They're the dotted line for Dickens to sign along, sir,' said the peeler.

'Good thinking!'

The peeler dipped the quill in the ink well and handed it to Eddie. He was about to sign when he stopped. 'I'll sign this, but only if you let me see Daniella first. I assume you're not letting her go?'

'Too right we're not,' said the peeler. 'She's a thief and an accomplice.'

'Then let me see her and I'll sign.'

'Promise?' asked the peeler.

'Promise,' said Eddie.

The peeler looked at the inspector. The inspector nodded. 'Very well, Master Dickens.'

*

When the door to her cell opened, the last thing Daniella expected to see was Eddie. 'Don't say they're bangin' us up in 'ere togever, two to a cell?' she groaned.

For a fleeting moment, Eddie was all excited at the thought of being locked up with her, then felt guilty knowing that he was about to walk free and she wasn't. How brave and defiant she looked, her nostrils flaring like those of a cornered horse, her . . .

'You didn't come in 'ere just to dribble and gawp, did ya?' she asked.

'No,' said Eddie hurriedly. 'They are letting me go, though.'

'And are keeping me 'n' Harold banged up, I suppose? That'd be right. An' they've already got poor Skillet and Mr Merryweather. That sounds fair.'

Eddie strode over to Daniella and gripped her hand. 'If there's anything I can do to help from the outside, just tell me and it's done,' he whispered.

Daniella wiped her hand on the back of her dress. 'You're all sweaty,' she said. 'And, yeah, you can help. Send me a cake baked out of dynamite.'

Eddie's face reddened. 'I'd love to do that . . . but I meant *legally* . . . Anything that I can do to help within the law . . . and wouldn't a cake made of dynamite explode if you . . ?' His sentence

62

petered out and his face went even more red.

'Yeah, I was jokin'',' said Daniella. 'Get that Wolfe Tablet to agree that he *asked* to be tied up, to see how Harold does his escaping tricks, and get him to say that he leant us the balloon. That'd be a big 'elp.'

'But how can I get him to do that?' asked Eddie, fearing failure.

'You're the bright kid who realised that the Great Zucchini couldn't really get out of 'is coffin with all that soil on top of 'im. You'll find a way.'

A loud checked stomach appeared around Daniella's cell door, soon followed by the rest of the roundest of round inspectors. 'Time to go and sign that paper, Master Dickens,' he said.

'I will find a way!' said Eddie. He took Daniella's hand and gave it a squeeze. His heart pounded. He felt like a hero in an adventure story (being totally unaware, of course, that he *was* a hero in an adventure story . . . though probably not *quite* the sort of adventure he was thinking of).

'You've got dribble on your chin,' said Daniella.

63

Episode 6

Making Things Better

*In which Eddie is faced with raspberry jam, an
ear trumpet and a very large moustache*

Back at Awful End, repairs were already under
way to the damage caused by the gas leak.
Unfortunately they were being undertaken by
Mad Uncle Jack and his team of incompetent ex-
soldiers who'd fought under him during a few
fruitless skirmishes on foreign soil, many, many
years before. They'd been incompetent soldiers
and now they were incompetent *ex*-soldiers, but
they were extremely loyal to Mad Uncle Jack.

Most of the men under Mad Uncle Jack had,
not surprisingly, been killed – particularly those
who'd followed his orders. It was only those too

64

incompetent to carry out the simplest of orders – 'Catch the next shell as it comes over before it harms anyone, there's a good chap,' or: 'Ask that man over by that cannon to stop firing, would you?' or 'CHARGE!!!' – who'd survived. There had been seven survivors, but two had since died, which left five ex-soldiers, Dawkins and Mad Uncle Jack himself doing the building work. Gibbering Jane was in charge of refreshments.

Mad Uncle Jack was delighted at his great-nephew's return. 'So they let you go, did they? . . . Or did you escape? Escaping from cells isn't becoming a habit now, is it?'

'They were *rooms* at St Horrid's,' reminded Eddie, referring to his earlier adventures in a previous book. 'And, this time, the peelers let me go. I was innocent!'

'Of course you were, my dear boy! Of course . . .' Mad Uncle Jack placed his trowel on the brickwork he was supposedly repairing. 'You haven't seen my missing starfish have you, Edmund?'

'Why yes,' said Eddie, 'and I've discovered that he's rather partial to lollipops.' Sure enough, as Eddie carefully removed the starfish from his pocket, one of its five arms was clutching the lolly stick and Eddie could have sworn he heard the faintest slurping noise.

65

'Excellent!' said Mad Uncle Jack. 'I must return him to the rock pool I've built in my study.' He hurried off.

'He's built a rock pool in his study?' said a bemused Eddie, though nothing should have surprised him in that house.

'Yes, Master Edmund,' said a rather dusty and very incompetent ex-corporal still in uniform (without the jacket). 'We helped him build it the other week. Dug up the floor and everything.'

Eddie had a sudden thought. 'You weren't at Colonel Marley's side at the Fall of St Geobad, were you?' he asked. 'Any of you?'

There were murmurings of 'What's St Geobad?' as though he was somehow accusing them of knocking it down.

'Never mind,' said Eddie. 'Er, what are you using as mortar to bond these bricks together?'

'Your Mad Uncle Jack's special mixture!' said the slightly dusty and very incompetent ex-corporal.

'It's jam, isn't it?' said Eddie, running his finger along the raspberry-coloured goo between the new bricks.

'It might have jam *in* it, Master Dickens,' said the ex-corporal.

Eddie tasted it. 'It's *just* jam, isn't it?'

'Jam might be a part of your Mad Uncle Jack's secret bonding formula.'

'It's just jam and nothing more, isn't it? No preservatives. No cement. No mortar. Just raspberry jam.'

The incompetent ex-corporal nodded. 'Yes,' he said, 'from a seven-pound earthenware jar he found in the pantry.'

'And it's not really going to repair this huge hole in the side of the house, is it?' said Eddie.

'Well . . . er . . . no,' agreed the ex-soldier. 'But we are just carrying out orders.'

Eddie sighed and decided to go in search of his parents. He found his father, Mr Dickens, in the library. This was a fantastic room with shelves taking up every inch of every wall (except where there were windows, otherwise it would have been – you guessed it – pitch-black). Even the doors had shelves on them, with carved and

67

painted wood to look like rows of book spines.

Eddie's father was sitting in a high-backed leather chair and was reading a copy of *PUNCH*, a new periodical about bare-knuckle fighting. A periodical is just another name for a magazine. Bare-knuckle fighting is boxing without boxing gloves, which isn't much fun for the fighters – it hurts much more – or for the boxing-glove manufacturers, who don't get to sell so many pairs.

He looked up as his son entered. 'Hullo, Edmund,' he said. 'How was prison?'

'It was only a police cell, Father,' said Edmund, respectfully. There were no Social Services Departments back then, so children had to respect their parents in case they decided to lock them in a flooded cellar or tie them to the mast of a ship, without a social worker coming along saying 'Er, you can't do that!'

'Good, good,' nodded Mr Dickens. Although he'd had several baths since the explosion, he still had a pale and dusty look about him as though he'd been made up to look like a music-hall ghost. (Music hall was cheap theatre with plenty of songs.)

'How are you feeling, Father?' asked Eddie.

'Good. Good,' nodded his father.

'Oh, good,' said Eddie. 'I was looking for Mother. Do you know where she is?'

'Good. Good,' nodded his father. It was then that Eddie realised that he must still be very deaf after being blown up into the rafters just the previous morning.

'W-H-E-R-E'-S M-O-T-H-E-R?' Eddie repeated, very loudly and very slowly this time.

If this had been a public library, a stern librarian would have gone 'Sshh!' and pointed to a big sign which read 'SILENCE'. But this was simply a private library in Awful End so . . .

'Sshh!' said a stern man, pointing to a big sign which read 'SILENCE'.

So much for the all-knowing narrator. Sorry.

Because all the wall space was taken up by book spines – both real and wooden – the man had to hold up the wooden-framed SILENCE sign, which slightly lessened the effect.

'Who on earth are you?' asked Eddie, in loud amazement. He thought he knew all the strange people who worked on his great-uncle's estate.

'I'm your father!' said a puzzled Mr Dickens, whose back was to the man, so he'd neither seen nor heard him.

'Not you, Father,' said Eddie. 'Him.'

Unfortunately, Mr Dickens didn't hear his son's explanation, so was mightily confused, until the man came into view. He handed Mr Dickens what to you and me would have looked like one of those large brass horns that come out of the front of those old-fashioned wind-up gramophones you see in films . . . but which wouldn't have looked like that to Eddie or his father because wind-up gramophones and films were yet to be invented. The man stuck the small end of the horn into a startled Mr Dickens's ear.

'If I loan your father this ear trumpet then there is no need for anyone to shout,' said the man, speaking directly into the brass horn. 'I have been given the responsibility of cataloguing this entire library and I cannot be expected to do so, in the time allotted, if I am to suffer constant interruptions. Silence or, at the very least, hushed voices would, therefore, be very much appreciated.'

'I can hear!' said Mr Dickens, clasping the ear trumpet. 'I can hear!' he repeated, much louder this time. He gave a whoop of delight and, like any whoop of delight, it was LOUD, which greatly distressed the man.

'Please!' he begged. 'A little quiet.'

Eddie looked at him. He wasn't much taller than Eddie and seemed to be mostly moustache. He wore pinstripe trousers and a black waistcoat and jacket, both of which were a bit shiny with wear. He had very little hair on the *top* of his head – though the moustache more than made up for that lower down – and what little hair he did have, he'd tried to brush across his bald patch.

'I'm Eddie Dickens,' said Eddie. 'This is my father, Mr Dickens. We're the great-nephew and nephew of Mad Uncle Jack, who owns this house . . . Did *he* ask you to catalogue all these books?' There was doubt in Eddie's voice because he couldn't imagine Mad Uncle Jack arranging for something so sensible . . . not the man who was, at that very moment, supervising the repairs to his house using raspberry jam!

'My name is Mr Lalligag and I was employed by the lady of the house,' said the man.

If Eddie had been puzzled and surprised before, he was stunned now. Even Madder Aunt Maud had employed a librarian to catalogue all the books in the library? That was about as likely as her having a sensible conversation with him. She lived in a hollow cow in the garden! Her best friend was a stuffed stoat which looked more like a stuffed ferret! Eddie was surprised she'd even remembered there was a library in the house!

'When did you start?' asked Eddie.

'This very morning,' snapped Mr Lalligag. Eddie thought the librarian would have made a very good ventriloquist because he couldn't see the man's lips move behind that most enormous of enormous moustaches. 'Now, I would be most grateful if you would keep the noise down!' With that, he turned and walked behind a stack of books, which was where he must have been when Eddie'd first come into the room and why he hadn't seen him.

'What a strange fellow,' said Mr Dickens. 'Rude, in fact. But this ear trumpet could be useful. Very useful indeed.' He returned his attention to his copy of *PUNCH*.

'Where's mother?' asked Eddie.

'About eleven thirty,' said his father.

There was once a famous author named Charles Dickens – no blood relation to our Eddie Dickens in these adventures – who used to fill his books with masses and masses of characters with very silly names. Because his books were so long, it often became quite difficult to remember who was who, so he got around this by printing a list of all his characters at the front of each book, under the heading 'CHARACTERS' or 'DRAMATIS PERSONAE' (which is Latin for 'DRAMATIS PERSONAE').

What with all these different people, such as Mr Lalligag, getting involved in *Dreadful Acts* so late in the day, I'm beginning to wish that we'd had one of those lists at the beginning of *this* book, but who's to say that we can't have one over halfway through this adventure? Who knows, it might even catch on. In fact, it makes more sense, because you'll already have read about the people I mention whereas, if this went at the front, you'd have forgotten who half the people were by the time you actually came across them on the page. Good thinking, huh?

Excellent. That's settled then. We'll have our list right here . . .

DRAMATIS PERSONAE

EDDIE DICKENS – *the hero*

MR & MRS DICKENS – *his parents*

DAWKINS – *Mr Dickens's gentleman's gentleman*

GIBBERING JANE – *an unqualified chambermaid*

MAD UNCLE JACK – *owner of Awful End, where all of the above live*

EVEN MADDER AUNT MAUD – *his wife, who lives with Malcolm inside Marjorie in the rose garden*

MALCOLM – *a stuffed stoat, sometimes called Sally*
or
SALLY – *a stuffed stoat, usually called Malcolm*

MARJORIE – *a large hollow cow*

MR CHEVY – *a peeler*

THE GREAT ZUCCHINI – *an escapologist*

DANIELLA – *his lovely assistant*

MR SKILLET – *his props builder*

MR MERRYWEATHER – *his manager*

MR WOLFE TABLET – *the famous photographer*

MR COLLINS – *the ironmonger*

THE DETECTIVE INSPECTOR – *a detective inspector*

MR LALLIGAG – *who says he's a librarian*

PLUS

an assortment of ex-soldiers, and the escaped convicts up on the moors

Not bad, huh? It looks quite classy, if the truth be told, as well as being a useful reminder of some of the characters we met so long ago you probably forgot about them. Speaking of forgetting, wasn't Eddie supposed to be doing all he could to convince Wolfe Tablet to drop the charges, not looking for his mummy?

The next place Eddie looked was in the kitchens of Awful End. Ever since she and Eddie's father had been cured of a very strange and smelly ailment, his mother was very particular about what she ate. When Eddie walked into the large, basement room, he found her talking to Dawkins, his father's gentleman's gentleman.

'Hello, Dawkins,' said Eddie.

'Master Edmund,' said Dawkins, with a slight bow. He was wearing a blue-and-white striped apron over his suit and was drying Malcolm the stuffed stoat with an Irish linen tea towel. Eddie deduced that Even Madder Aunt Maud must be close by.

'Mother –' Eddie began.

'One moment, dear,' said Mrs Dickens, whose hearing seemed to have recovered a lot quicker than his father's. She was seated at the huge kitchen table, sorting broad beans into two separate piles: small and not-quite-so-small. She graded them by passing each bean through her wedding ring, which she'd slipped off her finger specially. Those that passed through the thin band of gold went on the 'small' pile. Those that didn't fit through, or might have done but could have got[ten] a little squashed in the process, went on the 'not-quite-so-small' pile. When Eddie arrived, the 'small' pile was not quite so small as the 'not-quite-so-small' pile – in case you're taking notes.

'I'm discussing tonight's menu with Dawkins, my love,' she said. 'I will be with you in one moment.'

Eddie was only too aware that his mother's conversations were inclined to get rather long and convoluted, which is a polite way of saying 'very confused indeed'. He tried to explain the urgency of his mission with a 'But I need to get Daniella and Mr Zucchini –' but Mrs Dickens would have none of it.

'Sssh! Edmund,' she said, raising both hands for silence. In the process, she sent her wedding ring flying towards Dawkins (who was carefully drying Malcolm's eyes with the corner of the tea towel) and sent a broad bean flying towards Eddie.

It hit him smack in the eye. Sure, it would have been more painful if it'd been a bullet or even a small rock but, boy, did it hurt.

'Ouch!' Eddie cried out, though he was probably thinking some very rude words inside his head.

'NO!' screamed his mother, as her wedding ring bounced off Malcolm's leathery nose and headed for . . .

You're not going to believe what happened next. Even if you'd actually been there, you might have suspected that the whole thing had been rehearsed a dozen times to get it just right. If you saw it on stage, you'd clap at the skill and timing of it. If you saw it on film, you might turn to the person next to you and say: 'I wonder how many times they had to film this sequence to get it right?' If you watched it on video or DVD, you might pause it to see if there was any trick photography or careful editing . . .

. . . because Mrs Dickens's wedding ring bounced off Malcolm's nose and went straight into the gaping mouth of Even Madder Aunt Maud, who'd, at that precise moment, entered the

77

kitchen yawning, following one of the many 'little lie-downs' she'd had since being hit by Wolfe Tablet's stolen hot-air balloon.

She was so startled that she let out a 'GULP!' of surprise and, with that gulp, she swallowed the ring.

'My wedding band!' cried Eddie's mother, not referring to Mrs Jonah Widdlington's – no sniggering, please; that was her name – String Quartet, who'd played at her wedding reception – but to her wedding *ring*, which was now on its long and unpleasant journey to Even Madder Aunt Maud's stomach and beyond.

'What are you trying to do?' Even Madder Aunt Maud demanded. 'Poison me?'

Seconds later, she found Eddie's mother's hands around her neck. Mrs Dickens was trying to make her cough up the ring, but Even Madder Aunt Maud didn't know that. As far as she was aware, someone had tossed some foul-tasting pill into her mouth the very second she'd entered the kitchen, and now someone was trying to strangle her.

What upset her the most, though, was that she was sure that the pill had come from the direction of Malcolm. Was Malcolm – her dear, beloved, Malcolm – in on the plot to kill her? Tears sprang to her eyes as Mrs Dickens continued to give her neck a good shake.

Dawkins placed the stuffed stoat on the table and did his best to separate the two women as politely as possible, being only too aware that these were the ladies of the house and he was merely a gentleman's gentleman.

'Cough it up, Maud!' Mrs Dickens was shouting.

'*Et tu*, Malcolm?' said Even Madder Aunt Maud – whatever that might mean – doing her best to out-stare the glassy-eyed traitor.

'Ladies! Ladies!' Dawkins pleaded.

Eddie left them to it. It was clear that he was going to have to try to persuade Wolfe Tablet to drop the charges against Daniella and the Great Zucchini *all by himself*.

Episode 7

To the Rescue

In which Eddie's attempt to rescue the others
results in him needing to be rescued too

Wolfe Tablet had travelled to the area by hot-air balloon, and that balloon had now been impounded by the police 'pending further investigations' and was going nowhere. 'Impounded' actually means 'held in legal custody' but, in this case, it meant that the peelers had it tethered to the ground on a small patch of grass around the back of the police station (where they usually played football) and were taking it in turns to go up and down in it. One or two lost their hats, a few were airsick but, all in all, they agreed that it was great fun.

Mr Tablet himself, meanwhile, was back in his rooms at the Rancid Rat, recovering from his ordeal, and it was to the Rancid Rat that Eddie was now headed. I've said it before and I'll say it again: Eddie didn't get out much. When he wasn't drawn into adventures that weren't of his own making, he spent most of his time at home. And home was now Awful End. He wasn't particularly familiar with the surrounding villages, towns or countryside. He didn't have a bike. There wasn't a local bus service, and there were no shopping malls or burger joints to hang out at with your friends back then. A trip to the ironmonger's to buy a hook for the back of the loo door was an event, and a very rare one at that. So Eddie would have to ask how to get to the Rancid Rat.

The best person to have asked would have been Dawkins because, as long as he had enough tissue paper, he seemed happy with life and was good and practical at most things. But he was still busy trying to calm Eddie's mother and Even Madder Aunt Maud. There was no point in asking Mad Uncle Jack for directions. He'd once started to draw Eddie a layout of the gardens, but it'd turned into a picture of a frog carrying a parasol, which he then proceeded to colour in with green crayon, cut out and pin to the wall of his study, with great pride – his original task completely forgotten!

Gibbering Jane was an ideal person to talk to if you had a query about knitting. What she didn't know about knitting could probably be written on the head of a pin, and still leave plenty of room for the Lord's Prayer and a list of your ten least favourite meals . . . but directions? Eddie wasn't 100 per cent convinced she knew up from down, let alone left from right, or how to get to the Rancid Rat.

As for Mad Uncle Jack's band of ex-soldiers . . . Eddie did another one of his sighs, and decided to set off and ask for directions from the people he met on the way . . . which is all fine and dandy, so long as you actually *meet* somebody.

An hour or so later, Eddie had to admit to himself what he'd been denying for the previous half-hour: he was well and truly lost. He wouldn't be able to find his way back to Awful End, let alone the Rancid Rat. He had somehow found his way up onto the moors.

If this was a film, I'd have a dramatic chord of music about now. If this was a book, I'd make it a dramatic end to an episode. Hang on. This *is* a book but, then again, Eddie didn't know that, did he? All he could see was miles and miles of grass, boulders, gorse bushes and the occasional blasted tree. (I'm not swearing. I don't mean blasted as in 'These blasted shoes are giving me foot-ache,' but blasted as in 'blighted or withered'. In other words, even the trees up on the moors were fed up and leafless.) He'd lost sight of St Botolph's and Awful End somewhere below, not only because the moors were undulating – went up and down a lot – and were hiding them behind a hill, but also because of the mist.

In books such as these (not, as I've just said, that Eddie had the slightest notion that he was in a book such as this, or any other such book) mist and moors seem to go together. In fact, misty moors are a must. Get a moor without mist and you feel hard done by . . . so Eddie got the full works, and completely lost.

If only someone would find me, he thought. He hated being up there on his own. But when some-one *did* find him, Eddie wished that the someone had been someone different . . . because out of the swirling mist loomed the most frightening human being Eddie had ever seen.

He was huge, for a start, with a neck as thick as his head, so you couldn't tell it *was* a neck, and a face covered in horrifying scars. They reminded Eddie of the stitching on Malcolm, where his saw-dust stuffing was showing through. This monster of a man had no hair on the top of his flat-topped head, but the hairiest ears Eddie'd ever seen, and chest-hair sprouting from the top of his crumpled suit . . . a suit which looked more like a pair of ill-fitting pyjamas, with arrows on them.

If the arrows weren't clue enough, the giant was carrying a huge, black metal ball – as big as a pumpkin – on a piece of chain, the other end of which was attached to his ankle with a manacle . . . Eddie was left in no doubt that this was one of the convicts who'd escaped from Grimpen Jail.

The convict bent down and looked poor Eddie straight in the eyes. 'You ain't going to scream, are ya?' he asked, his voice deep and gravelly. His teeth were small and yellow and his breath smelled sour.

'N-N-No, sir,' said Eddie, polite as always.

'Good,' said the convict, 'or I should have to snap your neck in two, like a dried twig.'

'He would, too!' said another escaped convict, appearing out of the mist to Eddie's right. He'd moved so silently that Eddie did that almost-jumping-out-of-his-own-skin thing that surprised people do. 'That's why he's called Bonecrusher,' said the second man.

This second convict was almost as thin as Eddie's Mad Uncle Jack and was almost as frightening as Bonecrusher, but in a different way. He had long grey wisps of hair coming from his head and pointed chin, and had hooded eyes, which somehow reminded Eddie of a bird of prey getting ready to pounce on its unsuspecting victim. Staring into those eyes, Eddie could imagine a sharp brain behind them, cogs turning, hard at work.

'What are you doing up here?' demanded Bonecrusher, grabbing Eddie's arm. 'You ain't spying for the peelers, are ya?'

'N-N-No, Mr Bonecrusher,' Eddie assured him. 'I'm lost. I'm trying to find my way to the Rancid Rat . . . My friends have been locked up by the police and I'm trying to get them freed.'

'How very interesting,' said the second convict, with a grin. 'Come with us.' He took Eddie's other arm and, between them, he and Bonecrusher led him away through the mist.

A matter of minutes later – though it seemed an endless journey to Eddie because he feared it might be his last – he found himself being led into a small cave in a rocky outcrop. It was there he met his third convict.

A tiny man – he was smaller than Eddie – he

had a shaven head, big bushy eyebrows and wide open eyes that made him look more than a little crazy. Add to this the fact that he was jumping up at Eddie, barking like an eager puppy held in place not by a leash but by his ball and chain, and Eddie was left in little doubt that the man *was* crazy.

'This is Barkin',' said Bonecrusher. Barking gave a happy yelp and snapped at Eddie's ankles.

'I'm Eddie Dickens,' said Eddie.

'Forgive me for bein' so rude,' said the tall, thin convict, with a sneer. 'I failed to introduce myself. My name is Swags . . .'

'Short for Swagman,' explained Bonecrusher, his sour breath close to Eddie's face again, 'on account of him being one of the few convicts sent to Australia to make it back here alive.'

This caused much laughter between the convicts – well, more 'happy yapping' in Barking's case –

as so often seems to happen between baddies in stories, when they have a new captive.

Eddie decided that he'd better show them that he wasn't too afraid, or impressed. 'I know a man who can escape from tanks full of flesh-eating fish, and from locked trunks set on fire and –'

'You know the Great Zucchini?' demanded Bonecrusher, picking up Eddie by the arm with one hand, as though he weighed no more than a chicken, and plonking him down on a rock in the middle of the muddy cave floor.

'Y-Yes,' said Eddie, uncertainly.

'How?' demanded Bonecrusher, pressing his nose right up against Eddie's. 'And no lies.'

The unspoken threat left Eddie feeling chilled to the bone. He told the convicts everything.

'So you don't know where the hearse is now?' asked Swags, once Eddie had finished. Eddie shook his head.

'But he could find it for us,' said Bonecrusher, with obvious excitement. He was breathing faster, his huge chest heaving in and out. Barking jumped up onto the boulder and growled.

'I'm sure I could,' said Eddie with genuine eagerness, because he'd rather have been anywhere else in the entire world – including frightening foreign places – than right there right then. Reading about this might be fun for us, but it wasn't much fun for him living it!

'But what guarantee do we have that you'll come back once you've found it?' asked Swags.

'Good point,' nodded Bonecrusher.

Barking just whimpered.

'Er . . . I could give you my word,' Eddie suggested, not convinced that they'd be too impressed with this suggestion.

'I can see that you're a gentleman and that,' said Bonecrusher, 'but gentlemen don't usually feel obliged to keep their word when dealin' with the likes of us.'

'Escaped convicts and suchlike,' Swags nodded in agreement. 'So we'll need more than that to make sure you return.'

'But why's the hearse so important in the first place?' Eddie asked. 'If you want to escape from the moors, surely any horse and carriage will do. A horse and cart, even?'

Eddie found himself being lifted up by the neck, something which'd only been done to him once before (by a not-so-charming woman called Mrs Cruel-Streak) and that hadn't been half so frightening as it was now, having it done by an escaped convict in a cave, up on the misty moors when no one knew where he was.

'Don't ask questions, boy,' said Bonecrusher. It was just Eddie's luck that he wasn't one of those monsters-on-the-outside, heart-of-gold-on-the-inside villains you sometimes come across. Mr Bonecrusher appeared to be nasty through and through.

'Hang on, Bones!' said Swags, suddenly. 'It ain't the hearse we need. The second coffin ain't in it no more. The boy said they buried it . . .'

'And Zucchini's people were then arrested . . . You mean, it's still in the ground?' gasped Bonecrusher. 'I'd have thought they'd have dug it up and 'idden it back in the 'earse by now.'

'But the hearse bolted and Zucchini's people were arrested . . . I'll bet it's still six feet under.' (Six feet was how deep in the ground genuine coffins were supposed to be buried, though some lazy gravediggers were quite happy to stop at four foot six.)

'Where did you say the coffin is buried?' demanded Bonecrusher.

'Mr Zucchini said it was buried right next to the churchyard at St Botolph's,' said Eddie, once Bonecrusher had let go of his neck and put him back down. 'I don't know exactly. I haven't been there myself.'

'Well, we need you to find it and dig it up,' said Bonecrusher.

'And not run away and fetch the peelers . . .' Swags let his voice trail off mid-sentence. 'Hostage,' he said, at last. 'Hostage. We hold the boy hostage.'

Bonecrusher scratched his bald head like people do in comic books when they're thinking (but very rarely do in real life). 'How can we hold Eddie hostage at the same time as sending him off to dig up the coffin? Surely we need *another* person – a friend of his – to hold hostage while he goes off and does the digging? Someone else whose bones I can break if Eddie tries to doublecross us.'

'No, listen, Bonecrusher. I have a plan. We send the boy's parents a note saying that we've got their boy and, unless *they* dig up Zucchini's coffin and bring us the sandbags, we'll do him some serious harm.' Swag's face broke into a gappy-toothed smile above his nasty pointed chin.

'That's good, that's very good,' agreed Bonecrusher, 'but there are one or two details we needs to work out, right?'

'Like what?'

'Like how we send this message and what we send with it, to show we really have the boy.'

Eddie was hardly listening. He was worrying about the part of the plan where his parents received the note and were supposed to do exactly as instructed!!! Exactly as instructed? No one at Awful End could carry out the most straightforward instructions. These were his *parents* they were talking about . . . and what if Mad Uncle Jack or Even Madder Aunt Maud got hold of the note first, or if it somehow ended up in Dawkins's tissue-paper collection before anyone had a chance to read it? He couldn't have the convicts sending a note that his life depended on to Awful End. It was as good as signing his death warrant!

'Er, I don't think this is such a good idea,' he protested. 'You see –'

But Bonecrusher, Swags and Barking were in no mood to listen. They were too busy pulling off his jacket, shirt and trousers . . . leaving him in no more than his long johns.

'We'll send your folks your clothes,' said Bonecrusher.

'That way they'll not only know that we really do have you, but they'll also bring us the sandbags double quick so you don't catch your *death* of cold,' grinned Swags. They laughed some more.

91

Episode 8

In the Grip of the Enemy

*In which Eddie is . . . in the grip
of the enemy*

'Let me get this straight,' said Eddie. 'You want to keep me hostage whilst' – people used words such as 'whilst' in those days – 'whilst my parents go and dig up the coffin with the sandbags in it?'

'That's right,' said Bonecrusher, with a toothy grin.

'Even though Awful End may still be teeming with peelers looking for evidence against the Great Zucchini and Daniella, after the theft of the hot-air balloon and the so-called kidnapping of Mr Wolfe Tablet?' Eddie added, breathlessly.

'Quiet, you,' said Bonecrusher, his expression becoming the even nastier side of nasty. 'You're not going to trick your way out of this.'

Swags stared straight at Eddie through his hooded eyes. 'The boy might have a point,' he said.

'And even if the peelers aren't there and the message reaches my parents, surely you're letting even more people know your plan . . .'

'Go on,' said Swags, not taking his eyes off Eddie for a minute as he began to circle him, his chain chinking behind him.

'I mean . . . I don't know why those two sandbags which you made for the Great Zucchini are so important to you, but I now know that they are. Surely the fewer people who know that the better?' Eddie had their attention now. He had to do everything to make sure they let him go, and not give the occupants of Awful End a chance to muck it up, or who knew what might happen?

'Then what do you suggest?' said Swags, coming to a halt. He put a bony hand on each of Eddie's shoulders and, pressing his nose against the boy's, stared deep into his eyes. 'And no tricks,' he added, his voice barely louder than a deep breath.

Eddie shuddered. 'No tricks,' he agreed, and he meant it. He wasn't in the convict-capturing business. He'd get them their sandbags and hope beyond hope that they'd let him go. 'If one of you was going to take my clothes to Awful End, along with a note, and risk capture anyway, why doesn't one of you come along with me while I dig up the sandbags to make sure I don't escape, instead?'

Swags and Bonecrusher switched into thinking mode, trying to see the fault in Eddie's plan. Barking seemed more interested in sniffing a patch of thistles by the cave opening.

'Hang on! Hang on!' said Bonecrusher. 'The 'ole idea of someone else digging the 'ole instead of us is that there's somethin' slightly suspicious-lookin' about a man with arrows on 'is suit doin' anything, ain't there? If we wasn't worried about that, we'd go 'n' do the diggin' ourselves!'

'But here's the clever part,' said Eddie, hoping there weren't any other loopholes in his hastily devised neck-saving idea. 'Instead of sending my clothes to Awful End, why not dress Mr Barking up in them? They'll fit him. That way, he can show me the way to the village – I'm lost, remember – and then we can go to the field by St Botolph's churchyard and dig up the coffin together . . .'

'And what if anyone stops 'n' asks what ya doin'?' said Bonecrusher.

'The boy simply says that he's part of the Great Zucchini's Dreadful Acts troupe, clearing up after a trick that was cancelled following the arrival of Mr Wolfe Tablet in his balloon,' said Swags, who appeared to be having his ear licked by Barking, who was beginning to behave even more like an excited puppy.

The three convicts looked at each other. Bonecrusher nodded. Swags nodded and Barking gave an excited yap.

'Passed unanimous,' said Bonecrusher. 'We go with your plan, boy . . . but not until morning.'

Eddie felt so relieved that he wouldn't now have to rely on his parents or, God forbid, Mad Uncle Jack and Even Madder Aunt Maud, but he was still in a very sticky situation. And he wanted to get it over with.

'Couldn't we go tonight?' he suggested. 'Aren't most crimes more easily carried out under the cover of darkness?' He'd read that somewhere.

'Too dangerous, sonny,' said Swags. 'When the mist's this bad, it's impossible to find your way round 'ere at night. You could both end up in the bog.' He wasn't using 'bog' as a slang word for the toilet/loo/lavatory/bathroom, so there were no schoolboy giggles. He meant bog as in boggy marshland . . . earth that could suck you up so fast you couldn't get out, and so deep your remains might never be found.

That was good enough reason to stay put until daybreak, but Swags had another one all the same. 'The search parties are out in force at night,' he explained, "cos that's when some of the other escapees are stupid enough to be on the move. If they catch so much as a glint of a lantern, they'll let the dogs loose.'

'Daybreak it is then,' grinned the huge mountain of a man that was Bonecrusher. 'That gives us a chance to get better acquainted.'

To make sure that Eddie didn't try to escape in the night, each convict wrapped the ball-end of his chain around him, so he went to sleep – or tried to – in the middle of a big metal knot. Barking lay curled up against his feet, like a young puppy, whilst Bonecrusher and Swags slept with their backs to him (one on the left and one on the right), all on the sandy cave floor. Swags was no fool. He used Eddie's bundle of clothes as a pillow.

It's doubtful that Eddie would have slept even if the chains hadn't been so heavy, the cave floor hadn't been so hard, Bonecrusher and Swags hadn't been such loud snorers . . . and Barking hadn't whimpered on and off throughout the night, and twitched his legs like a dog dreaming that he was chasing rabbits. No, the main reason for his wakefulness was fear.

Dawn couldn't come quick enough for Eddie, but the escaped convicts insisted he had breakfast before he and Barking set off to retrieve the sandbags. It consisted of a few mouthfuls of leaves and grass.

'You need to keep your energy up for the day ahead,' said Swags. 'That's what we've been livin'' off. P'r'aps you could bring us back some food too, yeah?'

'I'll do what I can,' said Eddie, spitting out the mushy green ball of chewed leaves, when he thought no one was looking.

Now all that remained was for Barking to dress up in Eddie's clothes and they'd be ready to go. Bonecrusher had already removed the uprooted gorse bush he'd wedged in the entrance to the cave, to keep it hidden from the casual observer on the misty moors in the dead of night.

Actually, it was more a matter of them dressing Barking. He struggled a little and was terribly

97

ticklish, which made it a bit like trying to change a nappy on an uncooperative baby (if you've ever tried that). Then there was the small problem of the ball and chain. They couldn't pull the trouser leg over the ball, so they pulled it up the chain and over his leg, leaving plenty of room for the remainder of the chain, and the big, big ball to hang out of the top, for Barking to hold, if he didn't want it dragging along the ground behind him.

(To tell you the truth, I wasn't sure how they did this, so – because that's the caring kind of narrator I am – I tied a piece of chain-link fencing to my ankle and tried to pull a second pair of trousers over the pair I was already wearing, without feeding the other end of the chain through, where the big metal ball would have been. Just then, the front doorbell rang and, because I was expecting an exciting parcel, I was in a hurry to answer it. Suffice it to say, I ended up in a terrible tangle, but can now see how they did manage to get Eddie's clothes onto Barking, ball and chain and all.)

It was time to go. 'Now listen up, lad,' said Swags. 'Barking here has an excellent sense of direction – a nose for it, ya might say – and he can outrun ya, ball and chain or no ball and chain . . . and he has a nasty bite too. So be sure to stick to the plan . . . and no funny business.'

'No funny business,' Eddie assured him, and they were off.

Swags was right. Little Barking could move at high speed. As he clutched the ball on the end of his chain, it did little to slow him down. Occasionally, he'd look back to check that Eddie was following and, if the boy did appear to be lingering, he'd yap at him. It wasn't that long before they were off the edge of the moors down into hedge-lined country lanes and, about an hour after that, Eddie suddenly realised where they were.

'I know the way to St Botolph's from here,' he said excitedly. Now it was his turn to lead the way, with Barking (wearing Eddie's clothes, remember) hot on his heels.

They cut their way through the churchyard, the morning dew dampening the bottom of Eddie's long johns, as they dodged their way between the tombstones littering the ground like broken teeth. Then they reached a low stone wall.

'There!' said Eddie, pointing to a mound of freshly dug earth over in the next field. He clambered over the wall and hurried to the spot. 'This must be it. It's about the size of a grave, and the amount of soil in the mound is about the amount of space the coffin must be taking up below.'

'*Dig!*' barked Barking, which was the first real word Eddie had heard him speak. If the truth be told, Eddie hadn't been convinced that Barking *could* speak.

But that wasn't what was making Eddie nervous all of a sudden. It was the fact that he'd just realised that there was a flaw in his plan. He didn't have a shovel or a spade or so much as a teaspoon to dig with.

'What with?' asked Eddie.

Without waiting to give an answer, Barking threw himself to his knees and began to dig with his front paws – sorry, that should, of course, be with his *hands* – like a dog desperate to dig up a treasured bone, small scoops of earth flying out behind him. Eddie started digging in a similar fashion down at the other end. This would take for ever.

This is hopeless, thought Eddie. He'd been digging for what seemed like ages and it was now the full light of morning, yet they hardly seemed to have made a dent in the ground.

'What in heaven's name are you doing here?' asked a familiar voice. Eddie looked up. At the moment he saw the Great Zucchini and the lovely Daniella in front of him, each with a shovel in their hands, he also felt something sharp in his back. Barking must have had a knife! One wrong word from Eddie, and Barking might do something very nasty indeed.

Escapes All Around

*In which people seem to escape, or to have escaped,
here there and everywhere*

'Hello,' said Eddie, trying not to sound scared for his life.

'Whatcha doin' 'ere?' asked Daniella.

'I was about to ask you the same question,' said Eddie, looking up at the camel-faced beauty from his crouching position. 'The last time I saw you both, you were locked up at the police station.'

''E's the world's greatest escapologist, ain't he?' said Daniella, proudly. 'No local prison cell can 'old 'im!'

The Great Zucchini accepted the praise with a

slight bow, then his eyes fell on Barking, grinning at Eddie's side. 'Are you going to introduce me to your colleague?' he asked.

Eddie felt the tip of the object being pushed further into his back, out of sight of the newcomers.

'Er, this is Mr Barking,' he said. 'He's a friend of my Uncle Jack.'

'Why ain't you got no clothes on?' asked Daniella.

'Er . . . fresh air and exercise,' said Eddie quickly. 'My great-uncle is very keen on me taking more healthy exercise. Mr Barking is my trainer. I'm doing an early-morning run –'

'*Exercise ball*,' said a voice. It was Barking's. He handed Eddie the ball on the end of his chain.

Eddie dropped it with a thud on the earth, hurriedly picking it up with an idiot grin. 'Running . . . lifting exercise balls . . . er . . . digging,' said Eddie, helplessly.

'But why dig here?' asked the Great Zucchini.

'And how comes 'e's wearin' your clothes?' asked Daniella.

'Shut up,' said Eddie, desperately. He was running out of excuses!

'What?'

'Nothing . . . I mean . . .'

The Great Zucchini stepped forward and sank his shovel into the soil. 'Much as I would like to stay and talk,' he said, 'I need to get my coffin dug up and in the back of the hearse before the peelers find us gone.'

'*We'll help you*,' said Barking. The sharp pain in Eddie's back suddenly stopped. Eddie's eyes met the convict's. The words 'no funny business' went through his mind.

Eddie took the shovel off Daniella and started digging with the Great Zucchini, with Barking carrying on with his front paws – *hands* – as before.

If Eddie had been very brave, perhaps he would have hit Barking over the head with the shovel, but that's easier said than done. It takes a lot to bash somebody that way. What if you hit them too hard and split their head open by mistake? What if you don't hit them hard enough and they grab the shovel and hit you? So Eddie concentrated on digging.

Daniella sat on the wall. Even the sight of her frilly petticoats wasn't enough to stop Eddie worrying about what Barking might do next.

By the time they reached the top of the coffin, all three were a lot hotter and a lot sweatier. Eddie's long johns were streaked with soil, the boot polish colouring Zucchini's hair trickled down his cheeks, and Barking's little head was glowing red with all the effort.

Zucchini lowered himself down onto the lid of the coffin and Daniella threw him a coil of rope.

Quickly and efficiently, he tied it to the coffin, then Eddie and Daniella gave him a hand out. They pulled the coffin to the surface and laid it on the grass. Zucchini untied the rope.

'Skillet and Merryweather should be here with the hearse and the rest of my belongings shortly,' he said. 'The peelers found the hearse on the village green. The horses were drinking from the pond . . . They were good enough to put it in the stable at the back of the police station. Most convenient!'

'Then what are you going to do?' asked Eddie. 'You can't perform your Dreadful Acts if you're a wanted man!'

'I will either find a way of getting Mr Wolfe Tablet to drop the charges –'

'Something which *you* promised to do,' Daniella reminded Eddie, who blushed. If only he could tell her about the convicts . . . about who the harmless-looking Mr Barking really was.

'Or I'll send a large hamper to your local police station this Christmas,' Zucchini continued. 'It's amazing what peelers are willing to forgive and forget in exchange for a few bottles of port, a goose and some plum pudding.'

'*Open it!*' yapped a voice in Eddie's ear. Barking rattled the lid of the coffin.

'Could we open the coffin, please?' Eddie asked the escapologist.

'What on earth for?' he asked.

'What are you two up to?' asked Daniella. 'See, I knew you wasn't just diggin' here by accident.'

'Please,' said Eddie, looking directly at Zucchini.

'Very well,' said Zucchini, 'but there are only a couple of sandbags inside. It won't give away how the rest of the trick was done.' He crouched down beside the coffin and, producing something that looked like a cross between a corkscrew and a screwdriver, he undid the screws around the edges and, finally, lifted off the lid.

They all four peered inside. Sure enough, there were two large hessian sandbags labelled:

GRIMPEN JAIL

Just then, a commanding voice cracked the silence like a whip: 'Hands up, then nobody move!'

Eddie gave a silent groan. First Barking and now – now what? He looked up and was amazed to see Mr Lalligag, the man from the library! There was something very different about him since their meeting back at Awful End the previous day. He was still wearing the pinstripe suit and black waistcoat, slightly shiny with wear. He was still as bald as he had been, with what little hair he had brushed over his pate. He still had one of the biggest moustaches Eddie had ever had the honour of being that close to . . . but today? Today Mr Lalligag was holding an enormous revolver.

'Not *again*!' Eddie muttered and, if you've read the book *Awful End*, you'll know why. He, the Great Zucchini and Daniella all let go of the coffin lid and put their hands in the air. The lid thudded shut on the coffin, then there was silence.

'This place is gettin' busier than Piccadilly Circus,' muttered Daniella.

'Who have we here?' said Mr Lalligag, at last. 'Mr Collins the ironmonger, Master Edmund Dickens from the big house, and who might you be, m'dear?'

'Me name's Daniella,' said Daniella, ''n' what I wanna know is, what's such a small guy like you doin' wiv such a big gun?'

Eddie was so proud of her! She didn't seem in the least bit frightened of Lalligag. She turned to him. ''n' you can stop dribblin' and all!' she said.

'And I am *not* Mr Collins the –' Zucchini began.

'And, as you may have guessed, Master Dickens, I'm not really a librarian,' Mr Lalligag interrupted.

Now, before one of you readers gets all nasty and says, 'But you said he was a librarian in the DRAMATIS PERSONAE and if you, the narrator, can't tell the truth, then who can we trust?' I urge you all to look back at page 74, but keep your finger in this page so you don't lose your place. See? What I wrote was:

MR LALLIGAG – *who says he's a librarian*

Now, I can't be much fairer than that, can I?

'And you weren't really hired by my great-aunt to catalogue the books, were you?' asked Eddie.

'No,' Mr Lalligag agreed. 'The great thing about a house like Awful End is that nobody seems to know who's who or what anybody else is up to. Did you know, for example, that there's a woman living under the main stairs? She wears the top left-hand corner of a knitted egg cosy on a piece of string around her neck?'

'Of course I know. That's Gibbering Jane. She came with us to live there.'

'Oh . . .' said Mr Lalligag, obviously a little put out. 'Anyway, as soon as I learnt that the Great Zucchini was in the vicinity, I used a false identity to get into the house and keep an eye on what was going on.'

'So who are ya, then? If you ain't a librarian?' asked Daniella, decidedly unimpressed.

'I'm someone looking out for other people's interests,' said Mr Lalligag. 'Now, if you'll be kind enough to step away from the coffin, I'll take what I came for. Forgive this –' he waved the gun in the air '– but I'm not sure who to trust, so keep your hands up, go over to the wall and lie face down in the grass. If any of you so much as looks up, I'll plug you.'

Though not familiar with all the euphemisms for shooting or being shot – a euphemism is a nice word or phrase replacing a nasty one so, for example, a euphemism for a three-hour exam might be 'a nice little test' – Eddie was quick to realise that 'being plugged' meant ending up with a bullet inside him; which is why he did exactly what Mr Lalligag had told him to do, and lay face down. Zucchini and Daniella did the same, which is why none of them saw what happened next.

They heard the cry, the barking and the clanking of chains, but it was only when they heard the excited yapping that they all looked up and worked out what had happened.

Standing in the open coffin was Barking, with a huge grin on his excited little face. Now *he* was holding the revolver, which somehow seemed even bigger in his tiny paw. Its previous owner lay slumped half in and half out of the coffin, and it was obvious that Barking had hit him with his ball and chain.

Mr Lalligag had opened what he'd expected to be a coffin containing nothing more than two harmless hessian sacks, to be confronted by a far-from-harmless convict, ready to pounce.

Now, the brighter readers amongst you – that's
37.2 per cent of you – will have been wondering
what happened to Barking all of this time and will
have been wondering whether I made a mistake. A
few of you might have been muttering things
along the lines of 'he must have got confused and
has suddenly written Barking out of the story altogether. One minute he has the ex-convict there.
The next minute it's just Eddie, Zucchini and
Daniella.'

Of that 37.2 per cent, 26 per cent of you
believed that I hadn't, in fact, lost my marbles and
that Barking had managed to slide down the hole,
unnoticed, as Mr Lalligag approached. Only 14
per cent of the original 37.2 per cent of you who

noticed that Barking wasn't around guessed that he'd hidden himself in the coffin before the others had time to drop the lid and put up their hands.

I'm told by someone who doesn't get out much, and whose room smells of – well, I'd rather not talk about that – that 14 per cent of the 37.2 per cent of readers who noticed Barking had gone is just 5.2 per cent of all you readers . . . so, if you were one of those who realised where Barking had been all this time, please accept this well-earned round of applause:

Clap! Clap! Clap! Clap! Cheer! Cheer! Clap! Clap! Clap! Clap! Cheer! Cheer! Cheer! Clap! Clap! Clap! Clap! Cheer! Cheer! Clap! Clap! Clap! Clap! Cheer! Cheer! Cheer! Clap! Clap! Clap! Clap! Cheer! Cheer!

Right. That's enough. We don't want it going to your heads. Let's get back to the action:

'Well done, Mr Barking,' said the Great Zucchini, scrambling to his feet and striding over towards the coffin, unaware that he was now facing an armed escaped convict. 'Well done!'

Eddie leapt to his feet and took Daniella's hand, pulling her up. Touching her skin made him feel all funny in the pit of his stomach.

'*Who Skillet and Merryweather*?' asked Barking. He must have remembered Zucchini talking of their imminent arrival before Mr Lalligag had burst onto the scene.

111

'My manager and my props man. They should be here shortly,' said Zucchini. 'You can put that gun down now, my good man. The bonk on the head you gave this Lalligag chap has knocked him out well and good.'

'*Into hole please*,' said Barking, pressing the revolver into Zucchini's stomach.

'I don't understand . . .' the escapologist protested.

'He wants us to get into the hole,' sighed Eddie.

'*No. You with me*,' Barking told Eddie.

'Barking is one of the escaped convicts everyone's been talking about,' Eddie explained. 'We'd better do exactly as he says.'

The Great Zucchini and Daniella climbed into the hole while Eddie dragged the unconscious body of Mr Lalligag over to them and passed him in.

He then squeezed into the coffin with Barking, his ball and chain, the revolver and the sandbags. The situation was clear: one peep out of those three in the hole and Eddie would end up filled full of lead, or any other euphemisms you can think of.

*

Imagine the scene when Mr Merryweather and Skillet rode up the track beside the field, in the hearse Eddie'd first seen in the driveway of Awful

112

End, what seemed like ages ago. They were expecting to be greeted by the Great Zucchini and Daniella, carrying the coffin, all ready to throw it in the back for a quick getaway. Instead, all they saw was the hole, a pile of earth, the deserted coffin, and not a soul in sight!

Being on the run from the peelers, neither Mr Merryweather nor Skillet wanted to attract attention by calling out their missing colleagues' names, so they decided to collect the coffin and put it in the hearse, *then* go looking for them.

Of course, when they reached the coffin, Barking (who'd been watching their approach across the grass through a gap between the lid and the side) jumped to his feet and trained his revolver on the new arrivals.

'Blimey!' said Skillet, who had spent one or two years behind bars himself, for stealing a coat button. 'It's Arthur Brunt, the billionaire burglar!'

'Actually, his name is Barking,' said Eddie, getting to his feet. He had a stiff neck.

'He *comes* from Barking,' said Skillet. 'It's a place.'

Eddie looked at his captor with new respect. Was this man really the billionaire burglar the papers had written about when he'd finally been arrested and tried a few years back? He was supposed to be some kind of criminal genius. A mastermind.

Barking glared at Skillet, but then his expression changed and all pretence was dropped. 'How clever of you to recognise me,' he said at last. Gone was the strange yappy voice he'd used until now, to be replaced by a voice as smooth as silk: a *gentleman*'s voice. He also looked different now. You know when a teacher says, 'Wipe that silly grin off your face.' Well, it was as if Barking had done just that. When he stopped grinning, his eyebrows lowered and he no longer looked like the puppy in the window of the pet shop which you just had to rush in and buy . . . He almost looked sophisticated; debonair.

'I do so hate the term *burglar*,' he said. 'It conjures up some sneak thief in the night. I usually stole from houses to which I was invited, and only the best jewellery from the best people. Whilst on the run, I thought it best to adopt a very different persona' (which means, 'I thought it was a good idea to seem a very different type of bloke.'). 'Do either of you have a knife?'

'What about the one you stuck in my back to keep me quiet?' Eddie demanded, still reeling at Barking's transformation.

'That was no knife, Eddie,' he said. 'It was a half-chewed carrot I found in your pocket when I put on your clothes.'

Eddie groaned. He'd been tricked by his own

114

whittling carrot! Skillet, meanwhile, cautiously handed Barking a pocket knife.

Barking lined up Eddie and the newcomers in front of the hole, so he could keep the gun trained on everybody. Crouching down, but without taking his eyes off anyone for a moment, he cut open one of the sandbags with the knife. And can you guess what poured out? Sand, of course – they were sandbags . . . but when Barking put his free hand into the sack, he pulled out a fistful of jewels.

True to form, the jewels glinted in the sunlight, just as all jewels should. He put in his hand again and pulled out more. There were necklaces, earrings, brooches, bracelets: gold, silver, diamonds, rubies, sapphires, pearls.

'How did they get into our sandbags?' gasped Skillet, Zucchini's props man, amazed that they'd been carrying around a fortune without even knowing it!

'The sandbags were made at the prison . . .' Eddie recalled. 'Zucchini said that they usually sewed mailbags but they'd sewn these sandbags specially for him –'

'Quiet, *please*!' commanded Barking. 'Mr Skillet. You look to me like a man who is good at knots.'

Several hours later, when the rector of St Botolph's was taking a short cut across the field to the church, he noticed someone had been digging near the churchyard wall.

'What a silly place to dig a hole!' he thought. 'Anyone might fall in!' When he peered inside he found the Great Zucchini, his manger Mr Merryweather, his props man Mr Skillet, his lovely assistant Daniella, and a man with a huge walrus moustache all tied together with a single piece of rope. Each had a gag in his – or her – mouth, made from what appeared to be a torn-off strip of hessian sacking. They were sitting on an empty coffin and were speckled with sand.

Having helped to free them, the rector was later horrified to discover that all but one of them was, for one reason or another, wanted by the police!

But what of Eddie and Barking (as Arthur Brunt the billionaire burglar from Barking now chose to be called)? They were in a hearse, rattling at breakneck speed towards the moors, the tiny convict cracking the whip like a mad circus ringmaster.

Episode 10

That Sinking Feeling

*In which most of Eddie's family cram themselves
into a basket*

Wolfe Tablet, the famous photographer – and
there were very few photographers back
then, famous or otherwise – stood in the police
inspector's office, looking out of the window at his
precious hot-air balloon.

'I'm very grateful that you retrieved my balloon,
inspector,' he said, 'but what I fail to understand is
why I cannot take it with me. I have a race meeting
to attend. I intend to photograph the galloping
horses from the air.'

'We need to keep it as evidence,' said Mr Chevy,

the peeler stationed at the door.

'Evidence,' said the inspector from behind his desk. Well, his loud-check-covered tummy was immediately behind his desk. The rest of him was up against the wall.

'But you have eyewitnesses who can swear in court who stole my balloon and it was your own men who got it back for me. Surely you don't need to keep it tethered here until the trial?' the photographer protested.

'The law's the law,' said the peeler.

'The law's the law,' said the inspector. If the truth be told, the police were desperate to hold on to something. Zucchini and his staff had escaped, taking the recently captured hearse with them. All the police had left in this whole case was the hot-air balloon, so they were more than a little reluctant to let it go. That and the fact that it was great fun to go up and down in when they had nothing better to do . . . which was why the envelope (the actual balloon part above the basket) was fired up and ready to fly. A bit of a giveaway!

'But the balloon is my livelihood!' Wolfe Tablet complained. He was an important man. An impressive man. A man used to having his own way. The inspector squirmed in his creaking chair.

At that moment, the door to the office burst open and in marched Mad Uncle Jack and Even

Madder Aunt Maud, holding Malcolm the stuffed stoat like a baby, closely followed by Mr and Mrs Dickens (still without her wedding ring).

'Is he here?' Mad Uncle Jack demanded.

'Is who where?' spluttered the inspector, struggling to his feet. 'What is the meaning of this intrusion?'

'My boy, Eddie Dickens. Have you locked him up again? He's gone missing,' said Mrs Dickens.

The inspector raised an eyebrow and looked across to Mr Chevy. The peeler shook his head. 'No, sir,' he said.

'No we haven't,' said the inspector, 'and the last time we locked him up he signed a piece of paper saying he didn't mind. Isn't that right, Mr Chevy?'

'Indeed it is, inspector,' agreed the peeler. 'He signed along the dotted line. I drew the dots myself.'

'It's not then we're worried about,' said Mad Uncle Jack. 'It's last night. He didn't sleep in his bed.'

'Well, his bed was blown up a few days ago,' Mad Aunt Maud explained, instantly making matters more complicated, 'but he wasn't in the bed he should have been sleeping in since his bed was blown up, if you see what I mean?'

The inspector obviously didn't.

'What matters is that my son is missing!' Mrs Dickens wailed.

119

'And Malcolm wasn't trying to poison me at all,' said Mad Aunt Maud. 'That was a misunderstanding. It wasn't a poison pill, but a wedding ring. It bounced right off his nose, you see?'

'Malcolm? Who's Malcolm? And what's all this about exploding beds and poison pills that aren't poison pills . . .?'

'My wife is a little confused,' said Mad Uncle Jack, in a whisper loud enough to wake the police-station cat, which had been sleeping under the inspector's desk. 'She is, of course, referring to Sally, who is stuffed.'

'I'd like to report my son missing,' said Mr Dickens, who hadn't heard a word. 'His name is Edmund Dickens.'

'Sometimes known as Eddie?' asked a smallish man, stepping through the open doorway. He wore a pinstripe suit, speckled with sand. Nobody saw his lips move because they were covered by a large walrus moustache.

'And who are you, sir?' sighed the inspector.

'He's the librarian –'

'The gas man –'

'The dog-catcher –'

'The tree-counter –'

You see, our Mr Lalligag had given himself a different cover story – a different identity – to just about everyone he'd met at Awful End. Now he spoke the truth. 'My name is Abe Lalligag from the Pickleton Detective Agency and I am on the trail of some missing jewels, stolen by Arthur Brunt the billionaire burglar.'

'From Barking?' asked the inspector. 'He's one of the convicts who escaped from Grimpen Jail.'

'And, I'm afraid he has taken Eddie Dickens hostage,' said the detective. 'I too was held prisoner until half an hour ago. I was rescued by a passing rector. There's no time to lose. We must save the boy and reclaim the jewels!'

'A passing what?' asked Mr Dickens.

'Rector!' said Mrs Dickens.

'Where do you think he's taken the boy?' asked the inspector.

'To the moors!' said the detective. 'In a hearse.' He caught sight of Wolfe Tablet's balloon through the window. 'That would be an ideal mode of transport. Come on!'

Before the inspector or his loud-checked suit had time to protest, everyone piled out of his office, down the corridor and out to the balloon.

Beating off the competition with her stuffed stoat, Mad Aunt Maud was the first into the basket, with a leg up from Mad Uncle Jack, who stepped in with ease after her. Mr Lalligag of the Pickleton Detective Agency was next on board and he was already untying the guy ropes as Mr and Mrs Dickens scrambled in after him.

The balloon basket was already off the ground as Wolfe Tablet made it aboard his own contrivance, but the police inspector and Mr Chevy the peeler were far too slow.

No matter how much they stood on the ground, shaking their fists and crying 'Come back!' the balloon was up, up and away on its rescue mission.

'How do you make this thing go left or right?' demanded Detective Lalligag. 'Is there some kind of lever?'

'Air currents!' said Wolfe Tablet, adjusting the flame in the burner under the hole in the middle of the balloon envelope, so that it made the air inside it hotter and so rise. (Hot air rises. Even hotter air rises even higher. So now you know.)

'We fly up until we find the air currents – winds – in the direction we want to go.'

'Which is over there!' Mr Lalligag pointed.

Mr Tablet was a skilled balloonist and it wasn't long before he had them flying over the moors.

'There!' cried Mad Uncle Jack, leaning right out of the basket and pointing.

'What is it?' asked Mad Aunt Maud.

'A gorse bush the colour of my favourite old waistcoat.'

'Oh, so it is! Look, Malcolm!' She held the stuffed stoat, nose first, over the side.

'Any sign of my poor Eddie?' Mrs Dickens wailed.

'Not yet, madam . . . but look! There's the hearse!'

Sure enough, there below them – looking no larger than two gerbils pulling a shoe box – were the black horses and the hearse, abandoned by Barking as he and Eddie had carried on by foot.

'Look!' cried Aunt Maud excitedly, and everyone piled over to her side of the basket. 'That stream looks like a wiggly blue snake from up here!'

'It is the boy and the convict we're after!' Mr Lalligag fumed. 'The boy and the convict!'

Meanwhile, Mr Tablet had opened a wooden box fixed to one of the sides of the basket and was putting together a piece of complicated photographic equipment which he called a camera.

'Photographs of the capturing of the billionaire burglar would be a sensation!' he declared.

'We've got to find him first . . . There!' said the detective triumphantly. 'That's them!' And, sure enough, it was. There below was Barking with Eddie close behind, running through a patch of ferns almost as tall as they were. Eddie was carrying a carpet bag and, by the way he was struggling, Mr Lalligag reasoned that it must contain the stolen jewels. 'Can you bring this balloon down ahead of them?' he asked.

'It might be a bit of a bump, but I can indeed,' said Wolfe Tablet. He fiddled with the burner, pulled a rope or two and they were soon going down all right!

'Wheeeeeee!' said Mad Aunt Maud. 'We're flying, Malcolm. Flying!'

If Daniella's landing in the rose bed at Awful End had been undignified, this landing was a total disgrace! Of all the places they could have landed, they hit a rocky outcrop on a slope and the basket tipped over, with everyone still inside it, and then the balloon dragged them along the ground. There were plenty of 'oohs!', 'arghs!' and 'oofs!' and each and every one of them who'd been through the experience now knew what it felt like to be one of a litter of unwanted kittens inside an old coal sack stuffed with rocks.

Wolfe Tablet clutched his beloved wooden box camera to protect it as best he could. Mad Aunt Maud hugged Malcolm and Mad Uncle Jack hugged her. Detective Lalligag and Mr Dickens held on to each other, and Mrs Dickens held on to the edge of the basket.

They'd all managed to get about as upright as they could when Barking came running out of the patch of ferns. The last thing on earth he'd expected was this extraordinary welcoming committee, and he came to a halt.

'Give it up, Brunt,' said Mr Lalligag. 'You're a gentleman burglar, not a violent man. You're outnumbered and would have to shoot us all in order to escape.'

Barking glared back at him. 'We meet again, Lalligag!' he said, because that's the kind of thing criminal masterminds always seem to say when finally face to face with the detective who's been tracking them down. 'I'm not going back to the stinking jail and I'm not giving up my treasure after all this time!' He looked furious. *Fuming*.

'Er, why are you wearing my son's clothes?' asked Mr Dickens, stepping forward. Lalligag put out a hand to stop him. Eddie's father, still being deaf from the blast, really had little if any idea who was what or what was going on.

Barking put his hand on the butt of the

revolver tucked into the waistband of his – yes, all right, *Eddie's* – trousers. 'I have a simple proposition,' he said.

Eddie found it hard to believe that this was the same man who'd been sniffing thistles and licking ears . . . or perhaps the ear-licking had really been instruction-whispering, all a part of Barking's – of Brunt's – pretence.

'If I let the boy go unharmed, then you, in return, must let me go with the jewels,' said Barking. 'If you follow me, however, I shall start shooting. I can't say fairer than that.'

Lalligag appeared to be considering the proposition, when a couple of newcomers arrived on the scene.

'First, tell me this,' said a voice from the top of a nearby hummock – or was it a hillock? (I always have this problem.) Everyone turned to look.

'Ah, the local ironmonger!' cried Mad Uncle Jack.

'Hello, Mr Collins,' Even Madder Aunt Maud waved. 'Coooeee! I've been racking my brains and I've remembered that I *do* like you!'

It was, if the truth be told, the Great Zucchini. He was riding a 'borrowed' carthorse bareback, with the lovely Daniella up behind him, frilly petticoats rustling in the breeze. 'How did your stolen jewels come to be in my sandbags?' he demanded.

'Daniella!' cried Eddie, dropping the carpet bag. 'You came to rescue me!'

'It was Harold's idea,' she called down. 'He didn't want to leave you with the likes of 'im!'

The likes of 'im – that is to say, Barking, or Arthur Brunt the billionaire burglar, if you prefer – pulled himself to his full (if somewhat small) height and looked across to the escapologist on horseback, but kept his hand firmly gripped around the revolver. Then a look of smug pride shaped his features.

'When I was tried, convicted and sent to jail, they never found the latest batch of jewels I'd stolen. They searched my house, my hideout and dug up half of Barking, but never recovered a single sparkler.' (No, he wasn't talking about fireworks. A sparkler is slang for a gem or diamond.) 'They never found them because I'd smuggled them into jail with me. And who'd think of looking for them there? When I, along with Bonecrusher, Swags and the others found a way to escape, I didn't want to risk being captured with the jewels . . . so when you came to the jail requesting we sew sandbags for your act, I came up with the plan to fill them with my ill-gotten gains –'

'So the stolen jewels "escaped" first, then you followed and came to get them back!' said Eddie.

'Exactly . . .'

127

'Why all the talking?' demanded Mr Dickens, who'd seen a lot of mouth-opening and closing, but hadn't heard an actual word that was said. 'We're only a few pages from the end of the final episode. What we need is *action*, not words!' Of course, no one had any idea what he meant, but his words did have some surprising results.

'One thing you should know, Brunt,' cried Lalligag, lowering his head and charging across the springy moorland grass like an angry bull in a bullfight, 'is that I never load my gun!'

Startled, Barking pulled out the revolver he'd taken off Lalligag earlier, and – to his credit, I suppose – fired it up in the air rather than straight at the oncoming detective, just in case the Pickleton detective was lying and it was loaded.

There was a resounding 'CLICK'.

Lalligag wasn't lying: the gun was empty.

Barking dodged the detective, grabbed the bag from Eddie, who was too startled by the speed of the snatch to put up much of a struggle, and darted off down the hillside.

The Great Zucchini and Daniella came thundering down off the tummock – that's it: it was neither a hummock nor a hillock – on the carthorse, galloping after him. Mad Uncle Jack, Even Madder Aunt Maud and Eddie's parents were also in hot pursuit, with Eddie close behind.

Only Wolfe Tablet stood his ground, because he was setting up a tripod and taking pictures.

'Nobody steals my great-nephew's clothes and gets away with it!' cried Mad Aunt Maud, who wasn't particularly clear about the escaped-convicts/stolen-jewels/escapologist side of things, but was fully aware that Eddie shouldn't be walking around the misty moors in next to nothing . . . and she dived onto the ground, throwing out her arms to catch the iron ball that Barking was now dragging behind him.

To us, it would have looked like something out of a game of rugby, but – although it was first played in the 1820s – no one had come up with any proper rules yet, so few people had been to a rugby match.

It didn't stop Barking, though. He just kept on running across the springing turf, with Mad Aunt Maud being dragged behind.

When she'd made that dramatic dive, Malcolm – or is it Sally? – had flown out of her hands and been caught brilliantly by Eddie, running alongside.

He was bursting with pride that his great-aunt had taken such direct action against a master criminal, and was inspired to act himself. He threw Malcolm as hard as he could towards the fleeing convict.

There was a loud 'THUD' of stuffed stoat coming into contact with back of human head, followed by a cry. Barking stopped running, but the carpet bag kept on going: it flew out of his tiny paws and burst open, its glittering contents spilling onto the ground . . .

. . . and what dangerous ground! Without even realising it at first, Eddie had just saved Barking's life, possibly a number of their lives. They'd been heading straight for the bog!

At first glance, the land just ahead of them looked as solid as the ground surrounding it, with tufts of grass and heather sprouting up, covering its dangerous secret. Just beneath the surface was mud deep enough to suck down a herd of wild deer – and certainly a tiny convict weighed down with a ball and chain – never to be seen again.

'Good shot!' cried Daniella.

'My jewels!' cried Barking, watching them sink without trace for ever. 'No!' And the cry transformed into the plaintive cry of a howling hound: 'Oooo-oooooooooooow!'

Eddie thought back to the night in the cave and wondered if there really was more of a doggy side to Arthur Brunt than the billionaire burglar himself realised.

'Well done, Malcolm!' said Mad Aunt Maud, struggling to her feet and retrieving her beloved stoat. She held him by the tail and brought him down on Barking's head for good measure.

'You're a naughty, naughty man!' she told him.

Mr Lalligag of the Pickleton Detective Agency stepped forward and handcuffed the defeated villain. He'd lost the jewels but got his man.

Eddie looked around him. He hadn't felt so happy in ages. His family had come to rescue him ... even Daniella and the Great Zucchini had come to his aid. And it was he, Eddie – with a little help from a stuffed stoat who was as good as family – who had finally stopped Barking. He wanted to remember this moment for ever. Fortunately, someone else had the same bright idea.

'Everyone smile, please!' said Wolfe Tablet. 'And don't move!'

There was a bright flash and a loud bang, followed by a smell of sulphur.

And that, once again, dear readers, is the end of another of Eddie Dickens's rather strange adventures. For those of you who don't like questions left unanswered and loose ends untied, let me try to put your minds at rest.

I should start by telling you that Wolfe Tablet was so pleased to have been in on the capture of the billionaire burglar that he eventually dropped all charges against Zucchini's troupe for tying him up in the Rancid Rat and stealing his precious hot-air balloon. The original photograph of Eddie next to the handcuffed Barking can still be seen in the Wolfe Tablet Museum in the West Country. (I forget where it is exactly, and I don't have my guide book with me today. I've been there, though, and they do very good cream teas.)

Eddie's father's hearing returned completely, eventually, and Mad Aunt Maud's injuries – from being hit by a balloon, dragged along in a balloon basket and pulled along the ground by a convict, whilst clutching his ball and chain – soon healed. Mad Uncle Jack bought a new waistcoat the colour of the gorse bush.

Malcolm was, I am pleased to report, undamaged by the part he played in the convict's heroic capture.

Eddie's mum, meanwhile, got her wedding ring back, but please don't ask me to go into details as to how.

The Great Zucchini and his escapology troupe moved on to tour the rest of the country, but not before a huge party was held at Awful End. Eddie found that he could speak to the lovely Daniella without dribbling and that girls are really just human beings after all.

Bonecrusher and the other escaped convicts were finally caught – all except for Swags, who somehow got away. Those of you who read the third and final book in this trilogy will run into him again . . . just as Eddie himself did.

Which leaves one final matter: that of the carthorse 'borrowed' by the Great Zucchini and Daniella when riding to Eddie's rescue. His owner eventually found him, chewing the plants in the rector of St Botolph's garden. You wouldn't know the man. Why should you? He was the local ironmonger. His name was Mr Collins.

THE END
until the next time

The Philip Ardagh Club

COLLECT some fantastic **Philip Ardagh** merchandise.

WHAT YOU HAVE TO DO:
You'll find tokens to collect in all Philip Ardagh's fiction books published after 08/10/02. There are 2 tokens in each hardback and 1 token in each paperback. Cut them out and send them to us complete with the form (below) and you'll get these great gifts:

> **2 tokens** = a sheet of groovy character stickers
> **4 tokens** = an Ardagh pen
> **6 tokens** = an Ardagh rucksack

Please send with your collected tokens and the name & address form to:
Philip Ardagh promotion, Faber and Faber Ltd, 3 Queen Square,
London, WC1N 3AU.

1. This offer can not be used in conjunction with any other offer and is non transferable. 2. No cash alternative is offered. 3. If under 18 please get permission and help from a parent or guardian to enter. 4. Please allow for at least 28 days delivery. 5. No responsibility can be taken for items lost in the post. 6. This offer will close on 31/12/04. 7. Offer open to readers in the UK and Ireland ONLY.

Name: ....
Address: ....
....
....
Town: ....
Postcode: ....
Age & Date of Birth: ....
Girl or boy: ....

Philip Ardagh Club
token

Awful End

Over two metres in height, with a bushy beard, Philip Ardagh is not only very tall and very hairy but has also written over fifty children's books for all ages, but nothing quite like *Awful End* . . . until now.

Currently living as a full-time writer with a wife and two cats in a seaside town somewhere in England, he has been – amongst other things – an advertising copywriter, a hospital cleaner, a (highly unqualified) librarian, and a reader for the blind.

'Philip Ardagh is a very, very, *very* funny man. I've been waiting for him to write an adventure story for ages, and here it is. It's brilliant, it's daft, and it'll make you LAUGH!'

VIVIAN FRENCH

by the same author
published by Faber & Faber

FICTION

The Eddie Dickens Trilogy
Awful End
Dreadful Acts
Terrible Times

Unlikely Exploits
The Fall of Fergal
Heir of Mystery
The Rise of the House of McNally

NON-FICTION

The Hieroglyphs Handbook
Teach Yourself Ancient Egyptian

The Archaeologist's Handbook
The Insider's Guide to Digging Up the Past

Did Dinosaurs Snore?
100½ Questions about Dinosaurs Answered

Why Are Castles Castle-Shaped?
100½ Questions about Castles Answered

PHILIP ARDAGH
Awful End

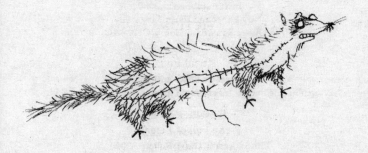

illustrated by David Roberts

faber and faber

First published in 2000
by Faber and Faber Limited
3 Queen Square London WC1N 3AU

Typeset by Faber and Faber
Printed in England by Mackays of Chatham plc, Chatham, Kent

© Philip Ardagh, 2000
Illustrations © David Roberts, 2000
Philip Ardagh is hereby identified as author of this work in accordance
with Section 77 of the Copyright, Designs and Patents Act 1988

A CIP record for this book
is available from the British Library

ISBN 978–0–571–20354–3

18 20 19

A Message from the Author

At no extra cost

Awful End was originally written in instalments, which explains why the chapters are called 'episodes' and not 'chapters'. These episodes were sent to my nephew, Ben, at boarding school, where they were – to my surprise – read out loud by his housemaster and housemistress 'Pa and Ma Brown'. This book is dedicated to them and (in alphabetical order) to: Cordelia, Francesca, Hattie, Henry, Isabelle, Katie and Ted Riley too. May their lives, and yours, be full of silly adventures.

PHILIP ARDAGH
England
2000

Contents

Crinkly Around the Edges

*In which Eddie Dickens is sent
away for his own good*

When Eddie Dickens was eleven years old, both his parents caught some awful disease that made them turn yellow, go a bit crinkly round the edges, and smell of old hot-water bottles.

There were lots of diseases like that in those days. Perhaps it had something to do with all that thick fog, those knobbly cobbled streets and the fact that everyone went everywhere by horse . . . even to the bathroom. Who knows?

'It's very contagious,' said his father.

'And catching,' said his mother, sucking on an ice cube shaped like a famous general.

They were in Eddie's parents' bedroom, which was very dark and dingy and had no furniture in it

1

except for a large double bed, an even larger wardrobe, and thirty-two different types of chair designed to make you sit up straight even if your wrists were handcuffed to your ankles.

'Why are you sucking an ice cube shaped like a famous general?' Eddie asked his parents, who were propped up against piles of pillows in their impressively ugly double bed.

'Doctor Muffin says that it helps with the swelling,' said his mother. In fact, because she had a famous-general-shaped ice cube in her mouth, what she actually said was, 'Dotter Muffin schez va it hewlpz wiva schwelln,' but Eddie managed to translate.

'What swelling?' he asked politely.

His mother shrugged, then suddenly looked even more yellow and even more crinkly round the edges.

'And why do they have to be famous-general-shaped?' asked Eddie. He always asked lots of questions and whenever he asked lots of questions his father would say: 'Questions! Questions!'

'Questions! Questions!' said his father.

Told you.

'But why a famous general?' Eddie repeated. 'Surely the shape of the ice cube can't make any difference?'

'Schows sow muck chew no,' muttered his

mother, which meant (and still means), 'Shows how much you know.'

His father rustled the bedclothes. 'One does not question the good doctor,' he said. 'Especially when one is a child.' He was a small man except for when he was sitting up in bed. In this position, he looked extremely tall.

Then Eddie's mother rustled the bedclothes. It was easy to make them rustle because they were made entirely from brown paper bags glued together with those extra strips of gummed paper you some-times get if you buy more than one stamp at the post office.

Postage stamps were a pretty new idea back then, and everyone – except for a great-great-great-aunt on my mother's side of the family – was excited about them.

One good thing about there being so few stamps in those days was that no one had yet come up with the idea of collecting them and sticking them in albums and being really boring about them. Stamp collectors didn't exist. Another good thing about there being no stamp collectors was that English teachers couldn't sneak up on some defenceless child and ask it* how to spell 'philatelist'.

* Teachers even thought of a child as 'it' back then. Some things never change.

3

Anyhow, even for those days, having brown paper bedclothes wasn't exactly usual. Quite the opposite, in fact. Bedclothes used to be an even grander affair then than they are now.

There were no polyester-filled duvets with separate washable covers. Oh, no. Back then there were underblankets and undersheets and top sheets and middle sheets and seven different kinds of overblankets. These ranged from ones thicker than a plank of wood (but not so soft) to ones which had holes in them that were supposed to be there.

To make a bed properly, the average chambermaid went through six to eight weeks' training at a special camp. Even then, not all of them finished the course and those that didn't finish spent the rest of their working lives living in cupboards under stairs.

The cupboard under the stairs of the Dickens household was occupied by Gibbering Jane. She spent her days in the darkness, alongside a variety of mops, buckets and brooms, mumbling about 'hospital corners' and 'ruckled chenille'. She never came out, and was fed slices of ham and any other food that was thin enough to slip under the bottom of the door.

The reason why Mr and Mrs Dickens had rustling brown paper sheets and blankets was that this was a part of the Treatment. Dr Muffin was always giving very strict instructions about the Treatment.

The smell of old hot-water bottles had almost reached 'unbearable' on Eddie's what-I'm-prepared-to-breathe scale, and he held his hanky up to his face.

'You'll have to leave the room, my boy,' said his father.

'You'll have to leave the house,' said his mother. 'We can't risk you going all yellow and crinkly and smelling horrible. It would be a terrible waste of all that money we spent on turning you into a little gentleman.'

'Which is why we're sending you to stay with Mad Uncle Jack,' his father explained.

'I didn't know I had a Mad Uncle Jack,' gasped Eddie. He'd never heard of him. He sounded rather an exciting relative to have.

'I didn't say *your* Mad Uncle Jack. He's *my* Mad Uncle Jack,' said his father. 'I do wish you'd listen. That makes him your great-uncle.'

'Oh,' said Eddie disappointed. 'You mean Mad *Great*-uncle Jack.' Then he realised that he hadn't heard of him either and he sounded just as exciting as the other one. 'When will I meet him?'

'He's in the wardrobe,' said his mother, pointing at the huge wardrobe at the foot of the bed, in case her son had forgotten what a wardrobe looked like.

Eddie Dickens pulled open the door to the wardrobe, gingerly. (It was a ginger wardrobe.)

Inside, amongst his mother's dresses, stood a very, very, very tall and very, very, very thin man with a nose that made a parrot's beak look not so beaky. 'Hullo,' he said, with a 'u' and not with an 'e'. It was very definitely a 'hullo' not a 'hello'. Mad Uncle Jack put out his hand.

Eddie shook it. His little gentleman lessons hadn't been completely wasted.

Mad Uncle Jack stepped out of the wardrobe and onto an oval mat knitted by children from St Horrid's Home for Grateful Orphans. Remember that place: St Horrid's Home for Grateful Orphans. There. I've written it out for you a second time. Never let it be

6

said that I don't do anything for you. Remember the name. You'll come across it again one day, and probably between the covers of this book.

'So you are Edmund Dickens,' said Mad Uncle Jack, studying the boy.

'Yes, sir,' said Eddie, because his first name really was Edmund.

Eddie Dickens's father cleared his throat. He used a miniature version of the sort of brush the local sweep used to clear blocked chimneys. This was all a part of Dr Muffin's Treatment.

'Edmund,' said Mr Dickens, 'you are to go with my uncle and live with him until your dear, sweet mother and I –' he paused and kissed Mrs Dickens on the part of her face that was the least yellow and the least crinkly at the edges (a small section just behind her left ear) '– are well again. You must never wear anything green in his presence, you must always drink at least five glasses of lukewarm water a day, and you must always do as he says. Is that clear?'

'Yes, Father,' said Eddie.

'And, Jonathan,' added his mother, for Jonathan was the pet name she called Eddie when she couldn't remember his real one.

'Yes, Mother?'

'Do be careful to make sure that you're not mistaken for a runaway orphan and taken to the

7

orphanage where you will then suffer cruelty, hard-ship and misery.'

'Don't worry, Mother. That'll never happen,' said Eddie Dickens, dismissing the idea as ridiculous.

If only he'd listened.

Mad Uncle Jack wanted to use the bathroom before he went and, being unfamiliar with the house, he found it difficult to get his horse up the stairs with-out knocking one or two family portraits off the wall.

The fact that he'd only nailed the portraits up there himself minutes before made it all the more annoying. He took the paintings with him when-ever he strayed more than eleven miles from his house. Because his house was actually twelve miles from the nearest place, that meant he always had them with him.

A key part of the Treatment was that neither Mr Dickens nor his wife Mrs Dickens should leave their bed more than three times a day. Because they had both already been up twice that day, and both planned to get up later for an arm-wrestling competition against their friends and neighbours Mr and Mrs Thackery, who lived over at The Grange, neither of Eddie's parents could get up to see him off.

Instead, the bed was lowered from their window

8

on a winch constructed from the sheets that were no longer in use since the Treatment began.

'Good luck, my boy,' said Eddie's father. 'Under such extreme circumstances, I would kiss you, but I don't want you catching this.'

'Get well, Father,' said Eddie.

'Be good, Simon,' said his mother. Simon was the name Mrs Dickens used when she couldn't remember that his real name was Edmund or that his pet name was Jonathan. 'Be good.'

'I will,' said Eddie. 'Get well, Mother.'

It had started to rain and the raindrops mixed
with the tears that poured down his mother's face.
She was busy peeling an onion.

Episode 2

Even Madder Maud

*In which Eddie first meets Malcolm . . .
or is it Sally?*

When Eddie Dickens climbed into Mad Uncle Jack's covered carriage, he found that it was already occupied. In the corner, an elderly woman was stroking a stoat.

'You must be Malcolm,' said the old woman, with a voice that could grate cheese.

'No, madam. My name is Edmund,' said Eddie.

'I was talking to the stoat!' snarled the woman, pulling the creature closer to her. 'Well?' she demanded, staring at the animal.

The stoat said nothing. It didn't even twitch or blink. The woman seized it by the tail and held it aloft (which is in-those-days language for 'up a bit'). It was as stiff as a board. 'Are you Malcolm?' she demanded.

It was round about then that Eddie Dickens realised that the woman must be completely crazy and that the animal must be completely stuffed. He took a seat opposite the woman.

'Put that seat back!' she screamed, so Eddie did as he was told and sat down.

Just then, Mad Uncle Jack stuck his thinnest of thin heads through the door of the carriage. 'Ignore her. She's quite mad,' he said gruffly.

'Who is she, sir?' asked Eddie.

'Sally Stoat,' said his great-uncle.

'Did she get her name from that stuffed animal she's hugging?' asked Eddie.

'It was the stoat I was referring to, you impudent whelp!' cried his great-uncle. 'That good lady is my wife, Mad Aunt Maud – your great-aunt – and there's most certainly nothing mad about her.'

Eddie's face went beetroot red. 'I do beg your pardon, Great-uncle,' Eddie spluttered. 'And you, Great-aunt,' he said, with terrible embarrassment. He hadn't even left the driveway of his own home and he had already managed to offend them both.

'Enough said,' said Mad Uncle Jack. 'I despise closed carriages so shall be lashing myself to the roof along with our luggage. I shall see you when we reach Awful End.'

'Awful End?'

'Our home. *Your* home, until your dear mother and father are cured of their terrible affliction,' Mad Uncle Jack explained.

Eddie's great-uncle clambered onto the roof where Eddie could hear him strapping himself into place next to his trunk.

'Drive on!' Mad Uncle Jack shouted.

Nothing happened.

'Driver!' he instructed. 'Drive on!' It was then that he must have remembered that they didn't *have* a driver. Eddie could hear him unstrapping himself and clambering across the roof above his head to take up position on the driver's chair.

Mad Uncle Jack gave a strange clicking noise that you sometimes hear people make to horses moments before they flick the reins and the carriage pulls off.

Eddie thought he even heard the flicking of the reins, but this was followed by silence except for the gentle patter of raindrops that were falling onto the stuffed stoat that his great-aunt was sticking out of the open window.

'Did you have a good war, dear?' she asked Eddie.

'What war was that, Great-aunt?' Eddie asked politely.

'How many have you been in?' she asked.

'None, as a matter of fact,' said Eddie. She was as tricky to talk to as her husband.

13

'Then don't be so particular!' she replied, pulling the stoat back into the dry of the carriage. 'Was Malcolm thirsty? Was he? Did he like his little drinky?'

'No horse!' called out a voice that Eddie recognised as belonging to his father, even though it sounded more yellow and crinkly at the edges than usual.

Eddie stood up and looked out of the window, across the driveway to his parents, who were sitting by the front door in their bed.

14

The weather wasn't doing their bedclothes much good. The brown paper bags looked a darker brown and were positively soggy. If his parents stayed out much longer, their bedding would soon turn to pulp. Eddie suspected that papier mâché wasn't a part of Dr Muffin's Treatment.

'No horse!' his father repeated, pointing to the front of the carriage.

Eddie climbed out, stepped onto the driveway and looked back at the carriage. He could see the problem. In the carriage sat Mad Aunt Maud with her stuffed stoat, by the name of either Malcolm or Sally, depending on who he was to believe. On the roof of the carriage were Eddie's trunk and his great-uncle's family portraits (that went with him always), and at the front of the carriage was his very thin and very mad Mad Uncle Jack, reins in one hand and a whip in the other.

But the problem was – and Mr Dickens had put it very well – that there was n-o h-o-r-s-e.

'Your great-uncle left him in the bathroom!' Mrs Dickens shouted, wiping away a tear from the corner of her eye. If the truth be told, what she actually shouted was: 'Yaw gway unk-le leff timinva barfroo,' because she had a whole peeled onion in her mouth.

A moment later, Mr Dickens's gentleman's gentleman led the horse out of the house and hitched him to Mad Uncle Jack's carriage.

'Thank you, Daphne,' said Mad Uncle Jack.

'Very good, sir,' replied the gentleman's gentleman. As a gentleman's gentleman, he knew that it was not his place to point out that he was not actually called 'Daphne' but 'Dawkins'. No, his place was a large basket in the kitchen with plenty of tissue paper, and he couldn't complain. Mr Thackery's gentleman's gentleman over at The Grange was far worse off. His place was on a small log behind a coal scuttle in the tackle room. Dawkins hadn't the slightest idea what a tackle room was, but had never thought to ask.

With the horse now in position, the carriage pulled away and they were off. Eddie waved out of the window at his parents until they became small dots in the distance. Perhaps this was part of their illness, or perhaps it was to do with perspective and it being a very long driveway.

'I think you should remove your clothes now,' said Mad Aunt Maud, as the carriage bumped along the wheel-ruts of an unmade-up road.

If Eddie Dickens had been beetroot red with embarrassment before, now he had gone blushing beetroot red. 'I beg your pardon?' he said, hoping that he hadn't heard her right.

He had. 'I said, I think you should remove your clothes,' she confirmed.

'Er . . . Why might that be, Mad Aunt Maud?' he

enquired as politely as possible, wishing that he was anywhere else in the whole wide world than in a carriage with this woman.

'If you wear all those clothes in here, you will have nothing to put on when we step out of the carriage, and then you will be cold,' said Mad Aunt Maud. 'I should have thought that was perfectly obvious.'

'But I'll be cold in here in the meantime, great-aunt,' Eddie was quick to point out.

Great-Aunt Maud glared at him. If looks could kill, he would have been seriously injured by this one. 'Have you ever thought of growing a moustache?' she asked suddenly.

'I'm only eleven –' Eddie protested.

'Quiet!' snapped Mad Aunt Mad. 'I was asking Malcolm here.' She gave the stuffed stoat a friendly rub between its glass eyes.

The stuffed stoat said nothing.

Eddie wondered if he'd be able to survive a whole journey sharing a carriage with this lunatic. At least she seemed to have forgotten about telling him to take his clothes off.

'Now, come on, young man,' said Mad Aunt Maud. 'Remove them at once!'

Eddie groaned.

To break the journey, Mad Uncle Jack stopped at a coaching inn called The Coaching Inn. It was in an unimaginative part of the countryside and to call

17

it anything other than The Coaching Inn might have confused both the locals and the passing trade.

Both the locals were there to greet Mad Uncle Jack's party. They were the landlord and landlady, Mr and Mrs Loaf.

Neither of them batted an eyelid when Eddie stepped from the carriage wearing nothing but his undershirt and a pair of long johns.

In those days, wearing nothing but your undershirt and long johns was considered being undressed. You couldn't really get much more naked than that. If there had been cinemas in those days – which there weren't – and they had shown a film of someone on the beach wearing nothing but his undershirt and long johns, there would have been outrage. Men with large beards

18

would have set up barricades and there would have been riots in the street.

Most people went through life without realising that they could actually remove their undershirts and long johns – they simply assumed that they were a part of them, like fingernails and hair. They simply assumed that these undergarments were their skin, made out of a different material from their face, hands and feet, and with buttons on them.

If anyone had appeared in just a pair of boxer shorts or swimming trunks, the womenfolk would have had 'an attack of the vapours' and the men-folk would have exploded in a rage at the indecency of it. What exactly 'an attack of the vapours' was is unclear, because there are no such thing as women-folk any more, and there is certainly no such thing as an attack of the vapours.

If a person did suffer from such an attack in Eddie Dickens's day, however, it seemed to involve a high-pitched squeal, a swooning, and a falling to the ground (or floor) with much crumpling of the dress.

The way to assist a gentlewoman after such an attack was to wave a small bottle labelled 'SMELLING SALTS' beneath her nose.

As with an attack of the vapours, smelling salts don't exist today either. Nor do bath salts. Every-one uses bubble bath or shower gel instead, which is all very interesting.

As a result, when Eddie stepped out of the carriage outside The Coaching Inn coaching inn, he felt as naked as you would if you were completely in the nuddy (except, perhaps, for your watch), despite the fact that he was wearing more clothes than the rest of us would wear on an ordinary day at the seaside.

He, therefore, expected both of the locals – the landlord and landlady, Mr and Mrs Loaf – to be horrified. But not at all.

'This is Master Eddie,' Mad Uncle Jack explained, climbing down and standing beside his great-nephew. 'Please arrange to have him stabled, and arrange for two rooms – one for me and my good lady wife, and one for my horse.'

'Very good, Mad Mr Dickens,' said Mrs Loaf. She obviously knew Mad Uncle Jack well, but it would be rude to call him 'Mad Uncle Jack' because she wasn't one of the family. 'This way, please . . . though I do wish you weren't staying.'

While his great-aunt and great-uncle – and their horse – were shown to their rooms by his wife, Mr Loaf led Eddie to the stables.

'You'll sleep in here,' he said. 'There's plenty of straw, so you should be warm and comfortable.'

'But why should I have to sleep out here, while the horse gets to sleep in the inn?' asked Eddie, trying not to sound too pathetic and helpless.

'Perhaps your great-uncle can only afford two rooms,' the landlord suggested. 'And then there's the fact that he's completely mad.'

'Good point,' nodded Eddie, shivering a little.

'You know, Master Edmund, that great-uncle of yours never pays his bill,' Mr Loaf continued.

'Then why do you let him keep on staying here?' asked Eddie.

'Well, he sort of pays, see, but not with money,' said the man. He was carrying Eddie's trunk, which he now placed on a few bales of hay.

'He pays without money?' asked Eddie Dickens, frantically opening the trunk lid and pulling on the first garment he could find. It was one of Dr Muffin's chin-to-toe body stockings, which was knitted from coarse black wool and covered him up to his neck. He felt a lot less naked now. 'Then what does he pay with?'

'Well, usually with dried fish,' the landlord of The Coaching Inn explained. 'Two dried hake for a double room – per night – and half a halibut for a single room. I never asked him to pay in fish and I never said he could pay in fish, but pay in fish he always does.'

'So what do you do with all this dried fish?' asked Eddie, sitting on his trunk.

'I send it to your father and, knowing what rates I charge, and the method of fishology by which his

21

uncle pays, he then converts the fish into money and sends me the exact amount.'

'You know my father?' asked Eddie excitedly. He had only been gone from his parents for half a day and he was missing them already. This was only the third time in his entire life that he had been away from home and it felt strange.

The first time he had been away from home was when he had been sent to sea. That was from when he was a year old to when he was old enough to go to school. The second time had been from when he was old enough to go to school until his tenth birthday. No wonder it felt so odd in that strange stable.

'No, I have never had the honour nor the privilege of meeting your father in person, Master Edmund,' said Mr Loaf, 'but we do communicate by post.'

'Aha!' said Eddie. 'That would explain the strange parcels my father so often takes to his study. I thought they smelt of dried fish.' His eyes lit up.

'Your eyes just lit up,' said the landlord in complete and utter amazement.

'No,' said Eddie. 'That was just a figure of speech.'

'I thought it had more to do with the body's electricity,' said Mr Loaf.

There was a lot of excitement about 'electricity' in those days before electric light, electric fridges and electric eels. That last one was a lie. There were most definitely electric eels way back then. How can we be so sure? Because Mad Uncle Jack would always tip Mrs Loaf with a dried electric eel at the end of each stay at The Coaching Inn. He was nothing if not generous and, as Mr Loaf so rightly said, completely mad.

Episode 3

Mister Pumblesnook

In which Eddie is entranced
by a handkerchief

Eddie found that the warmest place to lie was inside his trunk, but he couldn't sleep a wink. It wasn't because he was longer than the trunk, which meant that he'd had to curl himself into a ball. It wasn't because every ten minutes or so Mad Aunt Maud would burst into the stable, lift the lid of the trunk and scream, 'Not asleep yet?' in that terrible grating voice of hers, with wax dripping onto his face from her upheld candle. It had more to do with the fact that a band of strolling theatricals were rehearsing a play in the far corner of the stable.

Strolling theatricals were a strange breed of men and women who used to roam the countryside forcing unsuspecting yokels – who are locals who say 'ooh aar' instead of 'yes' – to watch something they called 'performances'.

A band of strolling theatricals was always led by a man called an actor-manager. You could always recognise an actor-manager from his large frame, from the fact that he always carried a slightly chipped silver-topped cane, from his booming, ridiculous voice – an actor-manager always used twenty-two words when one would do – and his blooming ridiculous name. Most actor-managers were called Mr Pumblesnook, and Mr Pumblesnook was no exception. He sat on a bale of hay in the corner of the stable of The Coaching Inn, barking instructions.

'Woof! Woof!' he said.

'Oooh, you weally aw such a funny man, husband deawest,' laughed his wife, who had a number of extremely irritating habits including pronouncing her 'r's as 'w's. If you don't think that's irritating, just you wait. By the time you reach the end of the next page you'll probably hate her as much as everyone else did.

'Oooh, you'we the most humowus fellow to have walked this eawth, husband deawest. Thewe hain't no denying it!' she added, which is a good

25

example of three more of her irritating habits.

Mrs Pumblesnook began all her conversation with the word 'oooh' – usually with three 'o's – as well as sticking 'h's in front of words that didn't need them and – as if that weren't enough – she always called Mr Pumblesnook 'husband deawest' when she was talking to him.

So that deaf people weren't spared the irritation she caused, she had a number of awful visual habits too. Her face was covered with some of the reddest blotches ever to have graced the visage of any human being – this was in the days when people still had visages, remember – and Mrs P had the dreadful habit of picking at these blotches with her claw-like nails and putting any loose skin that came away in a special pocket sewn to the front of her dresses. Another awful habit was what she did with the skin later, but no matter how much you beg, you'll never get me to write that down. Never!!!

There was some disagreement as to how she came to have these blotches. Some of the strolling theatricals were convinced that she'd got them from drinking her husband's *Eyebrow Embrocation*, while others thought they were a result of wearing theatrical make-up every night for over forty years. What no one disputed was that collecting the flaky skin was quite the most repulsive thing imaginable.

But what of Mr Pumblesnook? He was busy

talking his theatricals through a difficult scene of their up-and-coming production.

'Remember! Attention to the smallest detail reaps the largest of rewards, my children!' he bellowed.

Eddie groaned. He was never going to sleep, so he might just as well give up. Bleary-eyed and more than a little grouchy, he climbed out of his trunk and wandered across the straw-strewn floor to watch the strolling theatricals at work.

'Observe closely the way in which I remove my kerchief from my pocket and give this simplest of acts new meaning and life,' Mr Pumblesnook pronounced. 'See how the production of said kerchief becomes more than a mere action and becomes an interpretation of the action itself.' Then, with a strange quiver, followed by a dramatic flourish, the actor-manager pulled a handkerchief out of his coat pocket.

The assembled company – including young Eddie Dickens – burst into spontaneous applause. Eddie had never seen anyone pull out a hanky in such a way . . . It had been dramatic . . . exciting . . . He had *cared* about that hanky.

'Oooh, we have han audience, husband deawest!' cried Mrs Pumblesnook, spying Eddie and breaking the magic. 'We have ha little gentleman hamong us!'

Mr Pumblesnook fixed a dramatic stare upon

the child. 'What is your name, boy?' he demanded.

'Please, sir,' said Eddie, 'it's Eddie Dickens.'

At that moment, Mad Aunt Maud marched into the stable and over to Eddie's trunk, a guttering candle clasped in her hand. She lifted the lid and, ignoring the fact that the trunk was obviously empty, shouted, 'Not asleep yet?' Without waiting for the reply that she wouldn't have received anyway, she dropped the lid with a 'thunk' then marched back out of the stable and into the night.

'Oooh, such a charming lady, husband deawest,' sighed Mrs Pumblesnook, looking after Eddie's great-aunt as though she were the beloved queen herself. 'Such wefinement and such bweeding.'

'Indeed,' agreed her husband. He turned back to Eddie. 'You are related to Mrs Dickens, I presume?'

Eddie nodded. For those readers who are concerned that we shall be lumbered with these oh-so-amusing theatricals for at least the remainder of the episode, fear not.

Fate would have it that a carelessly dropped match was soon to set fire to the surrounding hay and to the clothing of a number of the less important strolling theatricals.

Had this actually occurred during one of the 'performances', the show would have had to continue right through to the end, no matter the cost to human life.

One of the rules which such people lived by was that 'the show must go on'. This, however, was only a rehearsal, so, instead of Old Wiggins and Even Older Postlethwaite being burnt to a crisp, they fled into the courtyard of The Coaching Inn where their fellow theatricals beat out the flames with their jackets then proceeded to dunk them in the horses' drinking trough.

In the meantime (and in the stable) Mrs Pumblesnook picked at her facial blotches, and her husband practised rolling his eyes in a manner befitting a gentleman (for his upcoming leading role in *An Egg for Breakfast*).

Eddie had been quite forgotten in the excitement.

With a sigh, he climbed back into his trunk, closing the lid behind him. There he remained until daybreak.

Episode 4

On the Road Again

*In which Aunt Maud is even more
maddening than usual*

The journey to Awful End began bright and early next morning. Mad Uncle Jack and equally Mad Aunt Maud had breakfasted on devilled kidneys, six eggs, a joint of ham and several glasses of port wine, served up by a jovial Mr Loaf. Eddie had breakfasted on the lid of his trunk. He'd had a slice of stale bread and some mouldy cheese.

When Mrs Loaf had first appeared at the stable with his food, the slice of bread had been fresh – still warm from the oven where she had baked it –

31

and there hadn't been so much as a smidgen of mould on the generous slice of cheese. When Mrs Loaf realised this, she apologised most profusely (which means 'rather a lot' in the kind of language Mr Pumblesnook liked to use) and hurried back into the kitchen.

She returned with the stale bread and mouldy cheese, and apologised once more.

'Do forgive me, Master Edmund,' she said. 'I don't know what I was thinking. I can't have you go spreading stories about us treating our guests kindly now, can I? That way more people would come to stay and I'd never get a moment's peace.'

'I'm sorry?' said Eddie. He wasn't sure he understood.

'How would you like strangers sleeping in your house . . . and the moment one lot leaves another lot turns up?' she demanded.

'But surely that's what coaching inns are for?' began Eddie, only to be interrupted.

'It's all right for Mr Loaf. He doesn't have to do all that sheet-changing and washing and ironing. Oh, no. All he has to do is drink ale out of a pewter tankard at the bar and shout, "Time, gentlemen, please." That's all he has to do.'

'Then why do you work in an –?'

'So I don't want you feeling welcome, now do I?' she said, thrusting the stale-and-mouldy replace-

32

ment breakfast onto the lid of the trunk. 'Eat this and be grateful.'

Eddie Dickens noticed that the plate had a large crack in it, clogged up with at least six months' worth of grime. This woman certainly knew how to make a meal unappetising when she put her mind to it.

'Thank you,' mumbled Eddie, more confused than ever.

If it was possible, and despite breakfast, Mad Uncle Jack looked even thinner than he had the previous day. He helped his wife and her stuffed stoat into the coach, shut the door behind Eddie, then clambered up into the driving seat.

Mr Loaf led the horse out of the main entrance to The Coaching Inn and hitched him up to the carriage.

'Thank you, my good man,' cried Mad Uncle Jack, reaching into the pocket of his coat and pulling out a dried eel, which he tossed down to the grateful landlord.

'No, thank *you*, sir,' said Mr Loaf and winked at Eddie Dickens, who was leaning out of the carriage window, watching the proceedings.

Eddie imagined Mr Loaf parcelling up the eel along with the other dried fish his great-uncle had used to pay for the board and lodgings and sending them on to his father.

'Goodbye, Master Edmund!' beamed the landlord. 'Good luck!'

'Good riddance!' added Mrs Loaf, sweetly.

With a flick of the reins and a loud whinny – from Eddie's great-uncle, not the horse, which was still far too sleepy to be making conversation at that time of the morning – they were off.

Mr and Mrs Loaf ran alongside the carriage, shouting and waving at Eddie.

'Drop us a line, Master Edmund,' called the landlord.

'Drop dead!' called the landlady.

'Stay again soon,' cried the landlord.

'Stay away!' cried the landlady.

'If you're ever passing this way –' began the landlord.

'Keep going without stopping,' finished the landlady.

And so the comments continued until the carriage picked up speed and the Loafs were left behind them.

Eddie had to admit that Mrs Loaf really did have an excellent knack of making him feel unwelcome. He never wanted to go to The Coaching Inn again.

'What time is it?' demanded Mad Aunt Maud. She was looking directly at Eddie when she asked the question, so he decided that she really must be asking him and not the stuffed stoat.

'I'm afraid I don't have a watch,' said Eddie.

'Then borrow mine.' His great-aunt rummaged in a small patchwork sack she had on the seat next to her. She pulled out a silver pocket watch on a chain and handed it to him. 'Now, what time is it?'

He read the hands. 'It's three minutes after eight o'clock,' he said, passing the watch back to her.

She studied the timepiece in her gnarled hands. 'I couldn't accept this,' she said. 'It's solid silver.' She held the watch up to her right ear and listened. 'And it has a very expensive tick. No, I most certainly couldn't accept such a valuable gift from a mere child.'

'But it's yours,' Eddie tried to point out.

'No, I cannot accept it,' insisted Mad Aunt Maud sternly. 'We'll hear no more about it. What would your poor, crinkly-edged mother have to say about you trying to give away your treasured watch?'

Eddie sighed, but decided it was best not to try to argue with his great-aunt. He slipped the watch into his pocket.

'Thief!' cried Maud. 'Thief!' She brandished Malcolm the stuffed stoat by the tail, like a club. It was as stiff as a policeman's truncheon and made a frightening weapon. 'Return my property to me at once!' she demanded.

Eddie swallowed hard. He dug his hand back into his pocket and passed her back her watch.

Great-Aunt Maud grinned from ear to ear. 'What a charming present,' she said. 'How thoughtful. How sweet.'

Putting down Malcolm carefully on the seat next to her, she leaned to her left and opened the window of the carriage, then tossed out the silver fob watch. 'Useless trinket,' she mumbled.

There was a cry, followed by a bit of confusion and then the carriage lurched to a halt. Eddie was propelled out of his seat and – to his horror – landed head first in his great-aunt's lap.

Apologising, he got to his feet and caught sight of a bearded stranger through the open window of the carriage.

The bearded stranger was rubbing his head with one hand and holding Mad Aunt Maud's watch with the other.

Mad Uncle Jack jumped down off the now stationary carriage and was striding towards the man.

'Why did you cry out like that?' demanded Eddie's great-uncle. 'You frightened my horse.'

'Because one of your number assailed me with a projectile!' spluttered the bearded stranger, barely able to contain his rage.

'Who did what with a what?' demanded Uncle Jack.

'A member of your party assaulted me with a missile!' the bearded stranger explained. When it

36

was obvious that Uncle Jack still had no idea what he was talking about, he tried again. 'One of your lot threw this pocket watch at me,' he said.

'How very interesting!' said Mad Uncle Jack. Before the bearded stranger knew what was happening, Eddie's great-uncle had snatched the watch from his grasp and was studying it closely.

'This watch does indeed belong to my beloved wife Maud,' he mused. 'I gave it to her on the occasion of her twenty-first birthday. Here, read the inscription.'

He thrust the watch under the bearded stranger's chin. When the bearded stranger managed to disentangle the silver watch chain from his beard, he read the inscription:

To Maud

Happy 2nd Birthday

Jack

The bearded stranger frowned. 'Didn't you just say that you gave this to your wife for her twenty-first birthday?' he asked.

'What of it?' demanded Mad Uncle Jack, digging his hands into the pocket of his coat and clasping a dried fish in each.

'Simply that the engraving refers to her second birthday, not her twenty-first.'

Uncle Jack snorted at the bearded stranger as if he

was an idiot. 'It was cheaper to have "2ⁿᵈ" engraved rather than "21ˢᵗ",' he explained. 'You had to pay by the letter.'

'But the "1" of "21ˢᵗ" is a *number*, not a letter,' the bearded stranger pointed out.

'Then I was overcharged!' muttered Mad Uncle Jack. 'Thank you for bringing it to my attention, sir. After we have deposited my great-nephew at Awful End, I will visit the shop where I originally bought this watch for my dear Maud – some fifty-five years ago – and demand my refund of a ha'penny!'

'Yes . . . That's all very well, but that still doesn't explain the reason why I became the target of a watch-thrower!' the bearded stranger protested.

Mad Uncle Jack stuck his head in through the open window of the carriage – his beak-like nose narrowly avoiding poking Eddie's eye out.

'Maud, dearest?' he inquired.

'Yes, peach blossom?' she replied.

'Did you throw your watch at this gentleman?'

'Gentleman? Gentleman?' she fumed. 'He's nothing more than a beard on legs!'

'Did you?'

'I wasn't aiming at him,' said Maud. 'He simply got in the way.'

'That's solved then,' said Mad Uncle Jack, satisfied that the truth had been reached. 'My wife was not throwing things at you, sir. She was simply

throwing things, and your head was in the way.'
With that, Mad Uncle Jack went to climb back up
into the driver's seat on top of the carriage.

The bearded stranger put his arm on Uncle Jack's
shoulder. 'Not so fast,' he said. 'This is a public high-
way and I have every right to be walking down it
unmolested,' he said.

Mad Uncle Jack pulled free of his grasp and
clambered up the side of the carriage. 'Your head
was in the way, sir,' he said. He liked the phrase, so
repeated it: 'Your head was in the way.'

'Then be very careful that this boy's head does
not get in the way of one of my bullets,' said the
bearded stranger.

He opened his coat and pulled out a revolver.
He pointed it through the open carriage window,
and aimed it straight between Eddie's eyes.

Episode 5

Big Guns

In which we learn that the bearded
stranger isn't either

Now, I don't know if you've ever had a revolver pointed at you, but even if you haven't, you probably know what one looks like.

First and foremost it's a gun. You pull the trigger and, if someone's remembered to put the bullets in it, one whizzes out of the end of the barrel and buries itself as deep as possible in the target.

If the target is just that – a target – then it makes an impressive 'bang' followed by a 'twang' and everyone hurries forward to see how close the bullet hole is to the bull's-eye.

If the target is a person, there's normally a cry of 'AAARGHHH!!!' as well as the bang, followed by a thud as the person falls to the ground with what looks like spaghetti sauce splattered all over his shirt . . . which isn't very nice, especially if your job is to wash the shirt afterwards. In case you haven't guessed it yet, guns aren't the safest of inventions.

The important thing about a revolver is how the weapon got its name. It has a revolving chamber. This means that once a bullet has been fired, the chamber revolves and the next bullet is lined up with the barrel and ready to go. This is jolly useful if you plan to rob a bank or something and want to fire lots of bullets into the ceiling to make people lie on the floor and be ever so helpful. It's amazing how happy even the most unfriendly bank manager is to open his safe when he has ceiling plaster in his hair.

Fortunately, revolvers are also jolly useful for sheriffs and marshals and people like that. They track down bank robbers and lock them away for a very long time for shooting innocent ceilings who never did anyone any harm in the first place.

Anyway, in Eddie Dickens's day, revolvers were one of the newest of new inventions. Before the revolver came along, most guns were flintlock pistols. They didn't even have proper bullets. You filled the barrel with gunpowder, added small metal pellets called 'shot' and hoped for the best.

One of the problems with a flintlock was that you had to reload it every time you'd fired it. This took about the length of time it took for the person you were firing at to come over to you and hit you over the head with the branch of a tree or whatever else he – or she – could lay his – or her – hands on. An even bigger problem was that a flintlock wasn't very reliable.

If people aren't very reliable, that isn't always the end of the world. They say that they'll meet you outside the cinema at three o'clock, then turn up at half past and the film's already started. It's annoying, but you'll live to see another day. If flintlocks are unreliable, you might not get to the 'living-to-see-another-day' part.

Sometimes, you might pull the trigger of a flintlock and, instead of the gunpowder firing the shot out of the barrel at the enemy, it would decide to blow up instead: BANG. Just like that.

If you were lucky, it would mean that friends would only have to buy you one glove for Christmas instead of a pair. If you were unlucky, it would mean that you'd never have to bother to buy a hat again . . . because you wouldn't have a head to put it on.

So that's why people who liked weapons thought revolvers were such a good idea – the person you were pointing the thing at was usually the one who got hurt if the trigger got pulled . . . which is why Eddie Dickens was feeling very, very nervous.

'I think you owe me an apology, sir,' said the bearded stranger. 'A simple "sorry" will be enough. Is it too much to ask for?'

'S-S-S-Sorry,' said Eddie, and he wasn't just being polite. He truly was sorry – sorry that he'd ever laid eyes on Mad Uncle Jack and Mad Aunt Maud and her stuffed stoat, Malcolm; sorry that he'd ever had to leave home and go on this dreadful journey to Awful End. Who on Earth would call their house Awful End anyway? His great-uncle and great-aunt, that's who. And why didn't that surprise Eddie?

'V-V-Very sorry,' Eddie added.

'It's not you who should be apologising, boy,' said the bearded stranger. 'It is this gentleman, here, who has insulted me.'

Eddie was tempted to ask the man why, if he – Eddie – had done nothing wrong, he was the one having the revolver pointed at him . . . but he thought it best to keep his mouth shut.

'Put that thing away, you big bush,' snarled Mad Aunt Maud, clambering out of the coach with surprising speed.

She snatched the stranger's beard and, to everyone's complete and utter amazement, it came away in her hand. Only Malcolm the stoat's expression remained unchanged, which, if you think about it, is hardly surprising.

The bearded stranger, who wasn't really bearded at all, made a grab to keep his disguise over his face. As he did so, the revolver was no longer pointing at Eddie, but skywards.

Mad Aunt Maud, who obviously wasn't so mad when it came to dealing with would-be highwaymen, grabbed the stuffed stoat by the tail and swung its head against the man's legs.

There was a nasty scrunching noise as the stuffed animal's nose came into contact with the man's knees, followed by a loud wail which Eddie was to remember right up until his sixteenth

44

birthday. (How he came to forget the wail on that particular birthday has to do with a lady hypnotist called the Great Gretcha, and is another story.) The non-bearded bearded stranger pitched forward, dropping both his revolver and false facial hair to the ground.

As the gun hit the solid roadway, the trigger was knocked back and a small flag on a pole shot out of the end of barrel and stayed there. The flag unfurled and on it was one word.

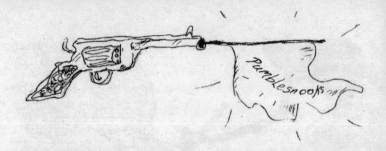

If you thought that the word was BANG then you'd be wrong. That word was PUMBLESNOOKS so you can guess how little the letters had to be for all of them to fit on a flag small enough to fit in the barrel of a gun. But they were big enough for Eddie to read them from where he was standing.

The man with the pretend beard had been threatening them with a *pretend* revolver! Now that the beard was gone and he was rolling around in the mud clutching his knees, Eddie recognised the insulted stranger instantly. He was no stranger at all. He was none other than Mr Pumblesnook, the actor-manager of the band of strolling theatricals.

It soon became apparent to Eddie that his great-uncle and aunt also recognised Mr Pumblesnook, but instead of being outraged, their behaviour amazed Eddie for the zillionth time since he'd left home with them.

'Oh, Mr Pumblesnook, you really are the most remarkable of men,' cackled Mad Aunt Maud, hoisting the mud-covered man to his feet with such force that he almost slammed into the side of the coach.

Uncle Jack, meanwhile, was bending down and retrieving the fake revolver from the road. 'You most certainly had me fooled, sir,' he confessed. 'I was already wondering how we should divide Eddie's belongings between us if you had shot him.' He handed the actor-manager his false beard, which now had a few twigs and a piece of an owl's eggshell in it. 'Where are you headed, Mr Pumblesnook? Might we offer you a lift?'

Eddie was furious. He was fuming with rage. Was he the only one who was outraged at some practical joker having pointed a gun at him? It didn't matter that the gun had turned out to be nothing more than a stage prop, the fear Eddie had felt had been real enough.

'What's this all about?' he demanded. 'Why is Mr Pumblesnook going about in disguise frightening . . . frightening poor, innocent children like me?'

'A *disguise*, my boy?' said Mr Pumblesnook, one eyebrow raised in a most dramatic manner (as far as eyebrows can be dramatic, that is). '*Criminals* wear disguises, my child. *Spies* wear disguises. This is not a disguise, Master Edmund. This is a *costume*. This is me in character.'

'But you're not on the stage now,' Eddie protested, quickly adding a 'sir'.

Now, actors love to quote the lines of a playwright called Shakespeare, not just when they're in the

47

middle of a Shakespeare play on stage, but whenever they get the chance. One of Shakespeare's lines that actors most like to quote is: 'All the world's a stage.' You may not think that it's the most brilliant line in the world – and that you could have come up with it – but Shakespeare came up with it first, and that's the main thing.

Who remembers the name of the second human being to set foot on the moon? Who remembers who came second in last Wednesday's geography test? Who remembers there was even a test? No, Shakespeare was the first one to write these words down and, because they're about acting, these are words actors particularly like to quote.

Think back to Eddie's words just then, and you can imagine how delighted Mr Pumblesnook must have been that he'd just heard them.

For those of you too lazy to look back a page, let me remind you that Eddie said: 'But you're not on the stage now . . . sir.'

No wonder Mr Pumblesnook's eyes lit up. Eddie's comment gave him the perfect opportunity to reply: 'But, in the words of the immortal bard, "All the world's a stage," my dear boy!'

And Eddie was impressed. He had no idea who or what 'the immortal bard' was – he had no way of knowing that it was strolling-theatrical-speak for Shakespeare – but he was impressed by a pertinent quote when he heard one.

'It is important for a great actor to get in character,' Mr Pumblesnook explained. 'It is important to develop a role long before it reaches an audience. Why, when I was preparing for the part of the salmon in *We Little Fishes*, I spent a whole month in the bath and ate nothing but lugworm and ants' eggs.'

He climbed up into the coach and sat next to Mad Aunt Maud, who was back in her original seat. Malcolm was back on her lap, none the worse for wear. 'I remember that time you were preparing to play the part of the kidnapper in *Bound Hand and Foot*,' she said, the admiration sounding in her voice. 'The way you managed to trick the genuine French ambassador down into your cellar and kept him hostage there was a stroke of genius! Such a shame you were arrested before the show could be performed.'

'Theatre's loss,' the actor-manager agreed, shaking his head sadly.

Eddie sat down and closed the door to the coach. He had a terrible sinking feeling. Mr Pumblesnook was obviously a close friend of his great-aunt and uncle . . . and that strongly suggested he was as mad as they were.

Episode 6
Orphanage

In which geese save Rome

Every story is told from a certain point of view. The storyteller – who is me, me, ME in this instance – tells a story in a certain way and sticks to it.

Apart from the occasional trip to Mr and Mrs Dickenses' bathroom, this story has been told from the point of view of staying with poor young Eddie. Wherever *he* goes, *we* go. When he got into the carriage, we went with him. When he spent the night in the stable of The Coaching Inn, we spent the night there too. When he was staring down the barrel of a fake revolver, we didn't run off and leave him there . . .

. . . but let's not be too proud of ourselves for standing our ground. If the revolver had been the genuine article and a bullet had been fired, Eddie would have been the one who was shot and bleeding, not us. I might be able to invent a book that fires a bullet at its readers when they turn to page 46, but imagine the mess it might cause in bookshops or public libraries.

No, the important thing is that nowhere in the story have I said 'meanwhile' and switched the action away from Eddie to somewhere else.

It's perfectly okay to do that in a book. There's nothing wrong with it. There are some really good stories where the author says 'meanwhile' and switches the action to somewhere else . . . but what a good storyteller doesn't do is suddenly change the point of view.

After all this time of not saying 'meanwhile' and switching the action to somewhere else, he doesn't suddenly say 'meanwhile' and switch the action to somewhere else . . .

Meanwhile, back at Eddie's home, his parents were in a state of panic. The reason why the Dickenses were panicking was the small matter of their house being on fire.

Nothing can spoil a late afternoon as much as having flames leaping out of all the upstairs windows, licking at the woodwork. This was a direct result of the latest stage in Dr Muffin's Treatment for their terrible ailment – even hotter hot-water bottles.

The Dickenses were only allowed to get up three times a day. They had to suck special ice cubes and they had to snuggle up in bed with piles of hot-water bottles. When this failed to achieve the desired results, the good doctor decided that their hot-water bottles couldn't have been hot enough.

He solved this by devising a new system especially for them. This system would heat the hot-water bottles while they were actually in the bed with the patients, and Mr and Mrs Dickens were the very first people he tried it out on. As it turned out, they were to be the *only* people he tried the system out on, because he guessed (correctly) that setting fire to those in his care wasn't particularly good for building a bond between any doctor and his patients.

(I say 'his patients' rather than 'his or her patients' because there weren't any women doctors in those days. They weren't allowed. It was something to do with the belief by the Medical Experts With Huge Beards Association that women's hair would somehow get in the way of their stetho-scopes when trying to listen to heartbeats. It was a pretty feeble excuse, but the governing body of the Medical Experts With Huge Beards Association really did have very impressive beards, so no one dared argue with them.)

Anyway, back to Dr Muffin and his hot-water bottle heating system. At his home, the doctor had a special tray on the sideboard of his dining room designed to keep food hot. Under the tray were three liquid paraffin burners with adjustable wicks to make the flames bigger or smaller. He took these burners to the Dickenses' house and put them under a bed.

The idea was that the flames would gently heat the mattress, which in turn would gently heat the hot-water bottles, which would, in turn, gently heat Eddie's parents. That was the idea. Of course, when the doctor did his first 'test run' on the bed in Eddie's room (because he was on his way to Awful End and wouldn't be needing it), Eddie's mattress burst into flames.

Fortunately for the doctor, he was holding a hot-water bottle, from which he whipped the stop-per and poured the contents onto the mattress and extinguished the conflagration (which is a twenty-eight-letter way of saying what 'put the flames out' says in fifteen).

Eddie's parents could smell the burning but couldn't investigate because they'd already been up three times that day – once to have a sword fight with the Thackerys over at The Grange, once to go shark fishing with the Trollope family who were renting a houseboat on a nearby lake, and once to throw an old boot at a cat that was yowling on top of the compost heap – so they knew they must stay in bed. Dr Muffin would be very angry with them if they got up a fourth time, and might refuse to allow them to pay him lots of money to treat them any more.

'Ish evwyfung awlwhy?' called out Mrs Dickens, who on this occasion didn't have a famous-general-shaped ice cube or an onion in her mouth, or both for that matter. The reason why 'Is everything all right?' came out sounding so strange on this occasion was that she had Mr Dickens's ear in her mouth.

Those of you with a squeamish nature, who feel sick if you tear a fingernail or see an ant walking with a slight limp, will be pleased to know that the ear was still attached to the side of Mr Dickens's head (which was exactly where it should be).

It was simply that Mrs Dickens had been sleeping moments before the goose in their bedroom smelled the smoke coming from their son's room and woke them up with its loud honking. Geese

were very popular in the days before battery-powered smoke alarms.

If you think that sounds crazy, go and find a
teacher – or some other kind of know-all – and ask
them the following two questions:

1. Are a flock of geese really supposed to
have raised the alarm and warned the
ancient Romans of an attack on the
Capitoline Hill by the Gauls in 387BC?

2. Did miners really used to take canaries
down the mines to warn them of any gas in
the mine shafts?

The answer to both those questions should be a
resounding 'YES!!!', so the Dickens family goose
smoke alarm wasn't such a crazy idea after all, now
was it? In fact, the very first battery-powered smoke
detector alarm was a bird, though it was a chicken
not a goose. Surely you've heard of battery hens?

So, where was I? Oh, yes: the smoke from Eddie's
burning mattress made the goose honk, which then
woke up Mrs Dickens. She had been dreaming that
she was eating a dried prune, which she discovered,
upon waking, was in fact her husband's ear. She
called out to ask Dr Muffin if everything was all
right and – lying – he assured them it was.

The doctor then refined the method. He realised

that what stopped the flames of the three paraffin burners from burning his food on the sideboard at home was that they heated the metal tray which, in turn, heated the serving dishes which, in turn, heated the food.

So what he did was turf Eddie's parents out of bed and make them sit on one of the thirty-one different types of chair designed to make you sit up straight even if your wrists were handcuffed to your ankles. (There had been thirty-*two* when Eddie left the house, but one had been completely eaten by a hungry woodworm since then. It must have been very hungry indeed, because Eddie had only been gone one night.)

While the Dickenses shared a chair, Dr Muffin rolled back their mattress and placed a number of trays and serving dishes he'd found down in the kitchen on the bed springs. He then rolled the mattress back into place with a satisfying crunch of china. He placed the three paraffin burners on the floor under the bed, made the wicks as big as possible, lit them, then ordered his two yellow-and-crinkly-edged patients back into bed.

'That should keep you good and warm,' he announced. 'You must both stay there until morning,' he said. 'Under no circumstances must you get up unless it is to go to the bathroom. Good day to you.'

56

With that, he left the bedroom, walked past Eddie's room, where the blackened mattress still smouldered, and made his way downstairs and out of the house. Not ten minutes later, the Dickenses' mattress was on fire.

'Perhaps it's supposed to be,' said Mrs Dickens, a trifle concerned.

'Surely not,' said Mr Dickens, the left leg of whose pyjamas had just caught alight.

'What should we do?' asked Mrs Dickens, the pom-pom on the end of her nightcap glowing like a golden Christmas tree bauble.

'Do? Why, nothing,' said Mr Dickens. 'The doctor has forbidden us to get up under any circumstances.' He had been brought up to respect the orders of a medical man.

'Under no circumstances, unless it is to go to the bathroom,' Mrs Dickens reminded her husband.

'Then let's go to the bathroom!' cried Mr Dickens.

'Good idea!' said Mrs Dickens and they both leapt out of bed seconds before all the paper bedclothes went up in a very pretty WHOOOSH of orange flame.

By the time they reached the bathroom – because they thought it would be cheating if they didn't really go there – it was on fire too. So were the stairs, their bedroom, Eddie's bedroom, the roof and just about everything else upstairs.

'Oh dear,' said Mrs Dickens. 'What shall we do?'

They decided to panic, which made perfect sense under the circumstances, because there wasn't a lot else they could do. The goose, meanwhile, had flown out of the window and was honking to her heart's content.

Talking of "meanwhile" – as I was earlier, if you recall – Eddie meanwhile was sitting on the edge of a metal-framed bed in a dank cell of a huge prison-like building called St Horrid's Home for Grateful Orphans.

Words his wise old mother had spoken came back to him. They were something she'd uttered before he'd set off with Mad Uncle Jack: 'Do be careful to make sure that you're not mistaken for a runaway orphan and taken to the orphanage where you will then suffer cruelty, hardship and misery,' she'd said.

And now here Eddie was . . .

What's really annoying is that we don't know how he got here. We were so busy with our meanwhile-back-at-home-with-his-parents that we missed the main action. Perhaps we'll never find out how he ended up in this godforsaken place. Perhaps we'll find out in the next episode.

In the meantime, we must leave Eddie frightened and alone in his cell, while his parents are trapped upstairs in a burning building.

Sometimes life can be really tough.

Episode 7

Escape!

*In which we finally get back
to poor old Eddie*

'Oh dear, Mr Dickens!' cried Mrs Dickens. 'Whatever shall we do now?'

'Do, Mrs Dickens?' said her husband. 'Why, we shall burn to death, of course.'

'Do you think that was Dr Muffin's intention?' asked Mrs Dickens, beating out the row of little orange flames that were licking at the bottom of her nightgown.

'Well, being burnt to a crisp would most certainly cure us of our dreadful illness,' Eddie's father pointed out.

Anyone eavesdropping on this conversation would never have guessed that these were the same two people who, moments before, had been in a terrible state of panic.

Anyone eavesdropping on this conversation would also have been very hot. The reason why Eddie's parents were suddenly so calm was that they were in the bathroom, and the bathroom contained a cabinet which contained a bottle which contained Dr Muffin's Patent Anti-Panic Pills. Mr and Mrs Dickens had both eaten a fistful.

The reason why anyone eavesdropping would also have been very hot was that the bathroom was now a wall of flame.

The Dickenses' alarm goose, meanwhile, had flown to the nearest house – The Grange, owned by the Thackery family – and was busy telling their alarm goose what had happened.

Here follows a rough translation of the conversation between the two birds:

Thackery goose: You smell of smoke, Myrtle.
Dickens goose: Hardly surprising, Agnes. The Dickens residence has gone up in flames.
Thackery goose: Oh dear.
Dickens goose: Yes. Such a shame.

Unfortunately, all the Thackerys' daughter – who

61

was sitting near the geese at the time – heard was:

Thackery goose:	Honk honk honk honk, Honk.
Dickens goose:	Honk honk, Honk. Honk honk honk honk honk honk honk honk.
Thackery goose:	Honk honk.
Dickens goose:	Honk. Honk honk honk.

Even if she had understood every word the two geese had spoken, this still wouldn't have been much use to the poor old Dickenses trapped in their burning home. Charlotte Thackery was less than a year old and, although she made a wide selection of exciting noises from 'goo' to 'ga' with a 'guck' thrown in for good measure, her doting parents couldn't understand a single word she said.

Fortunately for Eddie's parents, however, help was at hand. Those of you who can remember all the way back to page 4 will recall that the cupboard under the stairs of the Dickens household was occupied by Gibbering Jane.

 Gibbering Jane was a chambermaid who had failed the eight-week bed-making course and lived a life of shame in the darkness. She never came out of her understairs hideaway. Food was slipped

under the crack between the floor and the bottom of the door and, if you really want to know how she washed and went to the loo, I'll have to draw you a very detailed and complicated diagram which will cost you a great deal of money.

The only other person in the house – apart from Eddie's parents, of course – was Dawkins, Mr Dickens's gentleman's gentleman, who lived in a basket (with plenty of tissue paper) in the kitchen. He's also been mentioned before, but I can't remember the page he first put in an appearance. I do remember that the Dickenses often didn't remember Dawkins's name and sometimes called him 'Daphne', though.

One of Dawkins's duties was to feed Gibbering Jane. He was just passing through the hallway, making his way towards the cupboard under the stairs, when he noticed that the whole of the upstairs of the house was on fire.

Without a moment's thought for his own personal safety, Dawkins knew exactly what he must do. He dashed back into the kitchen and rescued his tissue paper from his basket.

He snatched the paper up in his arms and ran outside with it, leaving it beside a tree (weighed down with half a brick). Satisfied that this was a job well done, he decided that he'd better go back inside and see if Gibbering Jane or his master and mistress needed any help.

'Help!' cried Mr Dickens from upstairs.

'Help!' cried Mrs Dickens from upstairs.

'Are you talking to me?' Dawkins shouted.

'Oo aw yaw tawkin' taw, Dawkins?' asked Mrs Dickens, who had just stuffed another fistful of Dr Muffin's Patent Anti-Panic Pills into her mouth.

Dawkins was well used to his mistress talking with her mouth full and instantly translated this latest communication to mean: 'Who are you talking to, Dawkins?'

'Why, to both you and the master!' he shouted, then coughed as a cloud of smoke billowed down the stairwell.

'Well, we were indeed calling for help from anyone who might hear us and that most certainly includes you, Daphne,' cried Mr Dickens. 'Unless you can help us sooner rather than later, my wife and I are sure to end up dead before the end of Episode 7.'

'Before the end of what, sir?' shouted the gentleman's gentleman, who had no idea that he was a character in a story.

'Never mind, Dawkins,' yelped Eddie Dickens's mother (who, as you can tell from her voice, had now swallowed her pills). 'Just rescue us, will you.'

Dawkins thought this was an excellent idea, if only he could think how to rescue them. He heard some gibbering at ankle height and looked down to see Gibbering Jane. It wasn't that she was so small that she only came up to his ankles – that would be ridiculous. It's just that – apart from Eddie – she was about the most sensible person we've run in to in this adventure. She knew that hot air (which includes smoke) rises, so the best thing to do if you don't want to suffocate is to lie on the floor with a wet flannel over your face.

Gibbering Jane was lying on the floor, but she didn't have a flannel, so she was using a knitted ladder.

In all the years Jane had been in the cupboard under the Dickenses' stairs, she'd spent at least eleven hours and thirty-six minutes a day knitting. To begin with she'd made all the usual things – scarves, tea cosies, bobble hats – but, over time, she'd become more adventurous, knitting everything from fireplaces to ladders.

Dawkins saw the knitted ladder and, without so much as a 'May I borrow this for a moment?' he snatched it from Gibbering Jane's grasp.

This wasn't the sort of ladder Dawkins could climb up to rescue the Dickenses. It was all floppy and would need to be fixed in position upstairs in the first place . . . but if he could somehow get the knitted ladder up to them, Mr and Mrs Dickens could then tie it to something heavy, throw the other end out of the window and clamber down.

'I have a plan!' Dawkins shouted.

'This is no time to be frying eggs!' cried Mrs Dickens.

'He said "*plan*" not "pan",' said Mr Dickens.

'What plan?' shouted Mrs Dickens, whose eyebrows had just been singed off by a passing fireball.

Unfortunately, Dawkins had misheard his mistress's response to mishearing him. He thought she'd said: 'This is *now* time to be frying eggs,' so – being a very obedient servant who never questioned the Dickenses' instructions – he'd already rushed to the kitchen to prepare them a mouth-watering eggy snack instead of putting his rescue operation into effect.

Gibbering Jane, in the meantime, was gibbering – which should come as no surprise – and also crawling across the hall floor to safety. Parts of the upstairs of the house were now joining the downstairs by the quickest route, which was by falling from a great height in burning chunks.

Unless either Mr or Mrs Dickens could come up with a good plan and put it into operation within the next eight paragraphs, there was no way they'd come out of this alive . . . and that way Eddie would *rightfully* be in the St Horrid's Home for Grateful Orphans rather than because of some dreadful mistake.

It was then that Mrs Dickens had a brainwave. She

usually had one every sixteen years or so, so wasn't due to have one for another three. Luckily for them, though, she had this one early. 'The winch!' she cried.

'The what?'

'Follow me!' Eddie's mum shouted, and dashed back onto the landing, the fire raging all around her. Mr Dickens followed her into the bedroom. There, in the corner, was a coil of sheets. These were the same sheets as had been tied together and used to lower their bed out of the window, when they were waving farewell to dear Eddie and Mad Uncle Jack and Aunt Maud.

The reason why the sheets hadn't burnt to a crisp like almost everything around them was that they were soaking wet. It had been raining hard when Eddie's parents had seen his carriage disappearing into the distance. By the time Dawkins had winched the master and mistress back into the room and given them fresh brown paper sheets, the soaking wet coil of knotted sheets which had been used to hoist them up and down lay forgotten in the corner.

The heat of the fire had almost dried the sheets by now, and there was the hiss of the water turning into steam above them . . . but they were still just too wet to burn.

Mrs Dickens grabbed the sheets and tied one end to the nearest heavy thing that wasn't on fire.

Unfortunately for Mr Dickens, that was him and he had to struggle to free himself. He retied the sheets to the metal frame which was all that remained of their bed. The frame was very hot, and

he burnt his fingers, but there was no time to lose.

Meanwhile, Mrs Dickens had thrown the other end of the knotted sheets out of the window.

'Go!' said her husband, urgently, and she clambered down the outside of the house . . . to safety.

Now it was Eddie's father's turn. He had always been afraid of heights, and even felt a bit dizzy when he stood on tiptoe. Once, when he had stood on a chair to reach a book on a high shelf, he had had to be talked down by a team of passing philosophers, brought in by the fire brigade. One of the few things Mr Dickens was more afraid of than heights, though, was fire – so he was out of that window and climbing down the outside of his house quicker than you could say 'how now brown cow', which I've always thought was a rather strange thing for anybody to want to say anyway.

The result was that both Mr and Mrs Dickens escaped from the fire that had been caused as a direct result of Dr Muffin's Treatment. Unfortunately for Dawkins (sometimes known as Daphne), he wasn't so lucky. After trying to reach his master and mistress with the eggy snack that he'd made as a result of a genuine misunderstanding, he was forced back by the flames and had to retire to the garden. There he discovered that a burning ember must have floated through the air and landed on his tissue paper, setting it alight and reducing it to a very small pile of ashes. He burst into tears at this unhappy sight.

Gibbering Jane was equally unlucky. The results of all her years of knitting for eleven hours and thirty-six minutes each and every day were destroyed – except for the top left-hand corner of an egg cosy, which she was to wear on a string around her neck for the rest of her life.

'We're alive!' said Mrs Dickens.

'Thanks to your plan, my dearest,' said Mr Dickens.

'But no thanks to Dr Muffin!' said Mrs Dickens, beginning to have doubts about the doctor for the very first time since the Treatment had started.

Eddie's father was about to agree with Eddie's mother when he noticed that there was something different about her. At first he thought it must be the black soot that was smeared all over her face, but after he had rubbed it off her with the damp sheet that flapped at the bottom of the 'rope', he realised what it was.

'You're not yellow any more!' he gasped.

Mrs Dickens grabbed the sides of Mr Dickens's head and felt them. 'And you're not crinkly round the edges any more!' she said in amazement.

They then sniffed the air. It smelled of burning house and furniture.

'And we don't smell of old hot-water bottles!' they cried, in unison.

'We're cured!' said Mr Dickens and, taking his wife by the hand, they both danced around in a little circle.

'Dr Muffin is such a genius!' Mrs Dickens pronounced. 'I'm so sorry I doubted him.'

At that moment there was a terrible groan and their home came crashing down into a pile of brick and wood that looked nothing more than a giant bonfire.

'This calls for a celebration!' said Mrs Dickens. 'Just think, now that we're cured, there's no need for Simon to stay at Awful End.'

'You mean Jonathan,' said her husband, when, in fact, they both meant Eddie. You will recall that neither of them was terribly good at remembering their son's name.

'We'll send word to your Mad Uncle Jack to bring him back home!' smiled Mrs Dickens.

Little did she and Mr Dickens know that their dear beloved son had never even reached Awful End but was languishing in St Horrid's Home for Grateful Orphans.

Now, you don't really know what 'languishing' means and I don't really know what 'languishing' means, but it's what people do in prison cells or orphanages in books . . . and this is a book, and

71

poor old Eddie is in an orphanage, so 'languish' he must. That, I'm afraid, is the way of the world.

There was a book in Eddie's cell – sorry, room – in the orphanage. Written on the front in big gold letters were three words 'THE', 'GOOD' and 'BOOK', which, if you put them together, says: 'BOOK GOOD THE'. If you put them together in the correct order, they say 'THE GOOD BOOK', which is what I should have done in the first place.

As it was, this was the book that was going to help Eddie escape, but not until a later episode . . . and not until we find out how he ended up in St Horrid's in the first place.

Episode 8

Get On With It!

In which a chocolate could be
a mouse dropping

Things started to go from bad to worse for Eddie after the actor-manager, Mr Pumblesnook, joined him and Mad Aunt Maud in their carriage – not forgetting Malcolm the stuffed stoat.

Who could forget Malcolm? Not Eddie, that's for sure, because the stoat's snout was stuck in his ear.

'Why are we all squashed together like this?' he demanded, still angry with Mr Pumblesnook for having pretended to be a villain and pointed the revolver at him. 'Couldn't one of us sit on the other seat?'

This seemed a fair enough question, because all three of them (plus stoat) were sitting next to each other along one seat, while the seat opposite was v-a-c-a-n-t, which spells 'empty'.

'I am in charge of seating arrangements and I say this is how we shall sit!' roared Mad Aunt Maud.

'Did you not, in fact, spend a summer at the Young Ladies' School for Seating?' asked Mr Pumblesnook, who in Eddie's opinion was simply trying to keep in her good books.

'You are correct as always, Mr Pumblesnook,' Mad Aunt Maud simpered, and blushed like a young school girl which – with her age and wrinkles – gave her the appearance of an under-ripe prune. 'I did not, in fact, spend a summer at the Young Ladies' School for Seating . . . My knowledge of seating arrangements is instinctive. I was born with the skill!'

'But this is ridiculous!' said Eddie, who now had the misfortune of his great-aunt's elbow in his ribs, as well as the stoat in the ear.

'Quiet, boy!' screamed Mad Aunt Maud. 'When I was a girl, children were seen but not heard!'

'When I was in my early youth . . .' began the actor-manager, who, you will recall, used many words when few would do. '. . . When I was in my early youth, children were neither seen nor heard.'

'Just smelled?' suggested Mad Aunt Maud.

It was obvious to Eddie that Mr Pumblesnook hadn't been about to say 'just smelled', but he was too polite to say so.

'They were neither seen nor heard, just smelled!' Mad Aunt Maud screamed. 'Rubbed down with an onion so they just smelled!'

The mention of an onion reminded Eddie of his own dear mother, who had recently taken to popping whole, peeled onions in her mouth to improve the shape of her head. You guessed it. This was another part of Dr Muffin's Treatment. He sighed.

'Don't be sad, child,' said the actor-manager. 'Let us take advantage of the many miles and hours we share to see whether you have within you the potential to be a thespian!'

Eddie looked at him blankly.

'We've got time on our hands, so let's see if you can act,' Mad Aunt Maud translated. This was the first sensible thing she had done in the brief time he had known her. Eddie was stunned. So was Mad Aunt Maud. She seemed as surprised at saying something sensible as Eddie was.

'Me, act?' said Eddie, a tingling of excitement starting in his feet. Or perhaps it had more to do with wearing itchy socks.

'Indeed, boy, that is precisely what I indicated. Let us endeavour to establish whether you have the gift!' said Mr Pumblesnook. 'As you saw from my performance when hit by this dear lady's watch' – he nodded in the direction of Mad Aunt Maud, his forehead hitting her on the chin because all three were sitting so close together – 'it is vital to remain in character whatever the distraction.'

'Stay in character?' asked Eddie.

'To be the person whose character you are portraying,' explained Mr Pumblesnook.

Eddie still wasn't sure what he meant until Maud explained: 'Once you're pretending to be a character, don't let anyone put you off.'

For the second time in as many minutes, Eddie was stunned. If Mad Aunt Maud kept on being this helpful, they'd have to rename her Only-Mad-Some-of-the-Time Aunt Maud. What had got into her?

'Acting is so much more than pretending to be a character,' stressed the actor-manager, 'but, in essence, once you become that character you must not, as this fair queen just intimated, let anyone "put you off".'

Eddie did his best not to laugh at the idea of anyone calling his great-aunt 'fair queen'.

At that moment, there was a cry of 'Woooah, there!' from Mad Uncle Jack, and the carriage came to a halt. There was a scrambling sound as he clambered from the driving seat, and then his beakiest of beaky noses appeared through the open carriage window.

'A call of nature,' he said.

'I didn't hear anything,' said Mad Aunt Maud. 'What was it? An owl?'

'No, my dear, what I mean is –'

'Did either of you hear an owl?' asked Mad Aunt Maud turning to Eddie first, an action which led to her hitting him in the face with Malcolm's nose, then, turning to Mr Pumblesnook, hitting him with the stuffed stoat's tail.

'No,' said Eddie, nursing a nosebleed.

'Neither a terwit nor a terwoo, madam,' said Mr Pumblesnook, looking for the piece of tooth that had been chipped off into his lap.

'A badger call, then?' asked Mad Aunt Maud. Both Mr Pumblesnook and Eddie tensed just in case she turned to them again, bringing her stoat with her. Who knew what new injuries she might cause?

'No, my dear! By call of nature, I mean that I have to go to the . . . I must . . .' Mad Uncle Jack's face reddened, though it was so thin you wouldn't have thought that there'd have been room for it.

'Not an owl? Not a badger? Surely you don't mean that boring little bird that has a call that's supposed to sound like "a little bit of bread and no cheese"? Surely you didn't stop the carriage for such a commonplace call as that?' his wife protested.

Mad Uncle Jack was about to do some more explaining, when he could wait no longer and dashed off into the undergrowth. He appeared a few minutes later with a look of relief on his face.

77

'Did he find the eagle?' asked Mad Aunt Maud, as her husband climbed back up the side of the coach.

'Eagle?' asked Eddie.

'Children should be neither seen nor heard, just smelled!' she cried in indignation, as though she had just thought of it.

Eddie relaxed a little. There was something strangely reassuring about his great-aunt going back to being completely bananas.

'Eagle aside, young fellow-me-lad,' said Mr Pumblesnook, 'let us commence our experiment.'

There was a flick of the reins, a clomp of hooves and the carriage was in motion once more. It was agreed that Eddie was a fine little gentleman. Don't forget that Eddie's parents had spent good money on turning him into a little gentleman. (They'd tried to spend *bad* money on him, but it'd been sent back.) And, being such a fine little gentleman, might it not be a good idea to start his acting by playing the part of a child so different from himself.

'You don't mean a Foreigner?' said Eddie, shocked, when Mr Pumblesnook suggested this. This was in the days when all Foreigners were treated with a great deal of distrust, whether they were a prince or a pauper or anything else that did or didn't begin with the letter 'p'.

'Indeed not, sir!' said the actor-manager, clearly shocked. 'I would hardly ask you – an untrained

78

actor and merely a child, also – to assume the role of a Foreigner in the presence of a lady in such a confined space!'

'I met a Foreigner once,' said Mad Aunt Maud, a faraway look in her eye. 'I couldn't see him nor hear him, but I could smell him . . . someone had rubbed him down with –'

'An onion?' Eddie suggested.

'Good boy,' nodded Mad Aunt Maud. She tickled him under the chin and slipped a chocolate drop into his mouth. At least, Eddie hoped it was a chocolate drop. It certainly looked like one, but, knowing his great-aunt as he had come to, it could have been a mouse dropping.

Chewing the 'thing' somewhat nervously, Eddie leant forward to get a clearer view of the actor-manager past Mad Aunt Maud. 'If not a Foreigner,' he said, 'what part would you like me to play?'

'That of an orphan boy,' said Mr Pumblesnook.

Those of you with long enough memories, or at least half a brain cell, will see that this really marks the beginning of Eddie's latest troubles.

Episode 9

A Serious Misunderstanding

In which we meet the Empress of All China ...
Well, sort of

'What is the most important thing to remember when playing a character?' boomed Mr Pumblesnook, carefully wrapping a piece of one of his teeth in a handkerchief as he spoke.

The piece had broken off when Mad Aunt Maud had hit him in the face with the swing of her stoat's tail, half a mile or so back.

Eddie, meanwhile, was using his handkerchief for a very different reason – to try to stem the flow of blood pouring from his nose where his great-aunt had hit him with Malcolm's other end (during the selfsame swing). Eddie was beginning to suspect that Mad Aunt Maud could inflict more damage with that single stuffed animal than the average army could with wheelbarrows full of weapons.

'The most important thing to remember when playing a character?' said Eddie, thinking hard. 'To stay in that character, no matter what?'

'Ridiculous!' cackled Mad Aunt Maud, then slouched backwards in the seat of the carriage. She began rummaging in her handbag.

'Excellent!' said Mister Pumblesnook. 'Exactly, my boy. Exactly. There was one time when I was playing the character of a large hazelnut for a production of *Nuts All Around*. The costume was made from genuine hazelnuts, by my own good lady wife.'

'Lazy wife?' asked Aunt Maud, perking up. 'You should poke her with a stick or thrash her to within an inch of her life.' An inch is about two and a half centimetres, but this happened in the old days and, anyway, to thrash someone 'to within two and a half centimetres of their life' doesn't sound so good.

'My *lady* wife,' Mr Pumblesnook explained. 'Now, where was I? Oh, yes. I was playing the character of a large hazelnut when a family of squirrels – which must have been nesting in the roof of the barn we were using as a theatre that night – fell from the hayloft onto our makeshift stage . . .'

Eddie wished that the actor-manager would get to the point, but he knew that there was no point in trying to rush a man who used seven hundred and twenty-three words when eleven would do. (And don't go back and count them. That was just a figure of speech . . . and if you don't know what a figure of speech is, I wouldn't worry too much. I didn't know what a four-wheel drive vehicle was until I was knocked down by one when I was twenty-three years old, and it never did me any harm. Well, it *did*, in fact, harm me when it ran me over, but you know what I mean.)

'Thinking that I was a giant hazelnut, the squirrels proceeded to attack me, and nibbled at my outer shell,' Mr Pumblesnook continued. 'In such a situation a mere mortal would have slid out of the costume and fled the arena, but not I. I am an actor! I am a thespian! I was playing the character of a hazelnut in front of an audience, so a hazelnut I had to remain. It would take more than a marauding gang of tree rats –'

'Pirates?' interrupted Aunt Maud. 'You were attacked by pirates?'

'Not pir-rates, madam,' said Mr Pumblesnook with extreme patience. 'Tree rats . . . squirrels.'

Still dabbing his nose with his bloodstained hanky, Eddie was trying to work out why his great-aunt had suddenly started mishearing things. Why had she suddenly gone a bit deaf? She hadn't had much problem with her hearing for the first leg of their journey, so why now?

'So, the play continued,' Mr Pumblesnook went on. 'I remained in costume and in character, and behaved as a hazelnut would have behaved when under attack from squirrels . . . In character . . . The key to success as an actor, my boy!'

Eddie was about to ask how the average nut behaved when being eaten by squirrels – in a silent, crunchy sort of way, he supposed – when he was distracted by Mad Aunt Maud's actions.

Humming a tune so tuneless that it would probably be illegal to call it a tune in some very strict countries, his great-aunt was trimming her stuffed stoat's nostril hairs with a pair of gold-plated nail scissors. Nothing wrong with that, you might say. There are probably some teachers you can think of who could do with shaving their nose hairs or ear hairs (like Miss Boris, when I was at school) . . . but it was what Mad Aunt Maud was doing

83

with the trimmed hairs that had caught Eddie's attention. She was storing them in her own ears.

All thoughts about nuts had gone out of the window (like his aunt's watch in an earlier episode). No, that's not strictly true. All thoughts of Mr Pumblesnook dressed as a hazelnut had gone out of the window. Eddie was left thinking about another kind of nut: the nut who was sitting there with stuffed-stoat-nostril-hair trimmings in her ears . . . and he was going to have to live with this woman at Awful End until his parents were cured!

He shuddered.

'Are you ready to rise to the challenge, Master Dickens?' asked Mr Pumblesnook. 'Are you prepared to take on the character of an orphan boy and remain in the character – in that acting role – for the rest of this journey? In fact, are you prepared to take on this character and remain in the character until I tell you otherwise?'

'I guess,' said Eddie. It might help take his mind off what lay ahead: life in a strange house with a very strange great-aunt and great-uncle indeed.

'Do you promise to remain in character?' demanded Mr Pumblesnook, leaning across Mad Aunt Maud, who was busy returning the nail scissors to her bag, so – momentarily – letting Malcolm rest on her lap. The actor-manager seized the opportunity of this stuffed-stoat-free moment to look Eddie full in the face, without the fear of a furry sideswipe of tail, nose or paw. 'Do you promise on your family's honour to stay in character ?'

'Yes,' said Eddie Dickens, meeting Mr Pumblesnook's gaze.

'Family honour' was much more of a big deal way back then. In those days, if you punched a bishop or tickled someone collecting money for charity, it wasn't just you who were disgraced, but your whole family.

People would say: 'That's Mrs Harris whose boy ate that statue made out of lamb chops at the art gallery,' and they wouldn't sit next to her at church. Or people would cross the street to avoid walking on the same pavement as any members of the Munroe family, just because Mary Munroe had painted the entire Thompson family bright red while they were sleeping next door. No, family honour was important, so to swear on your family's honour was important too.

And Eddie Dickens had just sworn on the honour of the Dickens family that he would act the character of an orphan and keep acting the character of an orphan until Mr Pumblesnook told him to stop.

Now, Einstein wasn't born when the events in this story occurred, and he's dead now that you're reading this, but it's still worth saying that you don't have to be Einstein to work out what happened. If you've got a good memory, you'll recall that you were first told that Eddie was going to end up in St Horrid's Orphanage for Whatever It's Called as long ago as page 50-something, and this is page 86 . . . so it isn't exactly news. Now, though, we actually come to the moment when events headed in that direction.

Mad Uncle Jack pulled on the horse's reins and ordered: 'Whoa, boy.'

The horse, not used to his master giving sensible instructions, was so surprised that he actually stopped, which was exactly what Mad Uncle Jack had wanted. He had wanted to stop because there was a man with a very tall hat standing in the middle of the road. If Mad Uncle Jack hadn't ordered 'Whoa, boy' and the horse hadn't been surprised enough to stop, the man would probably have been wearing a very squat, crumpled hat by now, and would probably have been somewhat squat and crumpled himself. Mad Uncle Jack had wanted to avoid this because, even in the failing light of early evening, he could tell that this man was a peeler.

Now, you may be forgiven for thinking that a peeler is something you use to take the skin off potatoes, and you'd be right . . . but *this* peeler was a different *kind* of peeler. This peeler was named after a man called Sir Robert Peel and, if you think that this is beginning to sound like a history lesson, then you'd be right again – so I'll keep it short. As well as being famous for being a British prime minister, Robert Peel also founded the first proper police force in Britain, and the policemen were nicknamed 'peelers' after him. If his name had been Sir Robert Bonk, they'd have been nicknamed 'bonkers', so they should think themselves lucky.

So now you can see why Eddie's great-uncle was reluctant to run this man over with his horse and carriage. It was as true then as it is today: policemen get annoyed if you run them over. Especially if you crumple their tall hats.

This peeler's hat – like all peelers' hats – was very tall and thin. It was about as tall as three top hats, one on top of the other. This isn't a very helpful description if you've never seen a top hat. It's a bit like saying to someone that, when your mother sings in the bath, she makes a noise like a Greater Racket-tailed Drongo, when the person you're talking to has never even heard of a Greater Thingummy-Whatsitted Drongo, let alone heard the noise it makes. So, if you've no idea what a top hat looks like, tough luck. This peeler's hat was still the height of three top hats one on top of the other, whether you've seen a top hat or not.

'Good evening, sir,' said the peeler to Mad Uncle Jack. 'Would you be kind enough to step down from your seat?'

He didn't ask to see Mad Uncle Jack's licence and vehicle registration documents, because these hadn't been invented yet – and he didn't ask him to take a breathalyser test, because he wasn't interested in finding out whether Mad Uncle Jack, or his horse, was drunk. This peeler had more important things to do. 'I'm looking for an escaped orphan,' he explained. 'He ran away from St Horrid's Home for Grateful Orphans.'

'Ungrateful swine!' snarled Mad Uncle Jack.

'Exactly what I said,' agreed the peeler. 'I suggested that they change the name to St Horrid's Home for *Un*grateful Orphans, when I heard the news.'

'We must get up a collection to do that at once!' said Mad Uncle Jack, who, once he liked an idea, seized upon it and wanted to act quickly. 'It shouldn't cost too much to change. You simply need to find a local painter to add the letters "U" and "n" in front of the word "grateful" on the sign at the gate . . . I assume there is a sign at the gate?'

'Oh, yes indeed there is, sir,' nodded the peeler.

'Good. I would imagine that a "U" and an "n" would not be too expensive,' mused Eddie's great-uncle. 'I remember having an engraving made on the back of a watch for my beautiful wife some years back, and that only cost a farthing a letter . . . speaking of which, I imagine that St Horrid's has headed notepaper?'

The peeler nodded respectfully. This coach driver was no ordinary coach driver. He was obviously a gentleman.

'So the headed paper will need to be altered from "Grateful" to "Ungrateful", also,' said Mad Uncle Jack. 'No problem there, though. That could be a job for some of the ungrateful orphans themselves. Up at five in the morning, and write a few "Un"s before "grateful"s on the headed notepaper before going up chimneys or down mines or whatever it is the ungrateful little swine have to do for the rest of the day to earn their keep.'

'A splendid solution, sir,' beamed the peeler. After all, it had been his idea to change the name to St Horrid's Home for Ungrateful Orphans, and here was a true gentleman agreeing with him whole-heartedly.

'Let me give you a contribution towards the campaign for such a name change,' said Mad Uncle Jack.

'Well, sir,' said the peeler a little hesitantly. Like all policeman, he had to be very careful about accepting bribes. What one person might see as a genuine contribution towards a legitimate and important cause, an investigating panel might see as a bribe to do – or not to do – something. Then again, the peeler didn't want to upset this fine gentleman by not accepting whatever the amount was he was slipping out of his pocket. Ten shillings? A pound? Five pounds? A dried electric eel.

A dried electric eel?

'I'm sorry I don't have a halibut to give you,' said Mad Uncle Jack, 'but I spent my last one at The Coaching Inn coaching inn.'

The policeman gave him a sideways glance that police officers – men and women – are very good at giving. It's a look which seems to say: 'I don't know what your game is, but I know you're up to something and I intend to find out what it is.' The peeler had never been so insulted in all his life. A dried electric eel? This was the worst bribe he'd ever had. He'd been given half an apple once, but at least he could give that to the police dog back at the station . . . but a dried electric eel? And to think that he'd thought this man was a gentleman!

The peeler's attitude towards Mad Uncle Jack became decidedly chilly. 'I need to search the carriage for the orphan,' he said, dropping the use of the 'sir'. 'Do you have any objections to my doing so?'

'Not at all. Not at all,' beamed Eddie's great-uncle. He had no idea that he had offended the peeler and thought that they were still 'bosom buddies'.

'And who, might I ask, resides within the carriage?' the peeler continued, walking towards one of its doors.

'My wife Maud, the famous actor-manager Mr Pumblesnook and my nephew's son Edmund.'

'I see,' said the peeler. 'And no one else?'

'Just Sally,' said Mad Uncle Jack.

'A maid?' asked the peeler.

'A stuffed stoat,' explained Mad Uncle Jack.

'I see . . .' said the peeler. He looked through the open window in the carriage door to find one side of the carriage completely empty, and three figures and a stuffed stoat squeezed into the other.

He eyed the stuffed animal on Mad Aunt Maud's lap. 'Sally, I presume,' he said.

'Maud,' said Maud.

'I beg your pardon,' said the peeler. 'I was referring to your stoat.'

'His name is Malcolm,' said Mad Aunt Maud.

Eddie noticed the peeler raise an eyebrow, and that simple raised eyebrow seemed to say: 'Here's a group of people who haven't got their story straight. They must be up to something. They must have something to hide.' Of course, what the policeman had no way of knowing was that Mad Uncle Jack was mad, and always called Malcolm 'Sally'. Or maybe it was the other way around? Maybe Mad Aunt Maud was mad, and always called Sally 'Malcolm'. Maybe they were both mad, and the stoat's name wasn't Sally or Malcolm but Cornelius or Edna?

'I see,' said the peeler, slowly. 'And who might you be, sir?'

'I,' said Mr Pumblesnook, puffing his chest out

and looking very grand, 'am the Empress of All China.'

You can probably guess what had happened. While we were following the action outside the carriage with Mad Uncle Jack and the peeler, Eddie, Mr Pumblesnook and Mad Aunt Maud weren't sitting in silence until it was their turn again. Life's not like that. They carried on talking . . . and at the same time that Eddie had agreed on his family's honour to stay in the character of an orphan boy, the actor-manager had agreed to take on the character of the Empress of All China . . . and very good he was at it too.

Just because he was facing an officer of the law, Mr Pumblesnook wasn't about to go back on his word and back to who he really was. He had promised to play the Empress of All China, so the Empress of All China he would be.

He didn't have an audience larger than the peeler, Mad Uncle Jack peering over his shoulder, Mad Aunt Maud and her stoat, and Eddie the Orphan Boy, but they were an audience – and this cramped seat was his stage.

'I am the Empress of All China,' Mr Pumblesnook repeated. It's worth noting that, although China was no nearer or further away in miles then than it is today, it was much further way in time.

Today you can jump on a plane to China, or see

the country and its people on television. Back then, few people had been to China or met a Chinese person. Having said that, the peeler was in no doubt that this man was not the Empress of China. This man was a liar.

'I see,' said the peeler. So far he had been confronted by a coach driver who was trying to make a fool of him by giving him a dried electric eel, a stoat called Sally pretending to be a stoat called Malcolm, a woman claiming to be 'Maud', a grown man pretending to be a Chinese woman . . . which left a boy with blood all over his face, dabbing his nose with a hanky.

The peeler pulled a notebook out of his top pocket, and read what he had written only a few hours before on his visit to St Horrid's:

The Missing Orfan a nasti boy eskaped thur a brokun Winda. There wuz blud on the glass and he musta cut himself.

There was blood on the broken glass . . . and there was blood on the face of this boy, trying to hide himself between two bulky grown-ups.

'And who, may I ask, are you?' the peeler asked Eddie. 'The Czar of Russia? The Queen of Sheba?'

Eddie gulped. 'No, sir,' he said, trying to sound as orphaned as possible. 'I am a poor little orphan boy.'

The peeler leant into the carriage, slid his fingers

94

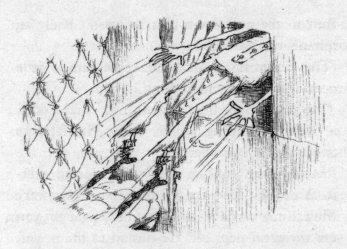

down the back of Eddie's collar and pulled him
out onto the road with one swift yank.

'Gotcha!' said the peeler, with a broad grin.
There's nothing a police officer likes more than
feeling a villain's collar and, in his book, escaped
ungrateful orphans were villains all right. In his
book, villains were probably spelled 'viluns' . . . but
what did spelling matter at a time like this?

'There's a nice warm cell waiting for you at the
police station,' he said. 'Then, after that, you can
go back to a nice cold one at St Horrid's.'

'But that's my great-nephew,' said a puzzled Mad
Uncle Jack, watching the proceedings with interest.

Eddie managed to twist his head around and
look back into the carriage. He looked to Mr
Pumblesnook, hoping beyond hope that he would
say that it was okay to be out of character now – to

95

admit to the policeman that he wasn't really an orphan – but no such luck.

The Empress of All China gave him a little imperial bow, but said nothing.

'I'm just a poor little orphan boy,' said Eddie, the worry sounding in his voice. His family's honour was at stake here.

'My mistake,' said his great-uncle, losing interest. 'You look just like Edmund and you were riding in my carriage, so I obviously thought you were my great-nephew.' He turned to the peeler. 'Feel free to take him away in shackles,' he said.

'But . . . But . . .' Eddie began to protest. Then the Empress of All China gave a stern cough behind him and he remembered his promise.

The peeler wasn't sure what shackles were. He seemed to recall from Sunday school classes that slaves went around in shackles, so he guessed that they must be those skimpy loincloths slaves were forced to wear instead of proper clothes. He thought he might get funny looks taking the escaped orphan back to the home in a skimpy loincloth, so he clapped him in irons instead.

'Come on, lad,' he said. 'Mr Cruel-Streak will be glad to have you back under lock and key.'

Funnily enough, Mr Cruel-Streak didn't sound like a very nice man to Eddie. And how right he was.

Oh Dear! Oh Dear! Oh Dear!

In which Eddie wants out

Eddie hated the cell in the police station, until he was taken out of the cell, popped into a cosy brown sack and ended up in his room at the orphanage. The room at the orphanage was more like a cell than the cell was. There most certainly wasn't enough room to swing a cat, not that any cats in their right minds would have gone into the room in the first place. They'd have been too afraid of the rat.

Notice that I said 'rat', singular. Not 'rats' as in 'lots'. Just the one . . . and Eddie was sharing his room with it. If it had been a cartoon rat, it would have been wearing an eyepatch and would have had a great big tattoo on its arm. It might even have been chewing a match in the corner of its mouth. Because it was a real rat, it was just enormous and very frightening.

It's true to say that, like wolves, rats have a bad press. Whenever three little pigs' houses are blown down, or a plague spreads across Europe killing millions of people, either wolves or rats get the blame. Rats are, given the chance, probably very nice, clean, friendly, lovable creatures who smell gorgeous and would give half their money to charity if they earned enough. This particular rat, however, was none of the above. This rat was the sort of rat who lived up to the motto of St Horrid's Home for Grateful Orphans.

Now, this would be a good time to tell you what that motto was. It would also be a good time to tell you who St Horrid was. Saints are, on the whole, good people. That's how they came to be saints in the first place.

There was one chap, called Kevin, who became a saint for sticking his hand out of a window. Well, there's more to it than that. He stuck his hand out of the window – probably to wave to a friend or to see if it was raining – and a bird landed on it and, thinking it was her nest, laid her eggs on it. All I can say is that he must have had a very hairy hand, or the bird was very short-sighted.

Anyway, the bird thought his hand was a nest, and sat patiently on her eggs, waiting for them to hatch. The man waited too. Rather than moving his hand he just stood there . . . He stood there until the eggs had hatched and the chicks had grown big enough to fly away. Then, and only then, did our man move.

You can bet your life that the first thing he must have done is rush to the toilet. He must have been there for weeks – with his hand out of the window, I mean, not sitting on the loo. You can be equally sure that he must have had terrible arm-ache. Think how tiring it is when you put your hand up to answer a question, and forget to put it down again (because there's something far more interesting going on just outside the classroom window). Well, he was made a saint.

Another good way of becoming a saint was by having terrible things done to you, but remaining true to your beliefs. Well, someone called St Horrid doesn't sound the kind of person who would be kind to anyone or be very saintly at all really . . . which is terribly unfair.

You see, over time, names change and mistakes get made. There was once a ship called the *Mary Celeste* which was found drifting at sea with no crew on board. It was all very weird and wonderful, and people still talk about it and write books about it to this day – except that nine times out of ten they call it the *Marie Celeste* (with an 'i' and an 'e') instead of a 'y' at the end. Even important reference books, and books written by very brainy people with huge dome-shaped foreheads and thick-lensed glasses call it the *Marie Celeste*, but they're wrong. It's easy enough to find the right name if you go far enough back in the records, but once the mistake was made, it was copied and copied and copied until the untruth became the truth.

The same applied to St Horrid. St Horrid's real name was St Florid, and even that's not strictly true. His real name was Hank, but when he became a saint, he was named St Hank the Florid, and this was shortened to St Florid. Florid isn't short for Florida, because no one had discovered North America yet, except the native North Americans, who were living there quite happily without Disney World or Burger King. No, the word 'florid' means 'having a red complexion' and, in even earlier times, it meant 'flowery'.

In Hank the Florid's case, both meanings applied. Hank was a young lad in the days when kings still had silly names such as 'Ethelred the Smelly' or 'Edward the Nutjob', and he was the son of a woodcutter. (His mother was the woodcutter.

The history books don't tell us what his father did.) If you were the son of a woodcutter way back then, you had two choices in life. You either grew up to be a woodcutter, or you died young.

There were a variety of different reasons for why you might die. Your lord and master might kill you for treading on his favourite patch of grass . . . or you might be sent to fight against some nasty foreign folk (who were probably really a lot nicer than your own lord and master, but you'd no way of knowing) . . . or you might die of some really unimportant ailment, such as a nasty cough, because there were no proper doctors or medicine.

But Hank didn't die young and he didn't become a woodcutter either. He became a saint. The lives of saints are always rather hazy because they were written down a long time after the events are supposed to have happened, but the story of how Hank became a saint is well recorded.

One day, Hank was out in the fields watering the goat – not that goats need watering, but the history books are very clear on this point so I thought I should mention it – and thinking about beards. Perhaps he was thinking about beards because goats have beards. Perhaps it was because far more people had beards back then, because no one had invented a decent razor blade yet (or, if they had, they hadn't told anyone else about it). Whatever the reason, Hank was thinking about beards, when he stooped to pluck a single flower from the grass.

He was putting the flower to his nose and giving it a jolly good sniff at exactly the same moment as a queen bee came in to land on it. The queen bee was out scouting for a new home and, if you know anything about queen bees, you'll know that where she goes, all the other bees follow. So, before Hank knew what was happening, a huge swarm of thousands of bees came and landed on his chin and set up home there . . . From a distance, it looked like an enormous beard.

Just then, a huge enemy army came over the hill, and its leader – some books call him 'Simon the Fairly Nasty', and others 'Simon the Not So Nice' – came galloping down towards Hank. The army had only recently landed, and Hank was the first person they had set eyes on from this country. When Simon the Whatever His Name Was saw this man with a huge, buzzing beard that seemed to change shape before his eyes, he turned and fled, taking his army with him.

He's supposed to have said something clever like: 'If the ordinary peasant in the field has such a magical and menacing beard, think how mighty his king must be!' What he probably really said was: 'Yikes! I'm getting out of here!'

Whatever he said, Simon and the enemy army were in such a hurry to leave that they all piled into one ship, instead of the five they'd arrived in, and sank to the bottom of the sea.

Four bees – again, the history books are very clear about this – stung Hank, then the whole swarm moved on (which doesn't usually happen once they've settled), leaving him with a red face and a crumpled flower in his hand . . . which is how he became St Hank the Florid. The saint part came about because he'd saved his country from an enemy in a mysterious fashion, and there were mutterings about 'miracles'. A passing monk had witnessed the whole affair.

Hank spent the rest of his life living in a very comfortable cave called a hermitage, selling pots of honey to passing tourists. All was fine until about 300 years later, when someone wrote down his name as St Hank the Horrid instead of Hank the Florid, and the name stuck. He became known as St Horrid. So people who were nasty and horrid themselves adopted him as their saint, and that must have been how St Horrid's Home for Grateful Orphans got its name.

The motto of the home was 'Work Hard. Get Very Dirty. Be Very Unhappy' and, from what Eddie could see of his room and the rat, it certainly lived up to it. Apart from the rat and his bed – and himself, of course – the only thing in the room was, if you can remember that far back, a large book with 'THE GOOD BOOK' written on the front in faded gold letters.

In Eddie's day, 'The Good Book' was the name that many people gave to the Bible, so that's what he expected it to be. But, when he opened the book, he found that it was full of pictures of . . . Go on. Have a guess. You'll never guess.

It was full of pictures of food. There were big, colourful illustrations of cakes and trifles and fruit salads and pies and every other mouth-wateringly slurpsious things you can think of.

Just looking at it made Eddie feel hungry, and he'd only been in the orphanage a few hours. He wondered how the other poor kids felt – the real orphans – if they had copies of the same book in their rooms. It was like torture, looking at all these good things (lots of them sprinkled with chocolate or with cherries on top), knowing that all you'd get to eat was porridge made from old wallpaper paste, or soup made up from boiling the remains of old leather shoes. (Eddie had been tipped out of his sack and dragged through the kitchens on the way to his room, so he knew what to expect.)

There were teeth marks on some of the pictures and, in a few instances, whole pictures appeared to have been eaten. Eddie imagined the previous occupant being so hungry that he'd been forced to scoff pictures of puddings rather than the real thing. The previous occupant was, of course, the genuinely escaped orphan for whom Eddie had been mistaken.

Because the bag Eddie had been delivered to the orphanage in was so dirty – it must have had coal in it before him – once he was tipped out of it, Eddie would have found it hard to recognise his own reflection. None of the staff seemed to notice he was the wrong boy, and he couldn't rely on his mad great-aunt and great-uncle to get him out of there. What should he do?

Eddie was just beginning to think that there was no hope, when he heard the scrape of a key in the lock and the door swung open. The biggest woman Eddie had ever seen in his life filled the doorway.

He looked up at her.

'Well?' she demanded, anger blazing in her cruel red eyes.

'Not very,' said Eddie. 'You see, there has been some terrible mistake . . .'

The woman hit him over the head with an enormous wooden spoon.

'WELL?' she repeated, but in capital letters this time.

'Ouch! My name is Eddie Dickens. There has been some terrible mistake,' Eddie blurted out, rubbing the lump that was already forming under his hair.

'You know that you are supposed to say "Good morning, good afternoon or good evening, Mrs Cruel-Streak," every time you have the pleasure of my company,' said the woman. She was trying to speak as though she was the Queen of England, but she sounded more like how Eddie imagined the rat would talk, if rats could talk.

'Good morning, good afternoon or good evening, Mrs Cruel-Streak,' said Eddie. 'My name is Eddie Dick –'

Eddie couldn't continue because he found he had an enormous hand around his throat and he was being lifted so high in the air that the bump on his head brushed against the filthy ceiling.

'Where's ya manners, boy?' snarled Mrs Cruel-Streak, dropping all pretence of being queen of anywhere except this terrible place. 'Thought you could run away, did you? Thought you'd get away with it?'

Eddie would have liked to explain that he hadn't run away from anywhere, but all he could say was 'ffrbwllfggghh', which reminded him of his dear mother, who was forever stuffing onions into her mouth, or sucking ice cubes shaped like famous generals. Tears poured down his cheeks.

Obviously delighted that she'd made the boy cry, and satisfied at a job well done, Mrs Cruel-Streak released her grip around Eddie's neck, and he fell back down to earth with a bump.

She then bent down to give the rat a friendly scratch between the ears, in the same way as you or I might pause to stroke a cat. This was a bad move on her part, because Eddie wasn't like the other boys and girls in the St Horrid's Home for Grateful Orphans. He wasn't weak from years of bad food, hard work and no hope. Anyone who could survive a coach journey with Mad Aunt Maud and a stuffed stoat wasn't going to let this bully ruin his life.

Without a moment's hesitation, he snatched up THE GOOD BOOK in both hands, raised it high above him and then brought it crashing down on Mrs Cruel-Streak's head. A look of complete and utter amazement passed across the enormous woman's face, before she slumped unconscious to the floor – and on top of the startled rat.

Eddie decided that it was best not to hang about. He closed the door to his room – let's be honest, it was a cell really, wasn't it? – behind him and turned the key in the lock. The key was on a large iron ring, and hanging from that ring were dozens of other keys. With these keys he should be able to unlock most, if not all, of the rooms in St Horrid's. He could go anywhere. He could free anyone. Yes. That's what he would do. He'd free the other orphans. He'd organise a mass breakout!

108

Episode 11

The Final Instalment

*In which we rather hope it's
all's well that ends well*

Less than an hour had passed since Eddie had fled his cell, leaving Mrs Cruel-Streak locked up inside it, but the change which had come over the orphanage was incredible.

St Horrid's was usually such a gloomy place that it would have been more fun to spend an evening in a coffin with the lid Sellotaped shut, or to gnaw through your own leg, lightly sprinkled with salt and pepper . . . but not any more!

There were laughter, whoops of joy and shouting as over a hundred very grubby-looking kids – who wouldn't have looked out of place in bags of coal, up chimneys or dressed as blackboards at a fancy dress party – were freed from their cells and were now charging all over the place.

Girls and boys who had spent their whole lives 'being grateful', working hard and having a generally rotten time, were now finding out what fun was for the first time. Not that any of them would have recognised the word 'fun' if they'd tripped over it. Reading and writing were actively discouraged at the orphanage. They were thought to be a bad influence.

What use were reading and writing to orphans? All they needed to learn was how to behave, respect their elders and betters, and live on as little food as possible.

In fact, one of the first places the escaped children rushed to was the kitchens, but not to eat. There was nothing you and I would really think of as being proper food in there anyway. No, they poured into the kitchen like a swarm of ants down a crack between paving stones, to give Cook a message.

Cook was a very large man with more warts on him than a toad . . . and the message the orphans gave him was a very simple one. They picked him up as if he weighed little more than a rag doll – there were lots of them, remember – turned him upside down and plunged him head first into a huge vat of bubbling gruel.

110

You may be sorry to hear that he survived this ordeal and, amazingly, the hot gruel actually cured him of his warts. But Cook didn't know either of these things would happen at the time. All he knew was that the horrible little children who were supposed to be locked in their cells – sorry, rooms – were on the rampage, and that he was now stuck in a cauldron. He was very frightened, and wished that they'd go away. And go away they did.

The army of orphans sensed that victory was in their grasp, but their army needed to arm itself. The obvious weapons were the famous St Horrid's Home for Grateful Orphans cucumbers. These were no ordinary cucumbers. The worst things you can really say about an ordinary cucumber are that it doesn't really taste of much, that it can make your sandwiches go soggy, and that slices can sometimes get stuck to the roof of your mouth.

Not the St Horrid's cucumber. That was a totally different animal . . . which is just a saying, like when some people say that something is a 'totally different kettle of fish'. They don't really mean that the thing is actually a kettle of fish, and I don't mean that the St Horrid's cucumber is actually an animal. When I say that it was a totally different animal, I mean that it was a totally different *vegetable*. Is that clear? Good.

These particular vegetables were grown in the poor, stony soil of the St Horrid's vegetable patch and they were very hard. In fact, they were very difficult to cut. In fact, they were almost rock-solid unless you plunged them into water, brought them to the boil and simmered them for about forty-seven minutes, stirring occasionally.

But the grubby army of escaped orphans wasn't interested in plunging them into water, bringing them to the boil and simmering them for about

112

forty-seven minutes, stirring occasionally. They were glad that these cucumbers were rock-hard, because they made very good clubs – rather like the truncheons carried by police officers, who, you may remember, were called peelers back in the days of Eddie Dickens.

Speaking of Eddie Dickens, what was he up to right there and then? Wielding a cucumber? Stuffing an upturned cook into a cauldron of his own gruel? No, Eddie was working on the next stage of his plan.

It was one thing to get the Grateful Orphans out of their rooms, but he had to try to help them escape from the orphanage altogether. It was all fine and dandy that they should want to get their own back on all the people who had been so horrible to them over the years, but Eddie was thinking beyond that. He had to get them away from this nasty, nasty place and hide them somewhere where they wouldn't be found and brought back.

This is why Eddie was now out in a yard with high brick walls on three sides and a huge locked gate on the fourth. The gate wouldn't be a problem because Eddie felt sure that one of the keys in the bunch in his hand would open it. He was more interested by what was in the yard. It was an enormous float.

I don't mean one of those things that people take into a swimming pool with them when they're learning to swim, or one of those things that bobs around in the top of a milk shake. I mean a carnival float – a large cart that had been decorated to use in a carnival procession. This float had been made to look like a giant cow.

Now, I wouldn't be surprised if the more sensible ones amongst you are wondering what a carnival float designed to look like a giant cow was doing in the locked courtyard of an orphanage. It's certainly the sort of question that would cross my mind if I was reading this story and not writing it. Well, I'll tell you.

The whole idea of the orphanage was to make money for Mr and Mrs Cruel-Streak, but Mr and Mrs Cruel-Streak couldn't really admit that, could they? They had to pretend that the whole idea of the orphanage was to care for the orphans. Now, there was a fairly popular belief at the time that strict rules, hard work and not too many baths were good for orphans, but people would have been horrified to learn that the Cruel-Streaks didn't really care what was good for the children and what wasn't.

St Horrid's Home for Grateful Orphans was paid for by public donations. This meant that people who felt sorry for orphans, or wanted to be seen to care about orphans, paid the Cruel-Streaks to look after them. What actually happened was that Mr and Mrs Cruel-Streak spent nearly all of this money on their own daughter, Angel, or on themselves. The orphans got next to nothing . . . but the public didn't know that.

When you rely on public donations, you have to have fund-raising events, and that's where the carnival float shaped like a giant cow comes in. For hundreds of years, the countryside had been seen as a rather nasty place, full of wolves and highwaymen and people trying to sell you life insurance for your sheep. People much preferred to live in the conurbations (which is a big word for towns and cities).

Recently, however, there had been a movement which said that the country air was good for you and that something equally good to come out of the country was milk. So the Cruel-Streaks had their slaves – the orphans, that is – build them a carnival float that was designed to make people imagine that St Horrid's was a lovely place somewhere in the country, where the lucky little kiddies got plenty of fresh air and milk. Just the sort of orphanage you'd want to give money to, in fact! The float was to be used in money-raising events across the region.

Less than twenty-three-and-a-half minutes after Eddie had first laid eyes on this giant cow on wheels, and discovered that it was hollow, he had rounded up all the orphans and they were piling inside it.

Some of the children were sorry to leave, particularly those whom Eddie had found in Mr Cruel-Streak's office, forcing the poor man to eat blotting paper. They left him tied to his own desk with a cord from his expensive velvet curtains, and with a large paperweight stuffed in his mouth – like a baked apple in a boar's head at a medieval banquet. He wouldn't be able to cry out for help in a hurry.

Now that all of the children were hidden inside the giant hollow cow, Eddie was frantically hitching the float up to a carthorse he'd found in a stable. The horse had obviously been far better loved and treated than the orphans. It certainly had better food. In its stable were a starter, main course and three choices of pudding, along with a selection of fine wines.

Finally Eddie was ready. He had to try several

keys in the huge padlock on the gate before he found the right one. It was dark outside by then, but there was still enough of a moon in the sky to see by. Flinging the gate wide, Eddie jumped onto the back of the horse. The giant cow on wheels clattered across the courtyard and out into freedom and the night.

The next morning, when Eddie's great-aunt, Mad Aunt Maud, awoke, she was confused. For some reason or other, she and her husband, Mad Uncle Jack, had spent the night sleeping in their carriage, rather than in some local hostelry, but – no matter how hard she tried – she couldn't remember why.

She had some vague recollection that it had something to do with the Empress of All China, or the actor-manager Mr Pumblesnook and, come to think of it, weren't they one and the same? Hadn't Mr Pumblesnook been pretending to be the Empress, and Eddie pretending to be an orphan?

Eddie? Now, what had happened to that nice young boy? That was it! It had turned out that he wasn't their great-nephew at all, but was really an escaped orphan. He'd been taken away by a peeler, that was it. It was all too confusing.

Mad Aunt Maud's head was in a spin at the best of times, but that morning it was in a whirl. Where was Malcolm? What had happened to Malcolm?

She frantically looked around the inside of the carriage in the early morning light. Her eyes fell on her stuffed stoat and her pulse returned to normal. There he was. Safe and well.

'Good morning, Malcolm!' she said, with obvious relief.

'My name is Jack,' Mad Uncle Jack reminded her, coming out of a light sleep.

'I was talking to my stoat, husband,' Mad Aunt Maud explained, the trimmed stoat hairs having fallen from her ears in the night and restored her hearing. What with her head in a whirl and having slept in an upright position, she had terrible neck-ache. It felt as if someone had stuck a hatpin in the side of her neck.

'But I thought your stoat was called Sally,' he protested. 'I've always called her Sally. Sally Stoat.'

'It is a he and not a she, and his name is Malcolm,' Maud pronounced.

'You never cease to amaze me, O wife of mine,' said Mad Uncle Jack with pride. Pulling a hatpin from the side of her neck, he kissed the spot where it had been.

The pain went almost instantly. 'How did that get in there?' she asked.

'You were snoring in the night and the Empress of All China stabbed you with it,' Mad Uncle Jack explained. 'These Chinese are full of all the

118

mysteries of the Orient. She called it acupuncture.'

'Did it work?' asked Maud with interest.

'After you stopped screaming and we stemmed the flow of blood,' said Uncle Jack. 'I'm surprised you don't remember it.'

'I must admit I'm feeling a little groggy this morning,' said Mad Aunt Maud. 'There's a lot I don't recall. Where is the Empress now?'

Jack looked down to the floor of the carriage and pointed. Mr Pumblesnook was asleep at their feet.

'Another Chinese custom?' asked Aunt Maud.

'More a lack of space,' said her husband. 'Now, if you will excuse me, I must get some air.' With that, he stepped over the sleeping figure of the actor-manager, opened the door and climbed down onto the rutted track . . . and can you guess who or what he came face-to-face with?

No marks for those of you who said 'a giant hollow cow on wheels'. He came face-to-face with Eddie's mother and father, Mr and Mrs Dickens. Their clothes look singed and their faces slightly sooty, but that wasn't what Uncle Jack noticed first and foremost.

'You're not yellow any more!' he said, in obvious wonderment.

'No,' smiled Mr Dickens.

'You're not a bit crinkly round the edges,' said Mad Uncle Jack, stunned.

He stopped and sniffed the crisp morning air with his beak-like nose. 'And you don't smell of old hot-water bottles!' he gasped.

'NO!!' said Mr and Mrs Dickens as one, with big happy grins on their faces. 'Dr Muffin is a genius! He cured us. All it took was burning down our home and everything in it. The combination of chemicals in all that smoke we breathed in was just what we needed. We're fine now.'

'Splendid . . . Splendid,' said Mad Uncle Jack, smoothing down his hair, which was sticking up all over the place after a night spent in the carriage. 'But what brings you here?'

'We're here to collect Eddie,' said Eddie's father. 'We expected you to have reached Awful End by now, but, as luck would have it, we've caught up with you already.'

'Eddie?' frowned Mad Uncle Jack, as though he was trying to remember where he'd misplaced a pair of spectacles or a rather unimportant piece of cheese.

'Our son?' said Mrs Dickens, cautiously, without so much as a famous-general-shaped ice cube or an onion in her mouth to muffle her speech. 'Now that we're cured, there's no need for you to look after him any more.'

'Precisely,' agreed Mr Dickens.

'Ah! I see,' said Mad Uncle Jack. 'The problem is that you were mistaken. The boy you gave over

120

to our care was not your son Edmund at all but an escaped orphan. He admitted it himself. I remember it quite clearly now.'

'Not Jonathan?' said Eddie's mother in amazement. 'I'm sure I'd know if he was my own son or not.'

'How unfortunate,' said Mad Uncle Jack.

At that moment Mr Pumblesnook rolled out of the open door of the carriage, landed with a 'splat' in the mud and woke up with a theatrical roar. 'WHO DARES TO KICK ME FROM MY OWN BED?' he demanded, in capital letters, in the same voice as he'd used to such great effect on the stage when playing Dr Pompous in the popular play *Royal Rumpus*. Then he leapt to his feet.

Eddie's mother and father had never met Mr Pumblesnook before, so were quite intimidated by this big hulk of a man with a barrel chest and booming voice.

'This is the Empress of All China and these are Edmund's parents,' said Uncle Jack, making the introductions. 'It seems that Edmund really was Edmund after all,' he told the theatrical. 'A most unfortunate mishap.'

'My name is Pumblesnook,' Pumblesnook explained. 'I have merely been in the character of the Empress this past day or so. It is indeed an honour to meet the parents of Master Edmund, a boy with obvious –'

'Forgive me for interrupting,' Mrs Dickens interrupted, 'but where is our boy now?'

'In some orphanage somewhere,' said Mad Uncle Jack. 'St Morbid's? St Solid's? St Poorly? I'm afraid I don't recall . . . I wouldn't worry. You can always get a new one.'

'A new one?' said Mr Dickens, puzzled.

'Another boy,' said Mad Uncle Jack.

'Oh,' Eddie's father nodded.

'What brings you to this neck of the woods, sire, madam?' asked Mr Pumblesnook, wiping the mud splatters from his jacket with the kerchief that had so impressed Eddie when he'd first laid eyes on the actor-manager in the stable of The Coaching Inn coaching inn.

'We sent Edmund to stay with my dear husband's

aunt and uncle because we were ill and didn't want him to catch whatever the disease was we had,' began Mrs Dickens.

'But now we are cured, there is no need for him to stay away from us, so we're here to take him home,' said Mr Dickens, taking up the story. 'We caught the train, and planned to walk the last mile or so to Awful End, which is how we came to catch up with the carriage so quickly.'

Mr Pumblesnook wiped away the last of the mud with a dramatic flourish, shook his kerchief and returned it to his breast pocket, where it sprouted from the top like some exotic flower. 'How were you cured?' he asked with interest.

'Our good doctor, the notorious Dr Muffin, burnt our house down with us inside it,' said Eddie's mother, the pride sounding in her voice. 'We don't know whether it was the fear of being burnt to a crisp or the effects of the woodsmoke but, either way, he cured us.'

'A truly remarkable tale!' boomed Mr Pumblesnook, obviously impressed. 'But I do have one question.'

'Yes?' said the Dickenses.

'You say that there's no need for young Master Edmund to stay at Awful End now?'

'Yes,' nodded the Dickenses.

'That he can come home with you after all?'

The Dickenses nodded again.

'But did you not most recently inform me that your house was, in your own words, if my recollection serves me correctly . . . was . . . burnt to the ground?' inquired the wandering theatrical.

Mr Dickens looked at Mrs Dickens. Mrs Dickens looked at Mr Dickens.

'By Jove!' he wailed. 'We hadn't thought of that!'

Eddie's mother let out a plaintive wail and crumpled to the ground. Her husband found that the easiest way to calm her was to fill her mouth with acorns. It reminded her of some of Dr Muffin's earlier attempts at remedy, and it strangely comforted her.

Mad Aunt Maud, meanwhile, was the last to emerge from the carriage. With Malcolm tucked firmly under one arm, the hatpin protruding from the stuffed stoat's nose, she walked around to the front of the vehicle.

Suddenly she recalled why they'd had to spend the night sleeping in the carriage, rather than being driven the last few miles home. They had no horse. It wasn't that Mad Uncle Jack had left the horse in a bathroom, or anything like that, this time. Early on the previous evening the horse had bolted, run away, legged it – call it what you will. Luckily for Mad Uncle Jack on top and the occupants within, the horse hadn't bolted with the

124

carriage still attached. It had somehow broken free and, before Uncle Jack had had time to catch the startled creature, it had run – in the words of a popular little ditty – over the hills and far away.

Note that I described the horse as having been a startled creature. Startled by what? By the Dickenses' faithful servants Gibbering Jane and Dawkins? Admittedly, they did look quite a sight. They'd travelled on the train with Eddie's parents, but, because they were servants, they'd travelled on the outside and were still covered with bits of gorse bush and splinters of telegraph pole that they'd rubbed up against as the train had gone hurtling along. But no, they'd only appeared on the scene the next morning. I'm talking about what startled Mad Uncle Jack's horse the night before.

Mad Aunt Maud knew what it was. She was staring at the culprit right there and then.

Just over a hedge in a field by the road was the largest cow she had ever seen in her life. The moment she laid eyes on it, she fell in love. It was like the first time she had ever seen Malcolm, in a shop filled with second-hand stuffed animals.

Ignoring all else around her, Mad Aunt Maud stumbled across the muddy road and up to the hedge. On tiptoe she could just reach the carnival float cow's black muzzle. She gave it a friendly pat.

'Hello,' she said. 'I shall call you Marjorie.' She followed the hedge until she reached a gate, then entered the field.

To say that Eddie's parents were surprised when Mad Aunt Maud emerged at the side of the carriage some ten minutes later, followed by Eddie and a crowd of some of the grubbiest children any of them had ever seen, would be an understatement.

Mrs Dickens rushed forward and threw her arms around her son. 'Wurdijucfrm?' she asked, her mouth still crammed with acorns. It was just like old times. I think she was saying: 'Where did you come from?'

Mad Aunt Maud looked far from happy. 'I caught them all climbing out of a cow's bottom,' she explained, a stern look on her face. 'Disgraceful behaviour, if you ask me. Poor Marjorie standing in that field, minding her own business . . . the

126

last thing she needs is a gang of children climbing out of her bottom . . .'

But no one – and I include Eddie – was listening. He was so excited to see that his parents were cured and to hear the news about the destruction of his home. Mr Pumblesnook was delighted by the arrival of the hundred-or-so orphans.

'Young blood!' he said. 'That's what my strolling band of theatricals needs. Young blood! You, children, are my future. Think of all the plays I will be able to perform now with you in the crowd scenes! The audience will love it! Think of the drama of the murder in *Julius Caesar*!'

The children, who had all had a good night's sleep in the giant cow – and hadn't even woken up when Uncle Jack's horse had spotted the monster and made a bid for freedom – were feeling excited and refreshed. They'd no idea what Mr Pumblesnook was on about, because they had no idea that he was an actor-manager, but at the mention of murder they all brandished their St Horrid's Home for Grateful Orphans cucumbers in the air, then brought them down on Mr Pumblesnook in a rain of blows.

'Excellent!' he cried, fending off his attackers with glee. 'You have such spirit!'

And that, gentle readers, is really an end to it and, though this story is called *Awful End*, it was not an awful one for the Dickens family. With their own home gone, Mr and Mrs Dickens and Eddie moved in to Awful End, the idea being that it would be a temporary measure until their own home was rebuilt. As it happened, their family still lives there today.

The escaped orphans did, indeed, join Mr Pumblesnook's band of strolling theatricals and, although they had to put up with Mrs Pumblesnook's irritating way of speaking, and the fact that she still picked the blotches off her face and kept them in the pocket of her dress, it was a good life. Because a big part of being a strolling theatrical is the *strolling* – they were always on the move. The peelers never caught up with them. One or two of the orphans grew up to be very good actors and, if you're ridiculously old, you might even be familiar with some of their names.

Mad Uncle Jack soon tired of sharing his house with Eddie and his parents, so built himself a treehouse in the garden. He made it from the dried fish that he hadn't used to pay his hotel bills. To begin with, he had trouble from the neighbourhood cats, but soon discovered that, once the fish were painted with creosote – which is designed to stop fences from rotting – the smell went and the cats lost interest.

Mad Aunt Maud lived in the garden of Awful

End too or, to be more accurate, she lived inside Marjorie in the garden of her former home. With Malcolm the stuffed stoat, of course. When she died at the ripe old age of 126, she was buried inside Marjorie under the rose bed. There she remained for over eighty-two years, until she was dug up to make room for a swimming pool.

And what of Eddie, the hero of this tale? Well, his adventures weren't quite over yet. History had more in store for Edmund Dickens, saviour of the orphans of St Horrid's. But that, as all the best writers say, is another story.

THE END
for now

The Philip Ardagh Club

COLLECT some fantastic **Philip Ardagh** merchandise.

WHAT YOU HAVE TO DO:
You'll find tokens to collect in all Philip Ardagh's fiction books published after 08/10/02. There are 2 tokens in each hardback and 1 token in each paperback. Cut them out and send them to us complete with the form (below) and you'll get these great gifts:

> **2 tokens** = a sheet of groovy character stickers
> **4 tokens** = an Ardagh pen
> **6 tokens** = an Ardagh rucksack

Please send with your collected tokens and the name & address form to:
Philip Ardagh promotion, Faber and Faber Ltd, 3 Queen Square,
London, WC1N 3AU.

1. This offer can not be used in conjunction with any other offer and is non transferable. 2. No cash alternative is offered. 3. If under 18 please get permission and help from a parent or guardian to enter. 4. Please allow for at least 28 days delivery. 5. No responsibility can be taken for items lost in the post. 6. This offer will close on 31/12/04. 7. Offer open to readers in the UK and Ireland ONLY.

Name: ....
Address: ....
....
....
Town: ....
Postcode: ....
Age & Date of Birth: ....
Girl or boy: ....

Philip Ardagh Club
token